THE DANGERS OF TRUFFLE HUNTING

Sunni Overend

HarperCollins*Publishers*
Australia

HarperCollins_Publishers_

First published in Australia in 2017
by HarperCollins_Publishers_ Australia Pty Limited
ABN 36 009 913 517
harpercollins.com.au

Copyright © Sunni Overend 2017

HarperCollins_Publishers_
Level 13, 201 Elizabeth Street, Sydney NSW 2000, Australia
Unit D1, 63 Apollo Drive, Rosedale, Auckland 0632, New Zealand
A 53, Sector 57, Noida, UP, India
1 London Bridge Street, London SE1 9GF, United Kingdom
2 Bloor Street East, 20th floor, Toronto, Ontario M4W 1A8, Canada
195 Broadway, New York NY 10007, USA

National Library of Australia Cataloguing-in-Publication data:

Creator: Overend, Sunni, author.
Title: The dangers of truffle hunting / Sunni Overend.
ISBN: 978 1 4607 5210 4 (paperback)
ISBN: 978 1 4607 0697 8 (ebook)
Subjects: Romance fiction.
Food photographers – Fiction.
Wine industry – Fiction.
A823.4

Cover design by Hazel Lam, HarperCollins Design Studio
Cover illustration by Agata Wierzbicka
Author photo by Sunni Overend
Typeset in 11/16pt Janson Text by Kirby Jones
Printed and bound in Australia by Griffin Press
The papers used by HarperCollins in the manufacture of this book are a natural,
recyclable product made from wood grown in sustainable plantation forests. The fibre
source and manufacturing processes meet recognised international environmental
standards, and carry certification.

For James

Whatever our souls are made of, his and mine are the same.
Emily Brontë

Marriage is a fine institution,
but I'm not ready for an institution.
Mae West

1

Pale winter sun shone through the bare oaks that lined the driveway into Gossard Range.

Kit had slowly decompressed over the hour's drive and now felt the remaining city weight lift as her tyres hit the unsealed drive.

The long, new, stone-gabion winery stretched grey-blue against the vineyards, filling a space once occupied by galvanised sheds.

Half a kilometre up the hill, brick-trimmed windows stamped the roughcast façade of a six-bedroom single-storey 1930s homestead. The Gossard family home was capped by a shallow-eaved, dark slate roof and fenced by the naked boughs of saucer magnolia.

Kit jiggled her feet and half yawned, half smiled as she got out.

'Kitty, Kitty Kat!' The call came from behind and her brother threw Kit into a soft, flannel hug before she turned around.

'Marcy Marc.'

'Where's Fifi? I thought he was coming.'

Marc had taken to calling Scott 'Fifi' since the engagement. It had begun as a bastardisation of 'fiancé' and because Scott had been irked by the emasculating tone, Marc continued to use it.

'He'll be here late.' Kit unloaded her camera gear. 'He had to finish a new prototype.'

'What is it?' Marc said.

'A stool.' Kit began walking towards the house. 'Yellow Perspex.' Marc laughed.

'Would you like one for the cottage?' Kit kept a straight face.

'If I ever own anything yellow *and* Perspex, shoot me.'

'I'd be happy to.'

'And don't call it the cottage anymore.'

'Why?'

'It's a house. A man lives in a house. A granny lives in a cottage. We know which I am.'

'Do we?'

'Didn't you call me a cad yesterday? Today a granny? What am I, Kitten?'

'So many things I wish you weren't.' Kit went ahead into the house. Marc tripped her, she grabbed him as she went down and they pinched and kneed each other in a tangle on the floor.

'Grow up.' Marc pulled himself up.

'Grow up.' Kit reached out and he pulled her to stand.

'Anyway. Come and look at my *house* soon. It needs a woman's touch and not of the kind it's been getting. Ha. Ha. Ha.'

'Yuck,' Kit said. 'Where's Annalese?'

'Town. Shopping. Don't call her Annalese.'

'*Mum.*'

'You know she's as bad to me as she is to you? I still manage "Mum".'

'Good for you,' Kit said, and they scuffled past the layers of oilskin coats in the vestibule.

The back of the house had been renovated a few years earlier, kitchen and living had been merged, and a once-dim space was now open to the north-eastern sun and the Gossard family garden.

Annalese, homemaker and matriarch, lacked imagination but she liked interior magazines and the space now appeared something like a Scando retreat cum Poliform showroom.

A long island bench divided living from kitchen and along the length ran domed glass lights and acrylic stools. Upholstered *bergère* armchairs met a clean, modern sofa in the lounge, and beech wishbone chairs penned a solid timber barn table upon which Kit laid her things.

'What are you shooting?' Marc said. 'I have work to finish down at the winery. Need help?'

'I love and hate you …' Kit squeezed his torso and Marc crushed her head until she gave out a suffocated laugh. Free, she reassembled her hair. 'I don't need any help, thank you. It's a drinks shoot. Gin & Elderberry Fizz, Honeysuckle Tea and a fresh Lemon Lime & Bitters. Is there citrus on the trees?'

'Heaps. I'll get you some bitters and gin from downstairs.'

Kit put on Annalese's mud-caked rubber and leopard Sperry Top-Siders by the back door, and took a basket and secateurs into the garden.

That her mother was a reasonable gardener still surprised her. Annalese didn't seem nurturing enough to make anything living … live.

That the plants had been allowed to go as wild as they had also seemed contradictory. Not that they were 'wild' but if Kit had met her mother for the first time and imagined her garden, the vision would have been of a barren parterre.

At this time of year, planter boxes overflowed with white and green, and cabbages, rocket, winter lettuce, onions and garlic all jostled for space.

Kit took the path that divided the lawn and citrus grove. She snipped fragrant fruit into her basket and picked early-flowering honeysuckle from the side of the house. The air smelled of clean, wet grass and the winery hummed in the distance.

'Oo, oo, oo!' Annalese was home. Kit hurriedly fired off a final round of photos.

She'd already gotten the requisite images and light was fading, but her mother's sudden appearance allowed what Kit called the 'final flurry' – a handful of thoughtless shots taken at the end of a shoot that invariably turned out the best.

Annalese laid her groceries on the bench. 'This looks pretty, darling!'

Kit embraced her mother carefully, unsure if she might break or explode – she was so good at both.

'Sippy-sip?' Annalese helped herself to a drink then gave a spectacular grimace. 'Oh *Kitty*.' She thumped the tumbler back on the table. 'How can someone with such an eye for food be so *dreadful* in the kitchen? Darling, I'll have to give you a cocktail lesson while you're here. Remind me before you go.'

Kit unsnibbed the door, tossed the contents of the glasses onto the grass then followed them outside, leaving her mother behind.

Escape or combat. They were the only two ways with Annalese.

The rectangle of caged stone that was the winery featured a large cutout in the centre, enclosing a view of grapevine-threaded hills. Tourists walked through this gravelled pass to the cellar door on the left, where greyed wine barrels housed healthy topiary, or a view of the winery on the right.

'Meg!' Kit waved to the manager as she made her way through the cellar to the offices, tucked in a second storey. 'Boys up top?'

'Yup! Still at it!' Meg smiled from where she knelt, restocking.

Wine, cheese, pickles and preserves: the walls to the stairs were lined with produce and Kit climbed to the offices at the top.

'Where's my son-in-law to-be?' Connor rose from his desk and brought his arms wide like a soft, tawny bear. Kit sank into her father's embrace. 'Friday night dinner's only a half hour off!'

'He might be late,' Kit said into Connor's shoulder.

'There's a *very* important little yellow chair at stake.' Marc pressed his palms together and nodded with feigned sincerity.

'He's a busy and important man,' Connor said without sarcasm, tucking his blue and white gingham shirt into his jeans.

'*Very* busy, *very* important,' Marc mocked, Kit yanked his hair and Connor hummed – appeared to enjoy the memories that came with watching his grown children squabble.

'That's enough,' he finally said. 'Kit, we need some bottles for tonight. Down in the cellar, far left, two reds, one white, make one a vintage – I feel like a treat.'

Marc shunted his sister towards the door and she delivered one last kick, which they both seemed to enjoy.

Back in the winery forecourt, Kit made her way towards the cellars, bunkered beneath the winery building.

There was another, smaller cellar beneath the homestead but this was the one the Gossards used most, big enough to accommodate both commercial and personal stores.

A coarse rope handle fastened the horizontal entry that led straight down into the ground. Kit unlooped the rope from the latch, pulled the trapdoor skyward, laid it open on the ground, and sensor lights flickered on as she descended the wide, steep stairs into the vault.

She folded her arms, inhaled the dank, grimy soul of the place and squinted into the gloom.

When her eyes adjusted, she took a few steps forward, knelt and settled her hands on the floor. She began combing her fingers through the fine layer of silty dust that covered the ground and the dense silence and utter familiarity made her want to cry in the way one only did when they felt they were truly home.

It had only been a week or two since she'd last come to the winery, but it had been perhaps years since she'd been down here, and here was the heart of the place, where the fruits of her family's labour lay quietly beneath it all. She swirled her finger in the dust, wrote her name, scuffed it out, then climbed to her feet.

What Connor wanted was towards the back.

The bottles were at the far left and Kit made her way through the rows, pulled out a bottle, returned it, selected another, returned that, then found the two she sought side by side and skipped two rows to find the last.

Two bottle necks in one hand, one in the other, she strode back towards the hatch and stood at the bottom of the stairs, gazing up.

The hatch space was dark.

Kit blinked, glanced behind her, back up, but all that was above were the darkened, cobwebbed timber beams that made up the rectangular exit, now closed.

'Fuck,' she said. She ascended the stairs until her head grazed the door. 'Hello?' She butted the door with her head and it rattled. She climbed two steps higher, tried to lift the door with her head, but it didn't yield and the hardness made her scalp hurt. The door had been fastened from outside.

Her shoulders fell and she shunted herself onto the stairs to bunt the door continuously with ease. 'Fuck, fuck you.' She butted the base of a wine bottle against the timber and called out again, not caring if the bottle broke, knowing she'd feel strangely vindicated if it did.

'*Hell-fucking-o?*' she shouted; the cellar wasn't located within particular earshot of anyone or anything.

The hatch suddenly swung wide and Kit blinked into the evening light. She tried to stand, slipped, caught herself, then clambered into the air to rest with relief on the ground.

'I apologise,' came a voice from above.

The voice wasn't one Kit knew and she let her eyes fall to the dirtied boots of a man.

'I didn't notice anyone go down there.' He had a hybrid accent Kit couldn't place. 'Someone left the hatch wide last week and some birds and rabbits got in. I thought the same had happened.'

'You could have called the fuck out.' Kit could predict already the stupidity of this transitory winery worker, another traveller passing through, and as she went to stand, her eyes flickered over dirtied moleskins, a worn leather belt, and a once-white T-shirt stained with grease from the sheds and debris from the vineyard. Their eyes met.

'Again, I apologise.' He was taller than expected and Kit found herself suddenly and unreasonably without words.

Ninety per cent of the winery staff were male, one hundred per cent knew who she was, and all treated her with a reverence she'd become used to. This man, however, hair dark, eyes to match, was gazing at her with – despite his words – an unapologetic fearlessness she hadn't expected.

His skin was mildly tanned, his face long but not thin, jaw defined, and any expression on his face converged on the small space between his eyebrows that was, right then, tightly gathered. He seemed to be internalising something. This dark reservedness cast a shadow over typically good looks, but he held a gravitas that could never be based on good looks alone. Kit's hand slackened, she heard a dull crunch as one of her wine bottles hit the ground, and she stared down at it then swore as she crouched but a red puddle was forming irretrievably on the gravel.

The stranger knelt, Kit smelled sweat, dirt, timber and vineyard, and she found the man watching her, expression complex. He blinked, seemed to be wanting to understand her in the way she was wanting to understand him. Kit sensed that her nervousness had taken him off guard, that he knew exactly who she was, and hadn't expected her to be like this, to be inexplicably disorientated.

His hand moved to brush something from her arm and Kit startled. 'I'll–I'll just get another–a bottle–' she tripped back

'–you're surely finished for the day, you go, I–' she faltered '–thank you, bye.'

She stumbled down the cellar stairs into the darkness.

The following morning, Kit stood with her fiancé, Scott, before a neglected white weatherboard guesthouse half a kilometre up from the winery homestead.

The Gossard Range wineries had been established early in the twentieth century by Marc and Kit's great-grandfather, an immigrant from a French viticulture dynasty on Connor's side. The portfolio included a Barossa Valley estate, but the Yarra Valley was the original and keystone vineyard where Connor, then Kit and Marc, were raised.

Kit stepped inside the cottage with its view over the vineyard.

'I can't believe how much better it looks,' she said.

After time spent studying and working in town, Marc, now in his late twenties, had returned to work on the winery and had restored the old cottage as his digs. Scott gave the space a disapproving once-over. Marc grinned.

'Save it, Fifi,' he said. 'Not interested.'

Scott clicked his tongue. 'Marc, you may live in the provinces but you do know it doesn't have to look like it?'

Marc switched on the coffee machine. 'I can't resist.' He held a straight face. 'Tell me, Fifi. How should it look?'

Scott swept his eyes over the living area. 'Boom. An epic print, right there. Boom. An *objet d'art* for that dank corner. Boom. Exotic cushions on that drab couch.' He leaned over to pinch the fabric between his fingers. 'Christ, Marc, is that *linen*? You're not middle-aged.'

'Ah, *Fifi*.' Marc smirked at Kit.

'Mate,' Scott persisted, collar buttoned high like a monk. 'I can offer you some chairs. I've got that prototype table in the studio ... take it. I will kindly gift your bland arse what others bust their Amex for.'

'I am *such* a lucky boy.'

'You're a tasteless hack.'

'Fifi, do you know what sex smells like? Would you like to? Come in to my room. The smell is fresh from this morning, and the morning before that, and the morning before that, and ...' Marc trailed off. 'I would say I'm joking but I'm not.'

Scott scowled. 'You're a child.'

'Oh and I should also have suggested that you keep off that middle-aged linen, there. Vaginas may have lingered ...'

Scott withdrew his hand from the couch. He smeared it on Marc's shirt. Marc grinned and Kit covered her mouth so Scott wouldn't see her smile.

On the way back to the homestead, Kit tried to agree with everything Scott said.

'That boy needs to grow the fuck up.'

'I guess.'

'He's a child.'

'Mm.'

'When's he getting a place of his own?'

'I wonder.'

Women flocked too easily to her brother's insouciance and well-formed face so Kit pruned his ego whenever possible.

This psychological gardening was generally ineffectual so she appreciated that Scott had ego enough to challenge Marc, too, despite it only acting to encourage.

They set the table for breakfast back at the homestead and Kit watched, unamused, as Scott relayed his version of Marc's interior, minus the sexcapades, to Annalese.

'Oh stop, Scott.' Annalese's laugh verged on flirtatious. 'Not everyone has your refined, urban taste. My son uses his hands, you use your brain.'

After thirty years with Annalese as a mother, Kit was still unsure of how conscious the woman was of what she said. As she'd aged, Annalese's insensitivity had worsened, as if retaining a sense of self meant shredding everyone else's. She also seemed to think that being critical gave her an air of intelligence, so she delighted in the shortcomings of others, actual or invented. Kit didn't know if this comment was meant to flatter or offend Marc, Scott, or both, but she knew it belittled them equally. Marc was highly intelligent and Scott liked to think he used his hands.

'Oh Kit … look at Kit go!' Annalese tittered as Kit carried a jug to the table. 'She can't cook but she knows where to put it. Look at those hips! Stop staring, Scott.'

'I wasn't,' Scott said and Annalese sighed.

'Well,' she said, 'I suppose they say shape *is* making a comeback … Thank God thin was in when *I* was working; boy, was *thin in*.'

Having modelled in the seventies, Annalese often found fault with and highlighted Kit's own anti-catwalk shape. Whether she was jealous, disappointed or plain confused by how she'd made a curvy daughter, the offence sat there – full-figured – between them.

Annalese suddenly clapped. 'How about a ride this afternoon?'

Kit hated the way she felt in jodhpurs.

Annalese bought her a new pair every season and they'd grown into a square Lycra tower in the cupboard of Kit's childhood bedroom.

Despite the likelihood that the gift existed to humiliate Kit, she wore them anyway, hoping that they were actually a sign of her mother's wish to connect.

Kit sat spread-legged on her pony, feeling the abundant stitching plague her upper thigh and thinking what she guessed her mother wanted her to: that riding was best suited to a certain breed of stick, sticks that sat tall and wore correct ponytails.

The others had made excuses.

Kit knew she'd soon wish she had too, but to decline the ride would also have been to agree to Annalese's contempt and disappointment. This was neither better nor worse than a ride, but at least this way, Kit could save the others.

Annalese spoke as they trotted away from the stables and ahead, the well-worn track forked towards the valley stream or up the north hill.

'Have you thought about the wedding, darling?' she said.

'I think you asked me that last week and I'm quite sure that I replied "no",' Kit said.

'No?'

'No.' Kit feigned a smile. 'No, I haven't thought about it.'

'Well.' Annalese smiled too. 'I think *I'm* quite sure that *I* replied that you weren't getting any younger, darling.'

'Yes, and I believe I replied "what a lovely thing to say, Mother".'

'Mothers weren't made to be lovely, darling, they were made to be helpful. Scott has a global élan and he won't last long here. Lock him down or he'll leave you behind.'

Kit wanted to laugh. When her mother wanted to intimidate or get her way, she spoke in a manner that verged on 'posh'. This tone told others who was in charge and if Annalese was really on her game, she'd add florid, unusual words.

'You're right,' Kit said. 'Scott's *global élan* is unmistakeable, I admit I find myself veritably daunted by it. Tell me, what should I do to orchestrate a wedding with such a man?'

Annalese flattened her lips into a thin line before prying them apart to let words snake out. 'Don't be silly, Katherine. If you think I'm kidding, I'm not. You're acting like you have time. You don't. Stop being naïve and make it happen.'

She cantered ahead, her horse kicking up dirt, and Kit felt the aura of her mother's delight: Kit had shifted an obstacle with humour and Annalese had repositioned it, with insult. This wasn't unusual: it was Annalese's favourite thing to do and she was good at it.

Kit straightened and cantered on, but despite her best efforts, Annalese's words clung. Kit sat tall, upped her pace, but posture wasn't going to cut it.

Kit was right where her mother wanted her – in her slipstream – and she rocked along, buffeted by insecurity. She wrenched off her too-hot helmet and a low branch swung overhead, snapping twigs into her scalp.

Annalese glanced back, saw what appeared to be Kit tearing her hair out, and said, gratified, 'Don't get upset, darling. Everything with the wedding will get sorted. *I'll* sort it.'

2

Piper rested against the table in black waxed skinny jeans, her red hair fizzing over the shoulders of the formless white shirt she was wearing with no bra.

Kit had studied photography but had segued into product styling and it had been on such a job that they'd met. Kit had since returned to freelance photography, now with food styling, and Piper had gone into magazines. Their friendship and collaborations had remained strong, and for the first time since Piper had become art director at best-selling food magazine *Hamper*, she'd called Kit in to freelance.

'What's wrong?' she said as Kit took a step back from the set.

Kit thought before she spoke. 'Does this magazine ever deviate from their bright-white-backgrounds-sparse-implements-minimal-mod-décor thing?' she said as she eyed the scene from afar.

Piper pushed off the table and went to stand beside her. 'What do you mean?'

Kit gazed with Piper at the set and began to scratch her neck. 'I mean exactly that,' she said.

Kit had been looking forward to shooting for the luxury glossy. She'd been prepared for and well accustomed to their clinical aesthetic but after the weekend at the estate, that strange man and her horse ride with Annalese, an irritating kind of itch had appeared and now, days later, resurfaced.

She strummed her throat, musing. 'It's all just feeling a bit … tight.' She fanned her fingers.

'Well, if *Hamper* had a subheading it would be "uptight".' Piper hummed, amused. 'Feel comforted by what you've managed with that fairy floss. It appears veritably wayward.'

Kit put on a smile but it slid off.

She stepped forward and for the fourth time swivelled the Turkish teacups, fluffed the Persian fairy floss and tweaked the honey-glossed sweets.

'Better?' Piper said.

'No,' Kit took off her jacket and toggled her camera's settings.

'Something else is wrong,' Piper said.

Kit fired off a round of shots, leaned towards her laptop and fiddled beneath her collar.

'You have eczema,' Piper said and Kit glanced to see if she was joking.

She wasn't.

Kit unfastened the top of her shirt and pressed the shutter button. 'Of course I don't have fucking eczema,' she said, as someone she didn't know sailed into the room.

'I heard we had a freelancer in today!' the woman said, and Kit recognised *Hamper*'s editor-in-chief. 'You're Scott Baldwin's fiancée, Kit?'

'I am.'

'Well I had to pop down and say hello,' the woman gushed. 'I'm a fan. A big fan of Scott. My husband and I have a Scott

Baldwin dining setting, it's the most refined piece in our home,' she laughed at herself. 'Tell him if he ever puts any kitchenware on the market we'll feature it in *Hamper* in a heartbeat.'

'I'll mention it.' Kit smiled and the woman clasped her hands, gratified.

'Set's looking good!' she said, then sailed back out the door.

Kit turned back to her laptop and watched the photos stream from her camera. The images made a grid on the screen. Kit rested her chin on her fist and cocked her head.

The successive little boxes of white on the screen harboured small clumps of pigment. White clutched at colour like a pale fist strangling something, mangling it into inorganic little squares.

'This isn't working,' Kit said.

Piper went to the laptop, peered close, then stepped back.

'I think they're actually exactly what *Hamper* want,' she said.

Kit swore quietly, undid a button on her shirt, and Piper smirked.

Kit turned back to the screen and leaned in. Piper laughed quietly.

'What?' Kit said. 'What's funny?'

'You.' Piper sighed. 'Your box.'

Kit couldn't be bothered asking what Piper meant and continued scrolling through the photos.

'Your vagina,' Piper elaborated, steepling her fingers. 'I think your vagina's upset and it's upsetting the rest of you.' A hand broke from the steeple to rest on Kit's shoulder.

Kit wanted to laugh sarcastically but didn't have the energy. 'For fuck's sake.' She went back to what she was doing.

'That's what I was thinking,' Piper said. 'But in lieu of a fuck, how about yoga tonight – a release?'

&

Kit climbed the stairs to Scott's split-level warehouse off Gertrude Street.

She didn't want Piper's 'release', she wanted clarity and containment, and knew the one place she'd find it.

Scott's new prototype sat atop his workbench and as Kit approached, Scott lowered it to the floor then shuffled it into position like a little throne.

'Sit,' he said.

Kit scanned the glossy, geometric seat and tucked the edge of her shirt into her jeans. She wasn't big but she wasn't tiny, either. Her body undulated in a notably female way that at times felt unwieldy in the carefully hewn arena that was Scott's studio.

She perched on the edge of his creation – a stool in yellow Perspex with sharp, single-sheet laser-cut legs notched in an octagonal top – and jiggled. It felt sound, but Scott leaned forward and checked the notches like a sailor might inspect rigging.

'Not unstable?' he said.

Kit rocked, wondered if there might be a squeak. 'Perhaps …' she said and Scott took her by the shoulders and settled her off to the side like she might be the cause.

He smoothed the seat of the stool, clicked his tongue, took the piece by the leg and lifted it skyward to view the underside.

Kit waited. She glanced around at the polished concrete floors, the lighting of Scott's own design and his clutterless, white birch benches. He held the stool high, tried to locate the deficiency in his design and as he did, his shirt rose, uncovering the shadows that led beneath his waistband. He wore a navy Loro Piana knit, his shirt was buttoned high to a cutaway collar, and red cotton skinny pants had been tailored carefully to his leg.

'I want you,' Kit heard herself say.

She wasn't sure if it was true but she felt tense from the day, wanted something, and knew that he was the closest thing to it.

Scott's gaze continued down the legs of his stool. 'I love that. Can you order dinner?'

Kit waited, hoped something else might happen, but Scott's eyes stayed on his chair and Kit turned to the couch and sank into it.

The first night they'd met, two years earlier, they'd had sex on that couch. The night had begun at a party and ended here, just the two of them.

Kit had gone to the party with low expectations and come home with the man who'd later propose to her. She hadn't known who he was at first, he'd talked too fast, kept his arms tightly folded throughout their exchange, and was overtly cerebral without seeming to feel a social obligation to tone himself down.

Their conversation had begun with Scott asking her what she did for a living and presuming her receptive to his musings – he'd plunged into an academic monologue about creativity.

Kit remembered him speaking of his 'struggle' to 'resist the easy path of doing what's been done before', and he'd asserted that 'most designers clutch at familiar sentimental comforts'. She'd wondered if he'd pause, allow her to contribute, but he hadn't. Finally he'd climaxed with, 'Kit – one can't accidentally "do" modern design. One has to have a certain level of intellectual rigour to continuously take the razor of rationality and functional logic to one's work.'

Kit had decided one might need intellectual rigour and a razor just to dissect what he was saying. That said, she was refreshed by a man who could think and reflect, despite feeling wary of his seeming lack of social self-awareness.

He was only two years older than Kit, reasonable looking, and that night, curiosity had led her back to his studio cum home. There, she'd realised he was prolific and acclaimed industrial designer Scott Baldwin and his apparent obsessiveness and oddity felt suddenly warranted.

At the time, Kit had been ready to meet the right person, and Scott's confidence, competence and dedication appealed. The more she got to know him, the more impressed she was with the way he'd structured his world and mastered his process. Kit was still searching for her creative identity and found herself drawn to someone who was so sure of his.

Though Kit's renewed love for photography had arrived before Scott, her subject matter remained broad, and Scott's confidence made her wish for the creative convictions he enjoyed.

Food was a subject her lens had long loved, but Kit had never been sure enough to commit to it. If Scott was anything, it was sure of himself and in that way he promised to keep Kit on track for a creative journey that had felt perpetually uncharted.

Kit wanted to couple her uncertain mind with his certain one.

Many around her seemed to be committing and settling. These social cues made Kit feel the pressure to do the same, and the result was a desire to do so. Life with a man like Scott was one that others would admire and respect, and the answer to his marriage proposal had seemed obvious.

Now Kit gazed at her laptop.

She tied her hair back, opened that day's *Hamper* folder and studied the photos as she tried to come to terms with them.

'What do you think of these?' she said. She didn't speak loud enough and turned towards Scott as she said it again.

'What?' he said.

'These photos,' Kit said. 'What do you think?'

Scott did one last thing to his chair then came over, yawning. He sat beside her, peered at the screen, then said finally, simply, 'Cool.'

Kit felt the itch at her throat flare. She took her hair down then put it back up again.

Scott slid the laptop towards him. 'I like them,' he elaborated. 'Polished, slick, pro. Are they the shots for *Hamper*?'

'Yes ...' Kit said. 'The editor came in while I was there ... told me how much she adores you.'

Scott gave a vague smile then folded his arms. 'The photos are good,' he said without doubt. '*Hamper*'s style guide suits you. I like their parameters, and I like what you've done within them. The work's tight,' he concluded. 'Really tight.'

Kit stared at the photos.

They seemed even more inhibited than they had earlier, like someone had pulled the food into Photoshop and applied a 'deny life' filter. *Tight* was exactly what they were; they felt restrictive and tight to the point of unpleasantness. Kit scratched her throat, stared at the screen and then up into the room.

'All good?' Scott said by way of indicating he wished to go elsewhere, and Kit reminded herself of his competence – his clean critical thinking that had always appealed to her. But gazing at the *Hamper* photos, she couldn't ignore it: her mind was beginning to turn.

For the first time, her understanding of things was diverging from his.

'All good?' Scott said again and Kit kept rubbing her throat as she contemplated the photos. To feel fundamentally opposed to Scott's creative opinion was to disagree with her only guide.

She tugged feverishly at her jumper, the shape suddenly too dense and small, and in a tangle of wool and hair, said, 'Thank you, thank you, Scott.'

Her jumper came off and a smile was forced on. Scott smiled in return and – duty done – walked away.

3

'Sorry troops!' Connor's delight was plain as he took the car over a deep rut and bounced Kit off the back seat.

'Christ, Dad.'

The G-Wagen leapt along the unkempt laneway between Gossard Range and the adjoining property. Kit put on her seatbelt and leaned forward to her brother and dad in the front.

'Have you seen all this yet?' she asked Marc.

'Some,' he said. 'Dad's keeping it pretty close to his chest.'

'Got to,' Connor said. 'Got to keep your strategy contained.'

The four-wheel drive crossed the fence line and careered onto the neighbour's land. When they reached a grove of trees, Connor stopped the car and got out.

'What sort of trees are these?' Kit said, gazing down the twiggy rows.

'Hazelnuts.' Connor knelt to pull up his socks.

Kit snapped a skinny branch and twirled it between her fingers.

'Cannock Chase has a total of one hundred and ten acres of fruit and nut orchard.' Connor paced forward to begin a monologue.

'We know. They're our neighbours,' Kit said and Connor dug his hand between the roots of a hazelnut tree and lifted the earth for her to smell.

'Does it smell like Nutella?' she teased.

'Nope,' he said. 'There's magic down there, kids, magic that commences our diversification. What it smells like … is *gold*.'

Marc looked entertained.

'This better be good,' Kit said.

Connor breathed in another handful of dirt.

'Black gold.' He grinned. 'Truffles.'

The old G-Wagen lurched along a low valley and back up onto an even ridge.

Kit rested her elbows on the back of the two front seats. 'Earl's really going to sell Cannock Chase?' she said.

'Yup,' Connor said. 'Shook hands on it, years back.'

'And when did *you* find out?' Kit asked Marc.

'About the sale? Start of the year. But Dad only told me about the truffles when pre-season began the other day, shifty old boy.'

Connor made a sound that meant he was pleased with himself. 'You're both going to inherit this one day and when you do, you'll learn to play your cards close to your chest, be a step ahead.'

'And you're going to buy it all?'

'Yup, one hundred and ten acres. We've got a near-on hundred-year-old family company and it's time we diversified, made the most of it. More than wine runs in our veins.' He smiled as they traversed deeper into the neighbour's perimeter.

'Old mate Earl toyed with the idea of selling the Chase about ten years back,' Connor continued. 'After a good think, I put my hand up. It took him a few years to mull it over but he agreed eventually and I said we could take our time. In the interim he let me stick a few thousand inoculated hazelnuts on that beaut bit of terroir he's got right on our fence line, perfect PH and incline. Five years on – huzzah! – our very own sizeable yield of Périgord truffles.'

'I can't believe you've been harbouring a truffle grove for *five* years.'

'Well they haven't been doing much – high chance it wouldn't have worked at all. And anyway, truffles are just the halo effect. When they're in season we can export them to restaurants and boutiques as a seasonal novelty under the Gossard Range umbrella, but for the big addition, well for that I'm digging *deep* into family heritage.'

Connor let his words hang in the air as a neat network of fruit trees came into view.

'You can see where this is going?' Marc turned to Kit. 'You know what they are?'

'Apples ...?' Kit peered through the window at the dormant grove.

'Apples,' Connor was only just containing his excitement. 'Of these one hundred and ten acres, sixty acres are apple trees, ten species, some rare.'

'Dad, you've been talking about this since I was a child,' Kit said, amused.

Connor reached to his side, withdrew a bright-skinned apple that he must have pocketed with this moment in mind, and rested it momentously on the Mercedes' dusty dash. 'Good things come to those who wait.'

Back at Gossard Range, Connor strode ahead to the cellars and called for Kit and Marc to hurry.

They tailed him, descended into the dim vault and not for the first time, Kit remembered that moment the other day. She glanced back at the light coming through the open hatch as she made her way down.

Connor was waiting for them by the family safe, deep in the western wall.

'It's all well under way, Kitten.' His stance was grand, something in his hand. 'It's not new to Marc, he's had the spiel, I've needed him, but this is otherwise all very much on the "DL" as you kids say,' he said with a grin. 'Are you ready to get on board?' He offered Kit an empty champagne-like bottle and she wiped the dust from the label with her sleeve.

'Maison Gossard,' she read. '1876 Cidre Bouché Brut de Normandie.'

'Yes!' Connor said. 'What your forebears at ol' Maison Gossard cut their teeth on, *cidre bouché* – cider under cork. What you hold there is an original antique that no one but our family has seen for generations.'

Kit polished the bottle with her hand. 'It's beautiful.'

'And would have *tasted* beautiful,' Connor said. 'Pure, organic sparkling cider from the Pays d'Auge, premium and indisputable French heritage that no upstart could imitate.'

Kit sighed. 'Is this about–'

'AGVM? Of course!' Connor rubbed his hands together. 'Nothing like a good old grudge to keep you in the game.' He reached again into the safe and retrieved a ragged, once-was rectangle of card. The yellow-lined thing was perhaps an old catalogue card, decorated with delicate French cursive. Connor passed it to Kit.

The piece was dated 1871, Normandy, and beside a lovingly sketched champagne vessel was a list titled *Cidre Bouché*.

'These are the last vestiges of Maison Gossard.' Connor reached across and gave the card a gentle rub with his finger. 'They date back well before Arenberg & Gossard – well before AGVM. I doubt Arenberg even laid eyes on the Maison Gossard cider relics. Gossard were well and truly winemakers by then.'

'AGVM don't have a cider range?'

'No. Arenberg may have pilfered most of Gossard's annals but they've ignored our real root heritage and now they'd love a crumb of history this rich. Our market has no interest in innovation. Heritage, legacy, provenance … *they* win this game.'

Marc yawned as Connor blustered on.

'It's all about the timing. When Cannock Chase came up I thought: it's fate. All I had to do was match those acres of rare, old-growth, unadulterated varietals with wild yeasts, honey, a few old-school techniques and ancestral secrets, and I knew we'd have a renaissance on our hands. A renaissance and an exciting new line that Arenberg & Gossard know nothing of.'

Kit smiled as she gazed at the relics. It was strange that Gossard Range had once been as one with their now nearest competitor.

Their forebears at Maison Gossard had partnered with American friend and investor Arenberg to establish Arenberg & Gossard in 1925. Arenberg had soon lost unsanctioned A&G investments in the Wall Street Crash of 1929. He followed this with a significant personal betrayal – Connor insisted that a woman was involved – and the partnership severed.

The fallout saw the then Gossard steward, Connor's grandfather, emigrate to establish Gossard Range in the Victorian wine region, while Arenberg & Gossard merged with Valcourt Mantel.

Now AGVM, Arenberg Gossard Valcourt Mantel, was a multinational that owned large chunks of the lifestyle sector, but despite this evolution and diversification, Arenberg & Gossard remained AGVM's flagship wine brand as well as Gossard Range's closest competitor. Both offered near identical product at similar price points.

'When was the last time AGVM tried to buy us out?' Marc said.

'Around the same time I had the idea for Cannock Chase. Elliott Arenberg just wants the Gossard name neatly under his AGVM umbrella. We're his missing piece, doing whatever we want with the name they think belongs to them – a sense of ancestral ownership that weasel can't shake. They'll try again when they hear about the cider. I'll never sell.'

'It's bottled in champagne bottles – the cider?' Kit gave the bottle back to Connor.

'As is tradition.' He turned the vessel affectionately in his hand. 'It's double-fermented like champagne – once in American oak, next in the bottle – and the high-pressure carbonation means it's corked and caged. The result will be like nothing you've ever tasted.'

'I'm excited,' Kit cooed.

'You should be,' Connor said, 'and all lips must stay sealed for now.' He squirrelled his treasures into the safe. 'Secrets and fun, secrets and fun …'

Following Connor's speech in the cellars, Kit sat in the stationary G-Wagen.

She messaged Scott that she was about to leave, started the four-wheel drive and reversed out towards the homestead.

A thump and shout from the tail bar made her brake and she stalled, glancing in the rear-view. She saw nothing then there was movement, and she turned to see a person shift behind the car.

'Shit,' said a man's muffled voice.

Kit swore, jumped out, found a man rubbing his leg by the back bumper and dropped forward.

'Oh my God I'm so sorry, sorry.' She searched for a bumper mark on his dirty moleskins, and repeated apologies as she glanced up.

The man was staring down at her and Kit's heart skipped, stopped, then doubled speed, and she slowly stood and thrust forward an unsettled, shaking hand.

'I'm Kit,' she stammered.

'Yes.' The warmth of his hand enveloped hers and they stood unmoving as car doors clicked shut, engines started, winery workers left for home. 'Raph,' he said.

'Raph, Raph,' she confirmed, 'Raph,' she said one too many times. 'I think we met the other week but I don't think we got to introduce ourselves.' She laughed, hoping it concealed her fixation. She didn't *think* they'd met, she *knew* they had. She quickly dropped his hand as her own grew clammy.

'I believe I locked you in the cellar,' he said with humour. Kit heard again the accent she couldn't place, and thought of that moment, weeks ago, that should have been forgotten but hadn't been. The memory had lingered, not just lingered but intensified: the sense of this man's eyes on hers.

Kit wanted to understand what the attraction had been and sensed that he held a strength – an indifference and independence that she found unsettling. She wanted to disregard him – walk away like she should have been able to – but something about this man was magnetic.

'Are you okay?' he asked, voice edged with concern.

Kit hesitated then nodded apathetically towards his bumper-scraped shin.

'I'm fine,' she said. 'There's first aid inside if you need it.'

'No, it's a bruise at worst,' Raph replied. He ran a hand through his dark hair and Kit smelled turf, oxygen, sunlight and labour, and thought how Scott only ever smelled like Comme des Garçons.

'Are you sure you're okay?' Raph asked again and Kit realised that she'd begun to tremble. 'I'll get you some water,' he said and he went to move by her.

Appalled that she'd run him down and now he was comforting her, she gathered her hair and tied it above her head in a move that she hoped emulated confidence. 'No, thank you, I'm fine,' she said. 'Be sure to have your leg checked.' She walked back around to the driver's side, climbed in and drove out.

❧

Scott was fussing over a new version of his stool when Kit arrived home.

She pulled off her jacket, tossed it with her bag on the lounge, and when she reached Scott where he leaned over his workbench, she pressed herself against his back and slithered her arms around his waist.

'Hello,' she heard him say. Kit slipped her fingers beneath the waistband of his jeans.

He turned to face her, smiling down, and she pressed her soft chest against him as she peered up into his eyes.

'You're in a good mood,' he said. 'How was the valley?'

Kit didn't reply but stood on tiptoes, kissed his mouth, slid her hands up under his T-shirt, and drew her palms across the skin of his back.

Scott's hand rose up to touch her head and he kissed her lips, their corner, her cheek, ear, the side of her neck, then his mouth reached her décolletage. He kissed her chest, his hands cupped her breasts and his mouth gave each a short, firm peck.

That seeming sufficient, he rose to kiss her nose before he turned back to his prototype.

Kit gazed at his back.

His lungs rose and fell under his shirt, and finally Kit let her hands slither back down from under it to hang by her sides. Then she walked to the couch, picked up a magazine and put on her headphones.

The pages of the magazine turned and she cranked the volume on her device, she began to flick the pages faster and pressed the headphones against her ears ... the smell of his sweat and the warmth of his hand on hers. The intoxicating enigma that was the winery hand grew in Kit's mind and no amount of bass or glam advertising was going to distract her from it.

Her energy climbed and Kit glanced up at Scott, wondering if he'd sense it and ask what she was thinking. He didn't, and Kit's eyes lingered on him, not seeing Scott but seeing *him*, Raph's fleeting smile, the grime that had covered him.

Kit offered Scott a second chance by patting the space on the lounge beside her and saying, 'Feel like a cuddle?'

He responded, 'Later … a bit much to do.'

'I might head over to the apartment,' Kit said.

The Gossard family's inner-city apartment sat unoccupied around the block; it wasn't unusual for Kit to spend the odd night there.

'Have you had dinner?' Scott said. 'I'm starving.'

'I've already eaten,' Kit lied, 'but I'll order you something.' She dialled for takeaway as her feet hit the pavement outside.

At first she power-walked, then jogged, then as the apartment neared, she undid the top of her jeans and began to run.

She unlocked the bottom door, ran up the stairs, unlocked the entry at the top, and inside, in the dark, she dropped denim, knickers, walked into the bedroom and alone, on the bed, came loudly, not once thinking of Scott until it was over and she was typing him a message.

'Your stool looked great. I ordered you Thai from our fave. K. Xx'

4

It was midday, and Kit had her camera poised over a grill-marked tortilla on the exposed aggregate floor of Scott's studio. She was almost finished when Scott arrived downstairs with his agent, Alexi Green. Kit waved as they appeared.

'Hey, Kit,' Alexi said. Alexi only ever wore high-waisted pants and monk shoes with expensive, oversize knits, and she hid a pretty face behind large glasses. Her hair was combed into a perpetual neat bun that sat just above her collar and her 'all business' vibe wasn't a ruse. She was the best at what she did and Scott owed much of his success to her combination of quality connections and industry nous.

Socially, Alexi seemed to like to talk work or nothing, but with Kit she tended to make more of an effort. 'Busy?' She came forward. 'Looks yum.'

'Thanks.' Kit glanced back at the viewfinder and took the shot.

There were two major components to being a food stylist. One was having an eclectic love for food, and the other, a good eye.

Kit had both, as well as the photography degree and a hard-to-source prop collection, and she'd begun to think it impossible to ever divide the roles of photographer and stylist again. The colour and composition of the subject was affected by the aperture and angle of the photography, and Kit felt she had to control it all to get the result she had in mind.

'So are you the new talent at *Hamper* magazine?' Scott said.

'I suppose I am ...' Kit replied, because despite unresolved feelings about the previous week's shoot at *Hamper*, she had, that day, taken a full-time position there. Piper had recommended her for the job, the editor had been happy with Kit's freelance delivery, and the position was offered.

'You'll be much happier there than as a freelancer.' Scott began to roll off the benefits though there was no need. His typically sound logic was what had made her accept the job earlier that day.

'I appreciate the encouragement,' Kit said.

'Well it's a no-brainer.' Scott glanced at Alexi for solidarity. '*Hamper*'s a leader, you'll have an assistant, there'll be a full studio, you'll have a salary, perks, and thank God you won't need to take photos here anymore ... Is that *oil* on my floor?' He walked to where Kit knelt.

Kit inhaled and let coriander and paprika fall across the barbecued corn and quesadilla on the floor. 'I'm almost finished,' she said. 'I'll clean it up, it's fine.'

Scott made a sound that meant he disagreed, then dropped something on the floor beside her. 'My sister thought you might like them,' he said.

A pile of magazines landed and Kit glanced across to see the solar-white teeth of a bride smiling up at her.

'Not long now?' Alexi said.

'Not too long, we hope.' Scott stroked the top of Kit's head. 'Alexi ...' He leaned towards the floor. 'You have concrete floors, don't you? Is this going to come out?'

Alexi peered down at the mess of food Kit had created on the floor.

'Maybe bicarb, if it's stained ...'

'Better not be.' Scott tapped Kit's crown, began to walk away, and Alexi followed him. Kit took another photo and when their voices were distant, she lifted a piece of buttered corn, freckled red with paprika.

She photographed a close-up, released the cob and it fell to land with a soft, oily, thud on the cover of the bridal magazine.

She gazed down at it, the butter spread and seeped, and when the bride's bright face was shrouded in a dark pool of oil, Kit picked up the food and wedding periodicals and gave them silently to the bin.

అ

The chopsticks were the disposable kind.

Kit snapped them apart, spread them in a vertical row like soldiers, then cocked her head to appraise the pile of rubbish out of frame.

Shreds of cheap Japanese paper packaging lay torn where Kit had discarded them and she squinted at the calligraphy print then retrieved it from the pile.

A bowl of miso (steaming), dried noodles (square), sushi (three rounds), daikon (shredded), wasabi and ginger (pickled), all appeared on a tray courtesy of Kit's assistant, Ellie.

'Have we got any of those little plastic fish-shaped soy sauce bottles?' Kit said.

'I'll see,' Ellie replied.

Kit withdrew a red plastic plate from her box of props and began to arrange the trimmings.

Ellie returned with a jar of mini plastic fish with red-mouth lids and brown soy filling.

'And spring onions?' Kit said and Ellie disappeared again.

Kit opened one of the soy fish and watched delighted as drops of brown spilled on the white backing. She added more, then flipped the box and tiny synthetic fish cascaded across the set.

'And the tofu you forgot.' Ellie returned.

'Thank you,' Kit said. 'Tip it into the broth.'

Ellie hesitated.

'Tip that into the broth,' Kit said again. The girl frowned. 'Just tip it, tip it all in,' Kit said with urgency and Ellie tilted the board, flinching as the food slid irregularly into the bowl.

'Thank you,' Kit said.

Two chopsticks in, scoop to the side, dried noodles square to chopstick soldiers, discarded wrapping in frame …

Kit reached for her camera.

'Spilled soy!' Ellie held up her hands in high alert.

Kit went to speak but Ellie plunged efficiently forward. 'No need!' Kit almost shouted as she blocked the paper towel in the girl's hand. 'No, that's how I want it – sorry, sorry, thanks – you can leave it.' She felt a kick of adrenaline.

Ellie stepped back and Kit grabbed her camera, took one photo, then paused. Ellie's mouth was opening and closing.

'What?' Kit said.

'I …' she stammered. 'The styling … it doesn't seem finished.'

'How?' Kit knew exactly how but she wanted the girl to say it.

'You've–' Ellie began. 'You've left the rubbish there and the soy's spilled and I think you should have left the chopsticks out of the soup. The wood's getting stained.'

Kit felt a small, desperate laugh rise up. She pressed her fingers to her lips, contained it, nodded in earnest and hoped it acted to validate the assistant's concern. It was day one at *Hamper*.

She stood motionless then slowly ran her gaze over the set, stopping at each element, one at a time.

'Yes,' she nodded. Her assistant was right. For *Hamper*, this *was* all wrong. She slid the tip of her tongue rapidly back and forth across her bottom lip, contemplating compliance and duty … conformity and correctness.

Ellie shifted, fidgeting, and Kit glanced over at her. She eyed her assistant's pretty little mouth, tight with doubt, then back at the wet, steaming broth.

'Grab those chopsticks,' Kit suddenly said. 'The ones in the bowl,' she clarified, and Ellie obeyed, seeming suddenly relieved, and Kit realised that the girl thought she was fixing things. She felt momentarily sorry.

Ellie held the chopsticks and Kit took a square of paper towel and stuffed it in the assistant's collar. 'Eat.' She wrenched the camera off the tripod and repositioned herself.

'We've not finished the photos–' Ellie appeared distressed.

'No, I know,' she said. 'I just … just … Eat.'

The girl peered uncertainly down at the soup.

37

'Chow down!' Kit said.

Ellie gingerly lifted the chopsticks and began to poke at the soup.

'Is that how you eat?' Kit said.

The assistant lifted the bowl, poked some more.

'What is this? Temple?' Kit grinned. 'Gobble for God's sake! Gobble!'

Ellie tittered – small, uncertain – brought the noodles to her mouth and Kit's shutter closed and opened as the miso sprayed across the girl's collar-napkin.

'Yes! More!'

Wet noodles flung, lips glistened and Kit contained a smile.

'I'm actually *starving*,' Ellie gushed as she chopsticked a piece of sushi towards her mouth. It broke, rice fell and Kit felt tense with delight as the camera whirred.

Four hundred photos later, the energy began to subside. Kit knew it was done. She drenched a piece of tofu in soy and sagged against the destroyed set, the protein salty on her tongue. 'I'm impressed. I liked your improv, Ellie.'

Ellie shook her head as she dabbed her mouth with her napkin. 'I am not complicit.'

Kit propped her keyboard. Steam, broth, little pink mouths, red plastic, wooden chopsticks, white rice, ragged wrapping, splattered soy and gaudy little fish. Photos made a grid on the screen. 'That's fine,' she said. 'Your mouth is anonymous.'

'Anyway,' Ellie said, 'you won't get them past editing.'

'We'll see,' Kit smiled.

'You won't.'

Later in the week, Piper sent Kit an email.

Subject: *High Five*
    Main: *One: Your first day photos: fucking hot.*
    Two: I must say however: what the fuck were you thinking?
    Three: In saying that, I'd argue it was your best work yet.
    Four: Sadly nonetheless, they were completely off brief and will never see the light of day.
    Five: … where did this come from?

5

Despite Kit's and Marc's childhood pleas, the Gossards had never owned a dog.

Though used to waking to roosters, tractors or Annalese yelling, dog barking was unfamiliar and when the sound woke her, Kit draped an arm over her face.

She had arrived at Gossard Range late the night before and pulled the curtains poorly together in her old room.

The dog barked again. Connor laughed, others talked.

The homestead's mint-green Aga pumped heat into the hydronic panels in the bedrooms and Kit slid from beneath the doona and pressed her legs against the radiant cast-iron heater as she pulled cashmere over her head.

Marc opened the bedroom door. 'Pants on, food in face, we're leaving.'

In the kitchen, Annalese had made stuffed croissants.

Kit took one from the counter, melted couverture filled her mouth, and she wondered again at the contradiction that was her passionless, uptight mother.

'Darling!' Connor walked towards the cellar door, ruddy-faced.

Kit waved, then knelt to pat the dogs. They began to lick croissant from her face.

'Meet Alfa and Romeo,' Connor beamed as he rubbed the animals' brown and white sheepy fur.

'Whose are they?' Kit said.

'Ours!' Connor clapped. 'They're our *Italiano* sleuths, lagotto breed, lake dogs from Italy! Good for one thing ...'

'One thing, Kitty Kat,' Marc tackled Kit from behind.

'What?' Kit asked.

Connor took his time surveying the day, then looked at Kit, eyes alight. 'Hunting.'

The old Merc bounced along the track it had taken a fortnight earlier and the lagottos scuffled in the back as Gossard Range ended and the orchards of Cannock Chase came into view.

'Mum didn't want to come?' Kit peered through the window at the overcast sky.

'Not if *staff* are coming, *please*,' Marc scoffed, and the car soon stopped at the thicket of hazelnuts, branches dense, an avenue of trees made dim and moody by the day.

Kit let the dogs out and their noses went to ground.

'You know they're also *trained* in Italy.' Connor jumped from the driver's side.

'Why didn't you just buy dogs locally?' Kit said.

'Because truffling is as much about the art and heritage as it is about the produce.' Connor marched to greet the arriving staff. 'We're doing this properly! With dogs *made* for truffling!'

Meg, the cellar door manager, waved in the distance. Marc twitched.

'What's wrong?' Kit said.

'What?' Marc twitched again then quickly hurried away towards the car.

'Stop, come back.' Kit began to laugh.

'No.' He continued towards the car.

'Yes.'

'No!'

'Marc, come here, come right back here.' Kit addressed her brother like a disobedient pet.

'No, Kit, save it.'

'Marc. You do not shit where you eat.'

'That's a feral saying, Kit!'

'Yours is feral behaviour, Marc. *Sleeping?* With *Meg?*'

'Shut the fuck up. I'm not talking about this with you.'

Kit folded her arms and peered skyward. 'What will Mother say? She's irked enough by us *socialising* with staff, how will she feel about you rutting with one?'

'I am the staff! Jesus, that woman is a snob and a brat and she won't find out.'

Kit watched him root around in the back of the four wheel drive. 'Is it serious?' she said.

'No.' Marc found something he'd been searching for and set it aside.

'*Poor* Meg, Marc.'

'What?' He withdrew his head and met her gaze. 'Why?'

'Marc, you know.'

'Kit, it's just fucking. Stop being such a prude.'

'*You're* just fucking, Marc, *you're* just fucking.'

'What?' he said again.

'You're just fucking. It's not "just fucking" for her.'

'Women like meaningless sex.'

'Not with guys like you! Meg's only having meaningless sex with you in the hope *you* make it become meaningful.'

The winery staff neared, and Kit and Marc quieted.

A dog had begun to look animated beneath a hazelnut and Connor gestured excitedly as he produced a small, copper-blade trowel.

The group gathered and Kit watched from a distance.

The dog dug, prodded, dug, prodded and Connor mimicked with the trowel until a gratified grin appeared along with a disfigured black ball.

A round of applause went up.

Connor congratulated the dog, put the truffle to his nose, handed it to the nearest onlooker, and when everyone shared their admiration, he clapped his hands and said, 'Hunting kits in the back of the car, kids. Go!'

A lagotto licked Kit's hand and she crouched to rub its ears as the gathering buzzed.

Trowels and baskets tumbled from the back of the G-Wagen and when everyone was equipped and heading towards the wood, Kit glanced up.

She hadn't noticed him, a dozen feet away.

He was tying his boot – head down, shoulders broad.

The dog nosed her hand. Kit sensed the man's form changing as he began to stand and she glanced down, frozen, eyes on the animal.

The dog started to fidget but Kit waited. She hoped Raph would do something, walk away, but she knew he was still there, motionless.

'Hi!' she shouted to provoke the adrenaline needed to stand.

His eyes were already on her and Kit watched his gaze rise with her movement.

'Hi, hello, how are you?' she said then stopped, stopped the speaking that was her unravelling.

'Hello,' he replied.

Kit decided she wouldn't speak again until he did.

There was silence, the voices of the group distant.

'Are you going to be using her?' Raph finally said. Kit blinked, and he clarified with a small smile, 'The dog. I'd like her on my side.'

He was dressed in well-fitted woodland wear, a navy waxed jacket with fawn kecks half tucked into boots of aged dark leather. The look was powerful, reminded Kit of armour, and she sensed that there was something intensely concealed about this winery hand.

The now familiar feeling began to spring up. Kit tried to check it.

It spread.

The feeling niggled powerfully, began to expand. It was the same feeling she'd been fighting since the day she'd first seen him – the feeling she'd felt the day of the 'failed' *Hamper* oriental shoot – and she knew that any new mistake from here on out would be because of it.

But there'd be no more mistakes.

She was in charge and she refused to let the mere aura of an otherwise inconsequential person bring her undone like this.

She dug deep, tried to contain the feeling, failed, wrestled, and as she struggled, sensed the feeling name itself, answer the question she hadn't asked.

Hunger.

Kit blinked it away.

The feeling was of hunger *beyond* hunger.

The dog nudged her leg. Kit blinked. A smile was on her face, and to conceal that nothing like a smile lay beneath, Kit smiled larger, then encouraged the dog towards Raph.

He crouched and stroked the thick, duo-tone fur, then asked Kit a question.

'Are you truffling?' he said.

'I'm–' Kit began and wondered if she should return now to the house, choose the challenge of Annalese over this challenge of being near to Raph.

He gazed up at her and again she saw a complexity she wanted to untangle.

'I am.' She turned to the car for tools. 'Good luck.' She strode by him into the trees.

A hundred metres up the alley of trees, Kit's heart slowed.

She dropped at the base of a trunk, and knees, elbows, hips, stomach, she fell forward then rolled onto her back to study the branches overhead.

There was a photo printed on canvas back in her father's office. A plaid-clothed farmer wore a felt fedora and stood beside a stout, spotted pig that scuffled in coloured autumn leaves at his feet. Kit had taken the photo for a food and travel magazine – traditional truffling, Umbria – and it had become Connor's favourite.

She gazed up into the branches of the hazelnut, waited for her body to stabilise, then sat up.

She picked up her trowel, disturbed the soft layer of soil at the base of the tree, prodded and probed, and finally hit something that made her pause.

She leaned forward, wished she had the dog, moved the earth with her hand, then suddenly, unexpectedly, she felt a weight land on her back. She paused.

The landing was soft … uncertain … but suddenly the weight began to move.

Kit screamed, ripped off her jumper and hurled it across the way.

She didn't hear footsteps or the dog.

She heard nothing but her adrenalised blood thump before a lagotto bounded from the trees with Raph in tow. She glanced up at them first, down at her bra, then at her jumper across the way, sequestered on the ground.

Raph came to a standstill as he tried to gauge the situation.

'Are you okay?' he said, brow furrowed, and Kit sensed that he was frowning only to conceal that he wasn't completely unhappy about the state she was in.

'Ah–' Kit's tone was high. 'M–my jumper.'

Raph followed her gaze, picked up the jumper, handed it to her. Kit leapt back, ashamed of her fear but not ashamed enough. 'Shake it, please? Shake it?'

He seemed uncertain, then seemed to understand and he

appeared amused as he gave the fabric three swift shakes. A small body dislodged.

Kit made an involuntary sound as the spider scuttled for cover.

Raph squinted after it then handed Kit her jumper. She promptly dropped it.

Raph smiled, seeming both surprised and taken by her vulnerability, and Kit felt angry as she swept her torso, arms, hair. She lifted the jumper from the ground and dropped it over her head.

'I didn't mean to smile,' Raph said, gazing at her in concern before reaching to touch her arm.

Kit pulled away and he paused, hand hesitating before he put it in his pocket and turned slowly to gaze again after the spider. 'What species?' he asked. 'Poisonous?'

Kit ran a hand over her hair to settle herself. 'A huntsman,' she said. 'Not deadly.'

'Huntsman …' Raph repeated the word. 'My mother's arachnophobic, I understand.' His eyes rested on her face and Kit glanced away, resisting the kindness.

Suddenly, she felt another tickle. Fear instantly overrode pride, and she did a three-sixty and said, high-pitched, '*Definitely nothing else on me?*'

'All clear,' Raph said without laughing. Kit knew he wanted to.

She met his gaze and his eyes flickered down to the discarded trowel, the hole she'd dug.

'Have you found anything?'

Kit flexed her hands, primed herself to speak. 'No, well, maybe, the spider–'

'I thought you were being attacked. By something much bigger.'

'I'm sorry I frightened you,' Kit said sarcastically, then regretted it.

The dog appeared excited. 'Pass me the trowel.' Raph dropped to his knees by the root of the tree.

Kit didn't do what she was told and Raph took the implement without invitation, adjusted his grip on the worn handle and began to dig. These peculiar fruits of the soil were rare and precious, near impossible to cultivate. Kit was desperate to unearth one, to reach in …

Raph slowly unearthed a huge, dark shape. Kit made a sound, reached to take it, and Raph pulled away.

'I want to see it.'

Raph resisted – enjoyed the tension.

'I found it,' Kit said, but Raph lifted the shape to his nose. Kit waited for him to speak but the smell of truffle stole his words and she nabbed the object from his dirty fingers.

The rough, gnarled lump smelled like nothing else and saliva sprang into Kit's mouth as she put the object to her nose. She inhaled again and felt a sudden yearning, a greed not limited to the food she held. She wanted less, *more*, no, less, *no*–

She dropped the wild intoxicant.

Raph picked it up. He turned it over and breathed it in again. 'Androstenone,' he said, slowly. 'Androstenone,' he said again as his gaze met hers. 'It's a pheromone that truffles and pigs have. It's why truffles are irresistible to them, they think it's mating season. Humans have the pheromone, too, that's why truffles make us–' he paused at a noise '–make us …'

Kit waited, mouth wet, but the noise became Connor, striding through the trees.

'What is *that* you've got there?' her father trumpeted.

Raph slowly lifted the truffle.

'*Phoar!*' Connor guffawed as he began to inspect it. 'Pick of the day so far! How many grams we reckon?'

'Three hundred? More?' Raph offered up the prize and Kit felt a pang, as if she didn't want their wild little discovery shared with anyone but each other. She wished he felt the same.

Connor's face was bright as he weighed the offering in his hand, and he said, 'This boy Rapha, I tell you …' He grinned at Kit, tossed the truffle high and snatched it like a baseball before he ruffled Raph's hair. 'No doubt about him.'

Connor walked off, whistling, in the direction he'd come. Despite not wanting to, Kit followed.

6

'I think it's coming together.' Scott stood back from a small stack of stools in his studio.

The yellow Perspex design he'd been working on had not only evolved, but had gained two twins. Three identical stools now sat atop one another, notched cleverly at the legs and seat so that they stacked in a tight, uniform cylinder that made them appear, all together, like a little sculpture.

'Wow,' Kit said. 'You've finished.'

Scott squinted and leaned forward, swatting at an unseen blemish on the stack as he made an unsatisfied sound. 'I'm not certain about it …' he said. 'I'm not sure.'

'What's wrong with them?' Kit said. The gaudy, postmodern aesthetic wasn't a style she was naturally drawn to, but she appreciated their originality.

Scott stepped forward, unstacked the stools, then rearranged them in a row. His dedication to perfection and function was his calling card and it was the reason he'd been chosen for this brief.

'I like how they look together,' he said. 'I put a lot of time into figuring out how they'd all work stacked in formation, but now I'm unconvinced that they're substantial enough on their own.'

Kit cocked her head, decided she agreed with him but didn't say so.

'They're going to be in a hotel lobby,' she said. 'They'll never be alone.'

'But they'll start at the exhibition,' he said. 'There it'll be up to the curator how they're displayed and I don't want just one stool on its own. The design only feels whole when the viewer can see the stool, as well as *stools* – stacked as one.'

'Then tell the curator that,' Kit said. 'Tell them that they're designed as a *set*, not individuals.'

Scott tutted as though she hadn't addressed his concern. 'Maybe ...' he said.

A collaboration between a design publication and a progressive London hotel, this commission had been a compliment. The hotel had stipulated eight new furniture items it required; the publication had gone forth and returned with eight designers, each of whom had been challenged to come up with a design for their designated product.

Once all the designs were finalised, each piece was to be exhibited at the London Design Festival, and then, at last, sent to its forever home as a feature in the hotel. Scott had been asked to design a stool and had welcomed the pressure that accompanied the challenge. Now the design was nearing completion and he'd soon travel to London to present it.

'Could you take a quick seat on one?' Scott frowned. 'I need some perspective.'

Kit sat down on a stool and, predictably, Scott changed his mind about wanting to see her on it. Despite design being generally for use by people, people were a designer's ugliest inconvenience – so the less there was to them, the better. Kit's person was curvaceous and distracting, the last thing a designer wanted anywhere near their independent masterpiece.

'I think I might head to bed,' Kit said as she stood.

'Thank you for the advice,' Scott kissed her. 'I'll follow you in.'

Once under the covers in his bedroom, Kit called out, 'Are you coming?'

'Yes …' Scott replied, '… soon.'

'Come warm me?' Kit smiled.

'Okay,' Scott called again, 'turn on the electric blanket 'til then …'

Kit lay staring at the resin pendant light that hung over the bed until her smile wore off.

Then, when forty-five minutes had passed, she rolled over and killed the light.

❧

The only inhabitant nowadays, Kit found the Gossard's Gertrude Street apartment a place of quiet repose.

The warm, open space had once been the upper level of two neighbouring townhouses bought by Connor back in the eighties, but when Kit then Marc had enrolled in university, their father had engaged an architect and created lodgings for his children in town.

The top floor had become one large apartment, and a sourdough bakery and bespoke screenprinters now tenanted two retail spaces below. With Marc back at the winery, Kit was the only one who stocked the pantry of the elevated four-bedroom flat.

The in-home pedicurist had arrived early and Kit sat on one of Connor's mid-century lounges, the woman's fingers between her toes.

Someone entered the door code and Kit filled the minutes until the guest arrived by picking up a scone, swirling the daub of butter and honey on top with her finger, then licking it.

'Well, well,' Piper appeared and came to stand over Kit, hands on hips.

'Home-baked scones with Gossard truffle butter and smoked honey.' Kit offered Piper the plate, and Piper slid off her shoes and jeans then sat beside Kit in her knickers.

'Thank you.' She smelled a scone before she poked her tongue in the top, took a bite, and the two sat silently as they turned the woody flavours over in their mouths.

'So the photos you delivered were interesting,' Piper said.

'Which ones?' Kit replied.

'The Taste of the Orient,' Piper said, and Kit thought of the assistant's pink little mouth, the splatterings of miso, the mottled napkin, spilled soy and stained chopsticks.

'Yes,' she said.

'Yes,' Piper said.

'I know, I know,' Kit said. 'I went a little off brief.'

'You did.'

'I'm sorry,' Kit said. 'It won't happen again.'

Piper watched the pedicurist smooth the edges of her toes with a little pumice.

'What happened?' she said.

'What do you mean?' Kit said.

'What happened with the shoot?' Piper said.

Kit frowned, feigning confusion in the hope Piper would give up.

She didn't. 'I mean what *happened*,' Piper said, 'to make you think that those feverish photos were suited to our famously conservative employer?'

Kit felt Piper's eyes slide to her face and offered her another scone by way of distraction.

It didn't work. 'No thank you. Was it Scott?'

'Was what Scott?' Kit said.

'Was it *sex*? Was it sex with Scott? Were you feeling liberated because Scott finally gave you the fucking you deserve?'

The pedicurist frowned.

Piper didn't care. 'Did he?'

Kit reached for some champagne.

'Scott *didn't*?' Piper sat tall, eyebrows high. '*Someone* did.'

Kit frowned at Piper's ability to intuit, to know beyond knowing. What Kit loved about Piper was now working against her.

Piper stared at her. 'I saw the real you in those photos, Kit.'

Kit gazed ahead. Hunger. The word, with its frenzied wish to unleash. She picked up her glass of champagne and drained it.

'Yes,' Piper said. 'The quicker that goes down the quicker whatever you're not telling me will come up.'

The yellow the pedicurist had used on Piper's toes looked better than the red she'd used on Kit's, and Kit considered the shades of poppy and buttercup as they clipped up the grey concourse towards the museum.

The mass of magazine awards attendees moved through the museum's glass atrium. Kit felt a hand land on her back as she and Piper joined the fray.

'Don't you look nice.'

Kit glanced back and saw that the hand and compliment belonged to Jimmy Hillinger, a freelance food writer and regrettable one-time lover.

He leaned in to peck her cheek. 'Little Lady Gossard.'

'What's news?' Kit hurried forward but Jimmy stuck close.

'News?' He smirked, long and lazy, in a slim-cut suit and ironic bolo tie. 'What's news with you? The estate?'

They hadn't dated long, a month at best – Kit's self-esteem had been low and Jimmy had been persistent. But even in that short time Kit had noticed that his regard extended beyond her to the winery.

Now, whenever they met, he angled for stories on the family or business, fascinated by the old-world luxury and affluence Gossard Range conveyed.

'And you've created a bit of a stir at *Hamper*,' Jimmy said. They'd arrived in a long auditorium. 'I hear you're showing them how it's done?'

Kit glanced at him and he appeared pleased to have gotten her attention. 'And I don't mean in a good way,' he said. 'I hear it was only day *one* when you rocked the boat.'

Kit turned away.

'Oops, I said the wrong thing.' He simpered. 'Now how's Connor? Planning a big move, I hear?'

Kit craned her neck as if searching for someone.

'A new *product line* …?' Jimmy leaned close.

'The only line he's making is a beeline to retirement.' Kit forced a yawn.

'Don't fib.'

'Have I ever?' Kit smiled and Jimmy's faded.

'People like knowing what you're up to out Gossard way. *I* like knowing what you're up to,' he called as Kit waved goodbye and strolled away towards one of *Hamper*'s tables.

Among other things, Jimmy also happened to be on *Hamper*'s payroll – the writer of their 'Industry Insider' column – but having never seen him at work, Kit had forgotten. She was pleased he wasn't at her table tonight.

'Was that as much fun as it looked?' Piper said.

Kit didn't reply as she watched Jimmy find his seat. Though she knew her first *Hamper* brief hadn't gone as planned, she felt unsettled knowing that someone at the magazine had been outwardly slating her.

Piper raised a bottle of wine from an ice bucket and mimed chugging it before she handed it to Kit. 'Down the hatch!' she prompted but Kit put the bottle back on ice and peered across the room.

'Dova Meyer ...' she said suddenly, standing up.

The woman was five tables away and Kit moved quickly towards her, hoping Piper wouldn't have a reason to follow. Dova was a hero of Kit's but even more importantly in that moment – the perfect escape.

'Dova,' Kit said warmly as she approached. The woman was talking to *Hamper*'s editor-in-chief. 'I recognised you from across the room and I couldn't help but want to come and introduce myself.'

Dova Meyer was a frequently awarded photojournalist, her work poignant, gritty and honest. Kit had never seen Dova in the flesh before. The woman was more round than she'd expected with a warm, open face.

'I loved your *National Geographic* photos growing up, I'm a long-time fan.'

'Oh, thank you so much!' Dova grinned.

'Now, this is Kit,' *Hamper*'s editor-in-chief said. 'She's one of our in-house photographers. We were just chatting the other day, actually, because her fiancé is *Scott Baldwin*.' The editor seemed to think no further explanation was necessary, and Kit was surprised when she was right.

'Oh *yes*,' Dova said. 'I have his candelabra, that very first one he did. Wasn't that a fabulous reinterpretation? I think that's what put him on the map, wasn't it?'

'It could have been …' Kit said. She had no idea.

'And what sort of photography do you do? Food – I'd guess?'

'Yes,' Kit said. She had the recent *Hamper* shoot on her phone but couldn't bring up the inglorious photos in front of the editor. Someone began to speak up on stage.

'Nice to meet you, Kit,' Dova said and the women broke to return to their tables.

❧

Kit phoned the estate.

Annalese anwered.

'I suppose you already know about Marc?' she said.

It was the morning following the magazine awards. Piper was at work with a hangover, and Kit was at a café, queued for coffee.

'Know what?' Kit said.

'The *rooting*,' Annalese replied.

Kit searched her viticulture vocab ... planting, stripping, spraying ... rooting?

'I opened the door of the cottage on Sunday morning and there's one of those young Italian backpackers sitting naked on Marc's lounge ... eating cereal!'

'Rooting,' Kit said. 'Oh.'

'Yes he's been rooting one – or all! – of those Italian grape-pickers.'

'Not the cellar door manager?' Kit frowned. 'Are you sure it wasn't the cellar door manager on his couch?'

There was silence on the other end of the line and Kit realised her mistake.

'Why?' Annalese said.

Kit tried to backtrack but was too slow.

'The *cellar door* manager?' Annalese's voice began to rise. 'He's rooting her, too?'

Kit stared down at the black and white tiling, breath held.

'Good God. I sent you children away to school for a reason and now look. Marc's back on the estate shagging every tart in sight. The cellar door manager with a cat's name? *Mog*?'

'Meg, and do not say anything.'

'My children do *not* sleep with staff. It's not how you were raised.'

'Jesus.'

'Gene pools are no joke, Kit. Marc's better than this.'

'Let's leave it to Marc.'

'Let's not. Let's not leave it to Marc.'

'Is Dad there?'

'No. Marc is. He's sitting next to me. He wants to speak to you.'

'Fuck,' Kit said and there was scuffling while the phone was transferred.

'Kitten!' Marc feigned delight.

'Hello!'

'I loved that conversation you were just having,' he said. Kit heard a door close.

'I did *not* say anything about Meg,' she said.

'Don't lie.'

'Well forgive my confusion. Recently you revealed to me your fuck buddy relations with cellar door Meg then our mother recounts a surprise sighting of a naked Italian who is *not* Meg but who also seems to have enjoyed your fuck buddy hospitality. I was therefore perplexed by this new information that suggests there's veritable fuck buddy conscription afoot and I was doing nothing more than seeking clarification.'

The person ahead in the queue swivelled to glance at Kit.

'I think it's best if women don't seek further clarification,' Marc said. 'Best if women knock on doors before opening doors.'

'Obviously I would have knocked.'

'Our mother did not.'

'Best not to entertain unclothed backpackers in your living room.'

'Best not to tell me what to do with my living room, nor, unsurprisingly, with my dick.'

59

'Please don't talk about your dick.'

'Neither you nor my mother should refer to my living room, dick, fucking, buddies or other. In return, neither shall I.'

'As long as you keep a raincoat on said dick I'll do my best to keep from speaking of dicks, as well as opening doors without knocking.'

'Dick is securely housed when required.'

'It's *always* required.'

Marc started to laugh. 'This conversation is over.'

'You're insolent, randy and vile.'

'Yes,' Marc said. There was silence.

'Well,' Kit said. 'Mother was thrilled.'

'I knew she would be.'

'Dad knows what you've been up to too, then?'

'Only because Annalese told him, but he hasn't said anything, probably because what I do with my knob is private and he's of the old school of thinking that private things are … private. It's refreshing.'

'Some may say refreshing, others – dull. Anyway, I was calling because I bumped into Jimmy Hillinger last night.'

'What a treat. He was a low point for you.'

'He seemed to know something about the cider. He was fishing, said something about a new product line. I didn't give him anything but I know how desperate Dad is to keep the cider and the Cannock Chase buy under wraps. Jimmy would break the news instantly if he got it. Should I flag it with Dad?'

Marc paused. 'Nah,' he finally said. 'Forget Jimmy. Dad's blood pressure's been up and I don't want to worry him about anything.'

'Blood pressure?'

'He hasn't said anything. A worker – one of the guys – mentioned it.'

'What did they say?'

'That Dad was struggling to keep up in the vineyard. Just one day. Had a headache, had to sit down. Haven't brought it up. Don't want Dad worrying that *I'm* worrying ... Raph, the guy, he'll help me keep an eye on him. Decent bloke.'

Kit stalled at Marc's mention of the name. The person behind nudged Kit forward and she hurriedly mouthed her order to the barista.

'I hope Dad's okay.' She shuffled to the side to wait.

'He's fine. I'll keep on at him about easing up.'

'And is he happy with him?'

'Who?'

Kit paused, wondered if she should say the name. 'With the winery guy ...' she said. 'Raph. Is Dad happy with ... him?' The question was benign enough, but not *enough* by any means. Kit had so ... many ... questions.

'Yeah. Capable guy,' Marc said. 'Leagues ahead of other lackeys we've got on the books. If I didn't like the bloke, I'd be feeling territorial. Dad seems to turn to him as much as he turns to me.' Kit had a vision of Raph standing in the hazelnut grove, gaze steady.

'Kit?'

'Yes, yes, great, that's great, as long as Dad's got decent people around ...'

'*I'm* around.'

'Yes. Good.'

'But you're the favourite. Come up and visit soon.'

'I plan to,' Kit said, and the coffees arrived.

7

'I've asked Piper to come,' Kit said. 'So you didn't feel like you had to.'

'Do you think I'm that much of a write-off?' Scott said. 'That you wouldn't ask me first?'

'I suppose … yes,' Kit said.

Scott sighed. 'Well, I'm coming. Your family will start to think that I think I'm too good for them otherwise.'

'No, they won't.'

'I've never even *been* to the Barossa estate,' Scott said. 'I'm coming.'

There'd been a large hailstorm the previous week, damaging areas of the Barossa Valley. Marc had already flown over to assess the damage at the Gossard's Barossa estate, but he and Kit had been earmarked for a weekend in the Barossa anyway, scheduled to host a midwinter staff party.

Kit had invited Scott to join them out of courtesy only. His self-imposed weekend work schedule allowed him only rare weekends away and she'd assumed this weekend wouldn't be one of them.

Scott debated while he watched his toast brown. 'I'll come,' he swiped the air and popped the toast. 'I'll just have to make up lost studio time when I get back.'

⋙

'Jesus,' Scott said as they waited to collect their luggage at Adelaide airport. 'Small town?'

'Quaint,' Kit said.

'Quaint implies charm,' he said. 'There's none.'

Scott was having withdrawals. Kit had anticipated it. His default state was of perpetual cerebral action – surmounting design problems and breaking new ground – so away from his work, Scott's mind became like an autoimmune disease, attacking itself and everything around it for lack of anything else to do.

On their trip to the Milan Furniture Fair the year before, Kit had had to wrench him from Venice to Tuscany to Verona to Lake Como, and it wasn't until they finally got to the fair that his cognitions revived and he became sociable again.

Now they walked towards the exit doors. Kit rubbed Scott's back with her free hand, hoping Marc wouldn't notice. He already thought Scott was high maintenance, and an inability to relax on holiday would only cement his disapproval.

Marc climbed out of the G-Wagen, the car's old bodywork awash with mud spray and hail dents. He grinned, threw their bags in the back, and jumped in the driver's seat. Scott motioned for Kit to join her brother in the front. Kit guessed that he wished to sit in the back and be ignored.

'So the hail really came down?' Kit tugged at her seatbelt.

'Golf balls,' Marc said. 'Did you see the dents? Parts of the estate took a hit. It's thrown poor Thomas into a fluster.' He paused to glance at Scott in the rear-view mirror. 'Scott, did you know that Thomas – our young, faithful Barossa manager – has a crush on Kit? Has done since he started – eight years ago?'

Scott gave a thumbs up.

'But don't let it worry you, I mean this guy lives in flannel.' Marc couldn't stop smiling. 'Hicksville compared to your smart red, city-boy pants.'

'Flannels are the ironic shirt du jour.' Scott looked boredly out the window. 'Chambray, too. Does Thomas like chambray?'

'Oh Fifi!' Marc said. 'You should work on *Project Runway*!'

Kit slapped Marc's leg.

Scott yawned, unperturbed. 'We can't all aspire to your fucking sartorial heights, Marcy Marc.'

'You know I love you, Fifi.' Marc dropped a gear, grinned at Scott in the rear-view then reached back to clap his future brother-in-law on the knee. 'You're a genius.'

Kit relaxed. Marc had said the right thing.

An hour and a half later, they reached the boundary of Gossard Range's Barossa estate. The four-wheel drive skidded through the bluestone entry and down the long drive, which was feathered with silver birch.

Marc brought the car to a halt in the large circular entry courtyard, rimmed by stone heritage buildings.

'Late lunch? What time's your friend getting here?'

Piper's flight wouldn't land until later. 'This afternoon,' Kit said and followed her brother towards Larder, the estate's restaurant. 'She'll get a car.'

Headed by a well-known locavore chef and housed in the estate's old stone stables, Larder's setting matched the rustic fare. Right now it was empty before Friday dinner service. Marc announced their arrival with a whistle.

'Get it yourself.' The new sous-chef appeared wielding a cleaver. Marc dodged it with a grin.

'Buddy,' he said, 'this is–'

'This is the woman Thomas can't shut up about!' The man beamed. 'Of course you're gorgeous, like Marc.'

'Stop flirting,' Marc said. 'But yes, this is my nasty sister and her debonair fiancé, Scott.'

'You're engaged?' the sous-chef said. 'Thomas will be crushed.'

'You're all fucking joking, right?' Scott said, too bored to be angry.

'A bird!' Kit pointed at the window. Everyone looked, no one cared, but it distracted them, and she said, 'A ploughman's lunch, please?'

'Three,' Marc said.

Their food soon arrived.

'It is beautiful out there,' Scott gazed out the window. 'How would it be for our wedding?'

Kit gazed up at the ceiling. Annalese had suggested the same thing more than once.

Scott touched her hand to draw her attention. When he had it, he stood and walked to the window – eyes on the landscape.

'At the right time of year this would be a stand-out venue …' he said slowly. Then, as if to himself – 'Strategic guests. Brilliant photographer. My designs part of the décor … we get the photos … and design publications.' He turned to Kit. 'People love a VIP view into artists' lives. Especially when they look this good. Make the whole wedding investment worthwhile?'

❧

The Barossa estate's guest housing was old and new.

Guest accommodation had grown from a cluster of old storage buildings that'd burned down. Architects had added black gabled timber uppers to the brick left behind, and well-appointed lodgings now stood amid turf and olive trees.

Kit pulled on her Hunters. The early morning sun sat low in cloud.

She buckled the collar of her leather jacket, stepped out onto the lawn, and the grass left wet streaks on the green of her gumboots as she ducked through the trees.

The chatter of breakfasters preceded the cobbled entry to Larder. Kit scrunched her hair into a bun, put on sunglasses, and despite clearing the largely unfamiliar eight o'clock tourist crowd, she kept the glasses in place as she slithered through the indoor tables to the bar.

'Avoiding someone, Gossard?' Larder's rough-and-ready barista, Cecile, grinned as she slid a jug of milk onto the steam wand.

'Everyone.' Kit rubbed an eye. 'Too early for tête-à-tête.'

'I agree. Coffee?'

'Espressos. Three.'

Cecile laughed. 'For you? Big night?'

'For guests. Marc, Scott.' Kit smiled. Piper had arrived late. She wouldn't be up for hours.

Kit took the pretty route back behind the entry circlet, coffees on a tray.

She'd just rounded the corner when she heard voices and froze. Two men stood twenty metres off. Kit pivoted and slunk back in the direction she'd come.

'Kit!' The ever-eager estate manager's voice had a familiar, regional twang.

Kit turned reluctantly back. Thomas grinned, then waved. Kit tried to do the same but the other man turned.

Raph's hands were in his pockets. Kit's hand froze mid-wave. She rebooted, laughed without reason and moved forward.

'Good morning,' she said and despite her hope that he wouldn't, Thomas stepped forward to kiss her. She laughed again, face colouring as Thomas tried to introduce Raph.

'I know, we know–' Kit stopped as Raph placed his hand on her arm and she felt his stubble brush her cheek as he kissed her, too.

'Hello,' he said, quieter than seemed appropriate.

Thomas nodded with amiable oblivion.

'Oh, yes, of course,' he said. 'You're both from over the border.'

'Yes,' Raph said.

'Well. We've had fun this week. Raph hasn't been over this way before so I've been giving him the grand tour, showing him the ropes, and he's been putting me to shame with his impressive know-how.' Thomas huffed good-naturedly. Raph accepted the praise by gazing into the distance as he folded his arms. 'And now the shindig! We're ready to party, Kit – are *you*?'

Despite being only twenty-eight, Thomas spoke like he was fifty-eight. Kit tried to smile to reward his keenness. Scott would be at the party. Thomas would be at the party. Scott and Thomas and Raph would all be at the party ... together.

Kit took off her sunglasses, hanging them on her collar as she marched doggedly towards what the men had been studying: the dropped branch of a massive oak.

'Branch problem?' she asked, as though it was a thing.

Raph's shirt was littered with bark like he'd been wrestling the bough. 'Yes ... branch problem,' he sounded amused. They all gazed at the damp, twisted log.

'What are you going to do about it?' Kit didn't care that she sounded bossy for no reason.

'The branch?' Thomas said.

'The branch,' Kit said. Raph said nothing and slowly ran his hand up the limb to a lone leaf. He snapped it off.

'We'll have to get the tractor, tow it,' Thomas said loudly as he gave the bough a solid rattle. 'We'll wait till after the weekend, give the tourists their time.'

Kit gave a nod that meant nothing. 'Great. I'll leave you to it.' She took her sunglasses from her collar and slid them on to her face. She turned to go.

'I'll see you at the party?' Thomas said, too hopeful, and Kit acquiesced before striding off towards the lodges, bog sucking wetly at her gumboots.

When she was out of sight, she tore her sunglasses off again, kicked the mud frenziedly from her boots and slumped against the side of the shed.

'You know Kit got naughty down here?' Marc called from below. They were descending a ladder underground and Kit took an extra step to kick his head. He swore.

Scott was last to reach the floor. Kit presumed he hadn't heard. Marc powered on the old filament bulbs.

'Naughty in what way?' Scott asked.

'You're an idiot.' Kit glared at Marc.

'What? You're going to marry the guy, doesn't he know you're a dirtbag?'

'God.' Scott nursed his third coffee. 'What now?'

'Don't worry,' Marc said. 'It's not a new one, it's just Thomas, the estate manager you've been hearing about.'

Scott's nod was apathetic.

'Thomas was twenty, Kit twenty-two. They scuttled down here like inebriated teenagers during the Christmas party–'

'Shut the fuck up,' Kit said.

'Kit left a bare arse print on the dusty countertop right there. Dad even saw it.' Marc howled and gave Kit a boisterous tackle. 'Don't look at me like that, it's funny, it's *funny*.'

'Let's get what we came here for,' Scott said. He wiped a finger along the dusty bench and peered at Kit.

'Kit?' The call came from the trapdoor.

'Hi!'

'Hello!' Piper's smiling face appeared before it was replaced by yellow gumboots as she took the ladder two rungs at a time.

'Sorry for the tardy rise.' She hit the floor and Marc did a double take in the way Kit had known he would the first time he met Piper. Her friend wore a filmy T-shirt despite the cold and her nipples caught the fine fabric as she lifted an arm to flick hair over her shoulder.

'You must be Marc,' she went to shake Marc's hand. Kit enjoyed for a moment seeing her brother lost for words.

'*Piper.*' She threw him a line.

'Piper, yes, Piper.' Marc pulled himself tall. 'Nice to meet you. I've heard so much.'

'Likewise.' Piper dropped his hand and slid hers into deep pockets. 'So ... wine? For tonight?'

'For tonight ...' Marc smiled in a way Kit didn't like then stacked crates of wine onto the old pulley-driven dumbwaiter.

8

'**K**it,' Piper said as they walked towards the restaurant, the boys ahead. The party was being held at Larder, which would be closed to the public for the night.

'What?'

'Your brother.' Piper's expression was strange. 'You never told me.'

'What?' Kit said again and Piper tucked hair behind her ear.

'His appeal. He has strong appeal in the corporeal sense.'

Kit laughed and said, 'No.'

'No?'

'Piper, no.'

'Please?'

'No,' Kit said again.

Piper bent to fidget with the fringe of her Marant Navajo boots. 'Fine,' she said. 'I understand.' She straightened. 'I will say though that I've just realised you're modest. You, your family, your winery … I don't think I've ever seen so much loveliness.'

'Don't be a sycophant. Marc is many things. "Lovely" isn't one of them.'

'I disagree,' Piper said

'He has a vague, distant, charm. At best.'

'He has an immediate, palpable magnetism. At worst.'

'Piper. No.'

'I won't say any more.'

'Yes you will.'

'I'll try not to. I won't look twice at him tonight. Can we get quite drunk?'

Kit stood in a corner of Larder, a glass of Gossard pinot in one hand, cracker in the other.

The interior of the converted stables was a mix of white and mint-green paint, original timber and leather-slung seats. She and Marc had embellished the space that afternoon with white bunting and foliage from the estate's garden.

Kit licked the soft cheese atop the cracker and checked the room.

'Why didn't you tell me that your friend was a free-breasted red?' Marc said.

Kit shifted the glass in her hand and fidgeted with her hair.

'Kit?'

'Sorry?' Kit met his gaze.

'What's wrong?' he laughed.

Kit frowned and took a sip of wine.

'Did you hear what I said?'

She shook her head.

'About Piper?'

'No.'

'I said that your friend is a free-breasted fucking red.'

Kit would have laughed less loudly had it not been for her nerves. 'Marc. *Marc.*'

'You've been secreting her from me.'

'No. But if I had, would you blame me?'

'Yes. You're supposed to want the best for me.'

'Marc–' Kit began but someone came through the door. It was no one she knew.

She glanced at the bar. Scott was still there … Raph was yet to appear.

'Marc,' she began again. 'The only way you play is bed then dead.'

'What?'

'Once you've bedded a girl, she's dead to you.'

'That's bullshit.'

'Is it?'

'I just haven't found the right one yet.'

'Bed or woman?'

'Woman.'

'Fucking won't reveal her to you.'

'It might …' Marc said with a grin.

Kit folded her arms. 'And Meg? The poor cellar door manager?'

'She's leaving.'

'Because of you?'

'Of course not,' Marc scoffed.

'How do you know? Maybe you hurt her.'

'She got a job managing a hotel … or something.'

'Lucky escape.'

They both watched Piper knock back a shot at the bar.

'Piper's too much for you,' Kit said.

'Don't be ridiculous.'

Kit slithered her arms around his waist. 'You're my hero. Now *I'm* protecting *you*.'

'You're protecting yourself.'

'I'm protecting all of us.'

Marc rolled his eyes. 'So that guy you brought is having fun,' he said.

Kit looked to Scott, now by the window with a glass of water and his iPad. 'He's trying to resolve something flat-pack. There's a problem.'

'*He's* the problem, he needs to cut loose and–oh–hold up–' Marc's eyes were on the opening door. 'Your night's looking up.'

Thomas closed the door behind him and Marc tickled Kit stupidly. 'You and Tommy! Old times in the cellar!'

Kit stood humourlessly until the tickling subsided.

Marc straightened. 'Okay. I know you're "too good" for him, or whatever. I have someone else you can play with. I had higher hopes for this particular guy but you may do.'

'What?'

Marc scanned the room. 'Actually, I don't think he's here yet,' he said. 'Sorry, I shouldn't offer you men until I have them on a plate. He'll be here.' He glanced at his watch.

'What?'

'I was thinking Raph,' Marc replied. 'For you. For fun.'

Kit twitched.

'Do I get a thank you?' he said.

'W-what?'

'Do I get a thank you for giving you my friend when you won't give me yours? Raph wants you and I'm letting you have him.'

'No, what? Wants–? Who? Stop it, Marc, you're so inappropriate. I don't even know who Raph is. Stop.' Kit began to sweat.

'You know Raph,' Marc said. 'He's that winery hand Dad and I like. I love the guy, except he gets this weird look whenever I mention your name. Aim *higher*, dude.'

'Shut the fuck up.'

'But seriously–' Marc sounded amused '–it's true.'

Kit swivelled towards her bag and withdrew her camera. She needed somewhere to hide and behind her viewfinder would do.

'What are you doing?' Scott was beside them and Kit's heart double-beat.

'I'm getting my camera … photos,' she stammered.

Scott glanced at the tablet in his hand.

'How are you going?' Kit offered.

He rubbed his face. 'It's screwing me.'

'You need a drink, a real one, I'll–'

'Nup. I think I'll have to call it a night,' Scott said.

Kit exhaled and touched Scott's sleeve like she was disappointed.

'You're welcome to come back with me.'

'I can't. We're hosting,' she said and he kissed her, said goodbye to Marc, and Kit watched the cardigan on his back disappear through the front door. She turned back to the room.

Thomas was there. 'Hello.'

Kit downed the last of her wine. 'Hello.'

'Can I get you another?' he asked.

'No, thank you.' Kit walked away. She felt bad for Thomas but worse that everyone knew they'd had sex. Her one-time escape from a tedious Christmas party had become a Barossa love story, 'Hope for the faithful manager and the boss's daughter'.

Kit fidgeted with her camera at the bar. Scott was one down, she'd escaped Thomas, and maybe Raph wouldn't show. She took her Negroni and prowled the room.

'Hey.' Piper had crept up on her, and so no one else could, Kit put her back against the wall. 'Why aren't you talking to anybody?'

'I am,' Kit said. 'I have been.'

'You haven't.'

'Aren't you looking for a man? Why are you looking at me?'

'Your brother piqued my interest but he's been vetoed–'

'The chef? Look. He has a beard, you love beards.'

'No, I hate beards. They remind me of steel wool, with food stuck in it.'

The door opened. They both turned and a man stepped inside, glanced about, then closed the door. He walked through the room and Kit noticed that he'd only half changed – clean on the top, dirty on the bottom – and as he reached the bar and asked for a drink, Piper said, 'Huh.'

The bartender set down a glass. Kit watched him fill it with Amaro Nonino.

'Huh,' Piper said again. The bottle was recorked and, 'Hmm,' she said.

Raph gazed into the tumbler, smelled, tasted and wiped his mouth on his arm. Kit glanced at the door. She could leave, no one would notice.

But it was too late. His head was turning. His eyes met hers and his head cocked before he gazed back into his drink.

'What was that?'

'What?' Kit said.

'What was *that?*' Piper said. 'That, that nod … thing. Who is that?'

Kit frowned.

'Who is it?'

Kit squinted like she was trying to figure out what Piper meant. 'I think it's some winery hand.' She gazed across the room like there was something better there.

'I'm going to introduce myself,' Piper said. Kit's hand landed on her arm and she glanced down.

'Sorry, sorry.' Kit let go.

'What's going on?' Piper said.

'I just thought you had food. In your teeth. You're fine.'

'I haven't eaten.'

'Okay. Go on.'

Piper began to laugh.

'Go,' Kit said. 'Go.'

Piper laughed again.

'Go! You'll miss him.'

'You're fucking him.' Piper made a hole with one hand and poked it with a finger.

Kit's laugh was loud. 'Who?'

'That guy at the bar.'

Kit began to tangle herself in sounds that should have been words. 'That's a fucked-up thing to say,' she finally said.

'It's not. Get outside.'

'What? No.'

Piper bumped the door open and shunted Kit into the cold. Their heels clattered on slippery cobbles. 'Who – the fuck – is that?'

'Who?' Kit tried.

Piper repeated the question, face straight.

'Raph,' Kit caved and Piper frowned, surprised to have gotten a name so soon.

'Raph?' she echoed. 'And who's … Raph?'

'I told you.'

'No you told me *what* he is – a winery hand – not *who*.'

'Piper, stop. It's freezing. He's an employee of Dad's. That's all.'

An Owlet-nightjar called out.

'You're cheating on Scott.'

'No. What's wrong with you?'

Piper scoured Kit's face. 'It would explain a lot … it would explain everything … your behaviour of late. I saw the way he looked at you in there.'

'What are you talking about?'

'He looked at you like he's fucked you … or plans to.'

Kit laughed, scared by the thrill that Piper's words delivered.

'This is ridiculous.' She turned to go inside.

Piper stopped her, face dark. 'Kit, I'm worried.'

'I'm one hundred per cent faithful to Scott, don't fucking worry!' Kit spat.

'That *is* what worries me,' Piper silenced her. 'You know I don't really like the … *way* he is … with you.'

Kit went to push past her friend.

'I'm right, you know I am,' Piper said. 'Scott has a very

particular, contained way of living. I would want something more, I would understand if *you* wanted something more ...'

Hunger.

Kit was so very hungry.

She'd chosen Scott. He would sate.

'Just please ... *please–*' Piper held Kit's arm '–trust your feelings.'

'That's the last fucking thing I should do.' Kit pulled away, skittered on the cobbles then hurried off into the dark, on towards Scott, and bed.

9

Four things sat on the table in Scott's dining room: drawing tablet, laptop, soda spoon and a lid filled with his white Jelly Bellies.

Near the sink was the jar of remaining Jelly Bellies, colourful because Scott had extracted the white. Kit picked up the soda spoon, swirled it in the jar, and the firm candy beans tapped together.

She found a buttered popcorn bean, put it on her tongue, and the flavour of caramel filled her mouth as she brought Scott's laptop to life.

She panned around a 3D render of a light fitting and remembered that once she'd felt in awe of Scott. The first time she'd seen this arrangement, she'd asked him what the white jellybeans were for and he'd told her he was conceiving a project.

The white jellybeans were part of the ritual. Scott hadn't even known what the flavour was, but he'd said that white gave him clarity of thought, and at the time this had made him seem deeply … something, to her.

The intercom buzzed. She let Piper up.

'Thank you for doing this.' She gave Piper a hug.

'Of course! It's my honour!' Piper sounded enthusiastic but appeared tense.

In spite of, or perhaps because of, their conversation in the Barossa, Kit had asked Piper to accompany her wedding dress shopping. Piper's reply had begun with silence and ended with an unconvincing, 'Yes please!'

Now she picked up a white jellybean and asked, 'Bonbonniere?'

'No. They're to help Scott think,' Kit said. Piper's mouth twitched like it wanted to laugh.

'Will your mum be joining us?' Piper wandered towards the window.

Kit tittered.

Piper turned back.

'No.' Kit explained. 'Annalese will *not* be.'

'Really? She's that bad?'

Kit laughed in reply.

❧

The bridal assistant stood beside Kit.

They both watched Piper ... and Marc.

Piper and Marc stood a metre away on the lime-washed boards of a designer's ready-to-wear store and Kit reflected on the reasons why she'd brought them.

Piper was good at being cool and pragmatic, and Marc was good at being honest and unaffected by emotion or lace. She thought she'd chosen them well ... she hadn't.

Flirting was all Marc and Piper seemed to be good at and the bridal assistant waved her hand at Kit's entourage until she drew their attention.

'Stunning, Kit!' Piper immediately exclaimed. 'Where do you get off having a body like that?'

Kit raised the corner of her mouth and took hold of the dressing room's tapestry drape. 'Do you like it?' Her voice sounded uncertain.

Marc took his time unfolding and refolding his arms. 'Assuming this will be a country wedding,' he said. 'You don't look right. It's too … princessy.'

'They're all princessy, Marc. That's what being a bride *is*,' Piper said.

Kit clicked her tongue as her gaze fell to the floor. Marc stepped forward to hold her shoulder.

'You don't seem happy,' he said.

Kit shrugged him off.

'You're not enjoying this.' He took her shoulder again.

'Of course I'm not.'

'What do you mean "of course"?' Marc frowned.

'Surely this isn't meant to be enjoyable?'

'Isn't it?' Marc smiled, uncertain. 'You're choosing something to wear for "the best day of your life".'

Kit's throat felt hot. Everyone's eyes were on her.

'Unzip the dress,' she said.

No one moved.

'Unzip it! Please!' she shouted.

'What? Now?'

'Now. I want it off. Get it off, please, please, please.'

Marc fumbled ineptly with the zipper then yanked it.

The shop assistant bumped him away, the zipper stuck, released, stuck again. 'This never happens!' the woman said and finally the dress slid from Kit's slightly sweaty frame. 'Would you like to try another?' Kit could hardly keep herself from laughing.

The three sat quietly at a café afterward.

Piper sipped her tea.

Marc stirred his coffee.

Kit used her serviette to dab at her upper lip, still damp from the in-store scuffle.

'Well,' Piper said.

'Good first go,' Marc added.

'Very good,' Piper said.

'We'll try again another day.'

'Yes,' Kit said twice and gulped her juice.

Scott was hunched over his computer when Kit got home.

The white Jelly Bellies had all gone from the lid, and there were no more in sight.

Kit touched his shoulder. 'All out of ammo?'

Scott didn't look up. Kit levered herself around so she was in plain sight.

'All out of white?' she asked. Scott's eyes were foggy when they met hers and Kit leaned forward to bite his nose. He tugged back with a grunt.

'How's it going?' she said.

Scott wiped saliva from his nose with his sleeve. 'Not well. I can't resolve it.'

'Shall I have a look?'

'No,' Scott said. Kit watched him move shapes about the screen.

'I went wedding dress shopping today,' she said.

'What did you find?'

'Nothing,' Kit replied and Scott glanced up at her, then back at his laptop.

'Why?' he said.

Kit let the question pass. 'Will you come with me next time?' she said.

Scott frowned. 'No, I'm the groom.'

'So?'

'I thought I'm not meant to see.'

'I don't care.'

Scott leaned in to eye the computer.

'I'd find it easier if you came, you're the only person I'm buying it for,' Kit said, and Scott's head slowly turned, his expression gentler as though her words had softened him. He took the back of her head and kissed her brow.

'Okay,' he said.

Kit felt suddenly like she'd won and lost all at once.

❧

'Round two wedding dress shopping next weekend?' Piper smiled.

'No don't worry, Scott's going to come with me,' Kit said. 'What was *Hamper*'s previous "Beginner's Guide To" web feature?'

Piper thought. '"Beginner's Guide to Kale". Kit, I'm more than happy to shop with you again. Next weekend?'

Kit leaned forward and carefully sliced a truffle in two,

exposing the organic, veiny inner to the clinical environs of the magazine's set. 'No. I'll be fine.'

She peeled back the wrapper from a prop she'd purchased at the Spring Street Cheese Cellars.

'Is that …?' Piper leaned in. The paper peeled open to reveal a velvet-rind brie-like cheese, sliced horizontally and filled with triple cream and black truffle.

'*Coulommiers Truffe.*'

'I didn't see it on the list,' Piper said.

'It replaced truffle oil. It's the only off-brief thing, I promise,' Kit said and despite a desire to do the opposite, she found a cloth, cleansed the white set of all imperfections and carefully began to arrange five meticulous scenes.

Truffle popcorn.

Truffle salt.

Truffle stored with eggs.

Truffle butter.

Truffle in Coulommiers.

'Beginner's Guide to Truffles.' She took out her camera.

Scott absently patted Kit's thigh as she stared at the ceiling.

He'd just come, was feeling content because of it, and his thumb slid across his phone as he browsed the web – his version of smoking after sex.

'That was nice,' he said.

'Yes,' Kit said, wanting it to be true and using her voice to make it so. The phone screen came into view as Scott held it out to her.

'How about this person?' he asked. 'He usually does fashion editorials so he'd be comfortable in an open space. It's probably a bit excessive but if we need one stand-out thing, it's a photographer, otherwise the rest won't be worth it.'

Kit peered at the screen, saw high-end fashion photos, and knew he was talking about a photographer for the wedding.

'Great,' she said.

'I'll send him an email.' Scott rolled over and leaned his back against her. 'How was *Hamper* today? Did you shoot the truffles?'

He'd been waiting in the bedroom for her when she'd arrived home – ready and waiting like she should have wanted.

'Yes,' Kit said. 'We shot the truffles.'

'Turn out well?'

Kit searched for the energy to lie again. 'Really great,' she managed.

'Good.' Scott didn't notice the tepidness of her reply and reached behind him to absently pat her thigh again. 'I'm glad you're coming around. *Hamper*'s aesthetic's good for you.'

'Yes,' Kit said.

The day's shoot had felt exactly like their sex: detached and prescribed.

10

Off-road was now rare for Kit.

She'd held onto her sixteenth birthday gift from Connor anyway, an old Land Rover Defender that felt like a part of the outdoors she could take home to the confines of the city.

The Defender knocked across the uneven terrain of Cannock Chase. Kit waved to Earl, owner and Gossard neighbour, as he passed, walking the other way.

'I have no idea where I'm going.' Kit put in a call to Marc.

'Where are you?' he said.

'About to pass the orchards, truffles are out to the right ...'

'Keep coming. Straight up the hill. When you cross the old rail, follow it east.'

Kit dropped into second gear, passed the orchards, continued on up a rise, and hit a terrace marked with rusted rail sleepers that ran in both directions.

The once public rail was now a dormant twenty-five-kilometre relic that snaked across the valley. An old station remained at Gossard Range and the rail continued on through Cannock Chase where grass grew over steel and gravel. The Defender straddled the track, which led to the dense arch of brick that marked the rail tunnel.

Kit came to a standstill then got out. The passage burrowed through the hillside. Greenery fell over the tunnel rim where timber battens sealed the way, and double doors marked an entry point. Marc stuck his head out and beckoned.

Inside, the world felt instantly cool and mossy.

The arching brick cavern glowed. Strings of cargo lanterns ran the length of the roof and branded oak barrels lay in racks along one wall. Hundreds of bottles slept in rows.

'So this is it,' Kit said.

'This is it,' Marc replied.

'Darling!' Kit heard her father, out of sight. He appeared, arms wide. 'Welcome to the cider vaults!'

Kit hugged him. 'It looks fantastic,' she said.

'It's supreme,' Connor replied. 'The conditions in here are just *supreme*.'

'I had no idea that you were this far along.'

'Yes, yes. The first batch has been on lees for what ... four months now?'

'Wow. And you're having fun?'

'Time of my life!' Connor hooted. 'With Marc, myself and one other bloke sneaking about, it's a veritable covert op, *guerrilla cider warfare*.'

'It's so exciting.' Kit grinned.

'It is liberating.' Connor sounded definitive and proud. 'It feels like we've at last dodged away from that old Arenberg & Gossard ... AGVM cobweb. They may have gotten the lion's share of our business back in the day, may be giants now because of it, but we've always held the lineage and the cider will make that known.' He strode forward, took a bottle from a rack and climbed onto an old rail trolley: greyed beams atop large rusted wheels, still on the track.

'And imagine when we sign on the dotted line for this. We can trolley cider by *rail* from Cannock Chase to Gossard Range. Now *that's* a renaissance ...' He popped the crown off the bottle and whooped as yeast disgorged on the ground. 'Let's see what four months tastes like, eh?'

'It's a bit dry.' Kit smacked her lips.

'Yes ... it's only half as good as it will be. Give it another couple of months, we'll add our secret liqueur at the last and it'll be a dream.'

Kit squinted. There was something unfamiliar parked near the tunnel doors.

'What is that?' she said as she moved towards it. 'Is it ...?'

'Is it one of the most *revered cars ever made*? Yes!' Connor hooted as he followed Kit along the tunnel. They reached the car and Marc ran his hand down the smooth rear taper of the old convertible.

'It's a 1963 Jag E-Type Roadster,' Connor whispered as he put his hand on the driver's side door and looked from Kit to Marc.

'I can see,' Kit replied, whispering without knowing why.

Connor grinned as he swung the driver's door wide. 'Get in!'

'Dad ... no,' Marc said.

'Dad, *no*?' Connor sounded appalled. 'There'll be no *Dad, no*, thanks. It's my car and I can do what I like with it. Get *in*.' Without hesitation, he climbed into the driver's seat and turned to see that his children were doing what they were told.

'Dad *bought* it?'

'He was excited about the cider, so he treated himself,' Marc said.

'Shush, shush, shush,' Connor said. 'We're not telling *Mum* yet. Open the tunnel, Marc.'

Marc opened the tunnel doors and sat reticently in the passenger seat.

'Hurry up, Kit!' Connor said.

'There's no room.'

'Sit on your brother's lap!'

Kit scrunched herself onto Marc's lap.

'We'll just do a nifty scoot around the property,' Connor said.

'Make it fucking nifty,' Kit said. 'This is so un-luxurious I can't believe it.'

'Do not say that,' Connor said. 'You're in the most beautiful car in the world.'

'Beautiful is not how I'd describe having my brother's knee up my arse.'

'It ain't glorious for me either, darlin',' Marc said.

Connor cheered as he accelerated out. He had a fatherly excitability that often ended in mishap. 'Excitement' and 'Dad' never gelled well and Kit sat rigid, watched branch, stone, stump and lump dance past the pristine exterior of the car as she held herself, face pinched.

The car lapped Cannock Chase, passed every possibility for calamity, and Connor finally began to slot the vehicle back into the railway tunnel.

When the engine was safely off, Kit popped the door and tumbled out.

'Arggh!' she screamed and fell backward on to Marc.

'*What?*' Marc clutched her. Kit gaped at a wild animal galloping from the shadows of the cider vault. 'Jesus,' Marc laughed and let her go. 'You scared the shit out of me.'

'*What is that?*' Kit grabbed his sleeve.

Connor opened his arms wide as the animal loped towards them. 'It's a dog,' he grinned. 'It's just a good doggie.'

The *good doggie* was almost a metre high.

It had mournful, shaggy grey fur, skinny legs, a long boxy snout and a slender tail that curved into a hook. It looked like it had been roaming the dark for centuries and had chosen this moment to step into the light.

'Fucking hell.' Kit leaned back against the car. 'It's a *dog?* Where the fuck did that come from?'

'Isn't he majestic?' Connor patted the animal's head. 'Such a good dog, such a good dog … it's Raph's deerhound.'

Kit blinked. 'What?'

'It's a Scottish deerhound. Graceful, old purebred. He's going to be a friend for Alfa and Romeo.'

'*Whose* is it?' Kit said.

'Raph's,' Connor replied. 'One of the winery men. It arrived by courier the other day, the man can't live without his animal, apparently. Long journey, been through quarantine and all, haven't you, poor boy?'

'Quarantine?'

'Raph's not from around here,' Marc said. 'Had the dog shipped.'

'Big trip, eh Sergeant …' Connor massaged the dog's ears.

'Why's the dog up here?' Kit said.

'Raph's been working with us in here, he's our third cider musketeer.' Connor grinned and Kit nervously combed her fingers through her hair as she stared at the dog.

'Raph? That winery worker?' she said.

'You've probably seen him around.'

'Yes,' Kit said, quietly. 'He was in the Barossa …'

'Yeah, I could do with five more of him, to be honest. He knows his stuff. It's taken him a bit to get used to the climate and our way, but he's indispensable now. It's not often you find someone who's *au fait* with the labour and understands the product and isn't a complete knucklehead.'

'How–' Kit hesitated. 'How'd you find him?'

'What?' Connor began. 'Oh, I didn't. He came to me. He'd done a stint in Margaret River and was on the hunt for something new down south. I was happy to have him, needed the extra hands, but I didn't expect him to deliver to the extent he has. I couldn't do the cider without him now.'

Marc's phone rang and he moved away.

Kit peered at Raph's dog. 'So where'd this come from?' she said.

Connor glanced up at her.

'The dog,' she said.

Connor thought, then shrugged as he huffed a laugh. 'Couldn't say for sure. Wasn't actually here when he arrived. Raph wasn't allowed animals at the place he was at in W.A. and when he mentioned he had a dog back home, I knew he meant overseas … he'd mentioned the States once, maybe … Anyway, I told him the animal was welcome. Want to keep the man around.'

'Is that where Raph's come from, you think?' Kit knew she sounded too interested and yawned to temper it.

'Not sure,' Connor sounded indifferent, too, and Kit felt annoyed. 'He seems to have gotten around. Think he's found his place here, though. Seems to be making himself at home now that's Sergeant's arrived, and they've bunkered down up at the shearers' quarters.' He patted the dog's head.

'What's that?' Kit replied but Connor didn't seem to hear. 'He and Sergeant have bunkered down where?'

'Oh, the shearers' quarters, back on Gossard Range.' Connor pulled a rag from his pocket and began to dust the rims of the car.

'What do you mean?'

'Raph's living up there.'

'What?' Kit said.

Connor began to manoeuvre the car's hood back in to place.

'Rentals are scant in the valley,' he said. 'Raph was having trouble so I offered the old quarters. No skin off my nose, nice having him close at hand, really. Always wanted more than one son ...' He glanced teasingly at Marc but he was on his phone.

'Aren't the shearers' quarters a ruin?' Kit said.

'Not at all,' Connor smiled, half serious, half not. 'I'd call them a bachelor's dream, and I'd give anything to live up there – peace and utter quiet. Raph isn't picky!' He chuckled. 'And in all seriousness, the man's become a real asset. He's loyal, someone I can rely on, and he's not that sort who's always on the lookout for the next best thing, you know? He and I have really built a rapport. It's fantastic having someone else I can trust on the cider here.'

Kit stared at her father as the huge hound pushed its head against her stomach.

'And now Gossard Range has another dog, eh Sergeant!' Connor fastened the hood. 'And Sherwood green, Kit? Do you think I got the car in the right colour?'

Raph was living on Gossard Range.

❧

Bulbs had begun to show among the cruciferous vegetables in Annalese's garden and chooks pecked near the delicate heads of snowdrops.

Annalese knelt in kneepads and rattan visor and Kit felt a sudden softness, one that came upon her unexpectedly at times when she watched her mother from afar, free from bluster and bravado.

A white cabbage moth lifted off a vegetable. Annalese's eyes followed it and she startled when she saw Kit. Her body stiffened and her armour began to click back into place like a Transformer.

'How long have you been standing there?' She coughed away a gentleness in her voice. 'You're earlier than you said.'

Kit had left the boys next door and had come to perform her subsequent valley duty: a ride with her mother. 'Not long,' she said. 'Shall we go?'

They tramped towards the stables and Kit felt the awkward seams of the jodhpurs cutting into her thighs.

She mounted her pony and, glad to have an audience, Annalese took her time brushing her horse, making long, thoughtful strokes while Kit stagnated astride.

'Scott called,' Annalese announced when they were finally mounted and climbing the rise.

'Called?'

'Called. Called me.'

Kit's mouth opened.

'He called about the wedding.'

Kit kept steady.

'He asked about having it at the Barossa estate.'

'I–'

'I said it was a wonderful idea, said that I'd always wanted one of my children to have a wedding there.' Annalese's ponytail bounced beneath her tan leather riding hat.

'He needn't have called. He and I will sort it all.'

'No, Kit, you're going to need my help.'

Kit's tongue began to click.

'I'm glad we have the venue down, now we can start–' Annalese came to an abrupt halt and made a short, clipped sound reserved for an inconvenience caused by staff.

A man walked along the track ahead. He stopped when he heard them.

'Don't stop, don't wait,' Annalese spat. For reasons that were nothing like her mother's, Kit thought the same.

Raph ran a hand through his hair as their horses halted in front of him.

'Hello,' he said. Kit took him in, hair unwashed, hands dirty, arms that clearly lifted much, often. She felt aware of her jodhpurs, tight across her legs and rump.

'Just passing!' Annalese didn't smile.

'Finished for the day?' Kit asked Raph and sensed her mother's displeasure.

Raph gazed up at her. 'Heading home,' he said.

'Home?' Annalese sounded tense and Kit felt her shoulders seize.

'Up the hill.' Raph nodded in the direction he was going.

'What's up there?' Annalese said.

'The shearers' quarters,' Raph said. 'I'm lodged up there where Connor–'

'On the *estate*?' Annalese's eyes were wide.

'Yes. Connor let me the shearers' quarters,' Raph said.

The twitch of Annalese's boot told Kit that her mother knew nothing of the staffer in residence.

'How are you finding it?' Kit said, quickly. 'Not too much of a ruin, I hope.'

'Does he look like he cares?' Annalese snapped. Her horse planted a hoof into Raph's shin. Kit froze, swore, then jumped down.

'I apologise,' Annalese said. 'He does do that to people he doesn't like.'

'Shut up, Mum. Raph, are you okay?'

Raph held his leg, crouched. 'There's some pain.'

'A lot?'

'A man can survive a horse kick, Kit, come on,' Annalese said. 'I'm cold.'

Kit put her hand on Raph's shoulder and felt his warmth through fabric.

'I'll ride you back to the shearers' quarters,' she said. Annalese grunted, condescendingly. 'Go, Mum, go. I'll get myself back.'

Annalese lifted herself in her saddle and cantered on.

'I'm fine,' Raph said.

He made to stand, winced down at his leg, laughed, and Kit was surprised by the humility she heard.

'I hit you with the car and now our horse has kicked you. Let me take you back, my girl's a quiet mount.' She stroked the horse's flank then hoisted herself up. Raph waited, then finally he glanced over his shoulder and boosted himself to sit behind the saddle.

'Are you too proud to ride behind?' she said.

'No.'

'Why did you hesitate?'

Raph didn't reply and as the horse began to walk rhythmically up the slope, Kit knew. She knew that he'd hesitated because, like her, he was nervous. The horse undulated and she felt exactly what she, and maybe he, had to be nervous about.

Closeness.

'Sergeant.' She said the word loudly to punctuate the silence and she sensed Raph smile. 'I met him earlier today. He was … terrifying.'

'He can be intimidating, at first,' Raph said. 'But he has a soft heart.'

'I doubt it. He looked fierce.'

'He can be, if he wants to,' Raph said, and the horse soon came to a stop by the shearers' quarters.

Once belonging to a neighbouring sheep farm, this part of Gossard Range was remote, the grass on the rise almost bald, the earth stony. The wind buffeted Kit's hair as Raph dismounted. The pocket of warmth they'd created between them was gone.

'Thank you,' he said.

'You're welcome,' she replied. She could now barely make him out in the twilight, he more dark and still than the relic just behind.

'I suppose I'll … see you soon,' he said.

'Yes, hope–' Kit almost said 'hopefully'. Her heart fluttered, and she sat motionless, the word hanging, begging to be finished.

Raph stood without speaking, Kit sat silently astride, and when she knew she'd remained too long, she raised her hand and turned to head down the hill.

11

Kit sat on the sofa in Scott's studio.

Her camera was on her lap, the latest issue of *Hamper* in front of her.

This was a career high.

It should have felt like it.

The cover photo was credited to her … her first cover.

She appraised it – the bland, neutered photograph of her own creation – and knew that she'd become too good at doing work that was not.

She examined the cover, then reached for her glass, swivelled the drink in her hand, and sensed the liquid rock back and forth.

She set the glass down then picked it up again.

She set it down and jiggled the magazine, hoping the movement would cause the cover to rearrange itself and become something she could be proud of.

It stayed still and she kept her eyes on the photo, didn't let herself look away from what she'd created. Bland and neutered.

That's what she was.

Bland and neutered was–

Scott coughed.

Kit glanced up. He yawned and tapped a pencil on the edge of his workbench.

She returned her gaze to the magazine, let it fall, picked up her camera, and set it to playback.

Larder, the Barossa estate, Amaro Nonino filling his glass at the bar.

She gazed at Raph, frozen in time, then up at Scott, moving real-time in the studio. The former seemed more alive than the latter.

Cold, inhibited and impassive: *Hamper* sat beside her like an unwanted friend. In her hands, inside the camera, was Raph.

Staring at him was like staring out the window and seeing his hound, circling her house.

The sight of it filled her with equal parts fear and freedom. She didn't know whether to lock the window or climb out. Raph called to Kit's wildness. He made it want to be set free and it was becoming too painful not to do so.

Neutered and bland, the magazine lay beside her.

In her hands, an escape.

She pushed the camera and magazine aside and descended into couch cushions.

Scott tapped his pencil.

Kit's chest rose and fell.

She lolled her head from side to side, saw her camera screen frame the man from the shearers' quarters then looked to Scott, saw his dedication and certitude, and sensed the way it contrasted with her doubt.

'I want to leave *Hamper*,' she heard herself say.

Scott glanced up. 'Don't be silly,' he said.

She was being silly. Scott had said it and Scott was usually right.

She turned the camera off, sat in silence and stared up at the exposed pipework on the warehouse ceiling.

Suddenly she sat up.

She reached for her laptop, began raking through Google, and finally she came across an online magazine platform she'd seen once before. Blank pages of a digital periodical twirled like real paper, and felt luxurious, tangible.

She wondered if this solution might be too insignificant and paltry, but it might be all she needed: a release. That was exactly all she needed.

Blank pages. Beautifully packaged digital storage. That was it.

She stared at the blank canvas and the world ahead felt suddenly hopeful. This would be a space in which she could safely explore her feelings, a place where she could offload the silliness that had become her distraction.

She glimpsed the *Hamper* cover and its limitations and disappointments seemed now distant.

Her duty was there, a chance for creation was here.

She glanced up and saw that Scott was absorbed.

She paused at the cover of her new magazine – an image, title? – and unsure of both, went on to insert a recent shot on page one, a shot that was the antithesis to *Hamper*.

Deformed, black shapes against faded wicker, red and white check cloth littered with soil from her home and the hint of a wild man's hand …

Truffle Hunting, Gossard Range, she typed.

＊

Everything felt almost fine now.

That she and Piper flew interstate to Byron Bay, scoured the hinterland's cheese rooms, produce stores, and farmers' markets for the best local fare and brought it all back to their hotel … felt almost fine.

That they spent the day in the moist valleys of the hinterland, scraped the sides of the foodbowl at farmgates, cafés and bakeries, and that they now had breads, dairy, carrots in four colours, heirloom vegetables, misshapen tomatoes and herbs they'd never seen, all in an incongruous, pillowed, four-star space … felt fine.

That the warm outdoors had made Piper and Kit feel expansive, revived, and that this feeling ended when they carted the tangle of food back to their air-conditioned hotel to roll out the lights and white backdrops of their employer … felt fine.

Kit cleaned fertile soil from the vegetables.

She erased flour dusted on the bread with a water spritzer.

She turned the 'best' faces of the vegetables to the front, made the food appear perfect like it wasn't and this all felt fine.

It felt fine because, despite the superficialities of her work, she had begun.

In a corner of the internet, she was cultivating an antidote, a release and it meant that sustaining this – maintaining conformity – was nothing. She trimmed back the bounty they'd collected to little more than white space, exactly how *Hamper* wanted it. It felt fine.

＊

Kit's pair of black leather cigarillo pants gave her a contained, invincible feeling of utility. Marc noted their noteworthiness as he passed her in the vineyard.

'Hello, pants,' he said.

'Hello.'

'One of the winery boys is going to hurt themselves if he finds you lying here in those. It's an OH&S hazard.'

Kit tilted her camera and snapped her brother's dark outline against the sky.

She'd returned from her *Hamper* sojourn and driven up to the winery with her camera, needing to purge her mind and memory card and fill it with something for her digital magazine.

Marc continued on into the vineyard, Kit lifted herself onto her elbow and reassessed what she'd been looking at.

She opened the aperture and brought a single grape into focus, dusty and purple with the beginnings of a sunset behind.

A shadow blacked out the light. 'Move, Marc.'

He didn't.

Kit turned and saw not Marc but him: the deerhound-man who circled her house.

She knew she should get up and walk away while she still could.

'What are you photographing?' he asked.

Kit answered by turning to the grapes on the bare winter vine.

'You've just hung them there.'

Kit laughed at herself. 'Yes, I'm faking the season,' she said.

He reached out, took one of the bunches from the vine and weighed it thoughtfully in his hand.

'Crush them,' Kit heard herself say.

'What?'

She watched his wrist and fingers flex, knowing what she wanted only when she said it a second time. 'I want you to crush them,' she said.

The grapes instantly became nothing.

Pulp and juice bled through Raph's fist and Kit's shutter clicked.

Raph opened his dripping, wet hand and wiped it across his white T-shirt. Kit hit the shutter again, caught the dark, wet pulp that spread across his chest.

Kit lifted another bunch and put it in his hand. 'Again,' she said and Raph crushed those too. He looked down at his hand then wiped it on himself.

Kit took a third bunch and heard herself apologise before she crushed them hard against him, feeling the wet beads explode between body and hand.

Raph gazed down at himself, then back up. He'd begun to frown and his hand suddenly rose, brushed Kit's face, and she touched her cheek ... felt the wet residue he'd left behind.

'A critter,' he said.

'Gone?'

He replied by pulling off his shirt and using it like a rag to dry her dirtied cheek.

There was silence. Kit would have felt uneasy had it not been for her new project. But, as it was, there was no problem. She had to take photos for her digital magazine and some of those photos would now be of him. No problem.

The sun had gone. The valley was cool and still. Cars started down at the winery building.

Kit reached out and dried her fingers on Raph's T-shirt, bunched in his hand.

'Here.' She gestured. 'Let me wash it.'

'That won't be necessary.'

'There's no washing machine at the shearers' quarters.'

'I can manage.'

'Let me take it home.' Kit stretched out her upturned palm. Raph assessed what he held then the damp piece of cloth filled Kit's hand. She resisted bringing it to her face to inhale.

'Thank you,' she said.

Raph said nothing.

'What are you doing tonight?' Kit asked.

'Nothing.' Raph searched her face. 'You?'

'I–' Kit wished she hadn't asked the question. 'I have a dinner with my–with Scott.'

'With *my* Scott?' Raph looked like he wanted to smile.

'With Scott.'

'With your fiancé, Scott.'

'Yes, my fiancé, Scott.' Kit began to walk away from him, down towards the winery.

Raph called after her. 'Your behind,' he said, 'it's dirty.'

Kit reached around, felt debris clinging to her leather-clad rear and brushed it gently away without stopping.

12

'I'm sorry,' Scott said over the phone.

Kit heard his agent, Alexi, pipe up in the background. 'Please tell Kit I'm sorry,' she said. 'It was the best I could do.'

'Alexi tried but it was the only day,' Scott said.

'So you can't postpone?'

'No. It's the only day this guy from Fermi can meet. He's not here long.'

'I've made appointments for us.'

'You won't have to cancel, your mother's going to go with you,' Scott said.

Kit wondered if she'd heard correctly.

'I asked Annalese to step in,' he added. 'She was happy to.'

Kit was waiting to meet Scott for wedding dress shopping, he'd just called to cancel, and unless she had misheard, he'd just said that he'd arranged for Annalese to go in his stead.

'You asked my *mother*?'

'Yes, she'll be there soon. You know how important this meeting is, otherwise I'd be there. I'm sorry.'

Annalese tilted her head from side to side, appraising Kit in the dressing room mirror.

'Are you going to lose any weight before the wedding?'

The shop assistant appeared startled. The only thing that startled Kit was that her mother hadn't asked the question sooner.

'She doesn't *need* to!' The shop assistant's nonchalance was morphing into hysteria. The woman had become so wound up that Kit knew she'd soon unravel. 'Do you know what other brides would do to have this shape? Dresses *adore* a curve.'

Annalese tittered, eyes on Kit. 'On your wedding day, darling, modesty is key. Think Jackie K., not Marilyn. You're all Marilyn in that gown. It's tacky.'

Despite Annalese being the only one who wanted to be there, it had been Scott who'd asked her to, ergo Annalese was performing a favour, ergo she was owed liberties, ergo a complete lack of censorship was the liberty she'd chosen to effect.

'Fucking Scott,' Kit breathed. The shop assistant strummed her fingers uncomfortably on her upper lip until Kit finally asked her to kindly relieve her of the Valentino.

'Look. It's a beautiful dress.' Annalese unfolded and refolded her arms. 'I think it's you, Kit, that's the problem.'

Kit gave a dizzy little laugh as the assistant helped her from the dress and hung it from one of Le Louvre's gilded mirrors.

'Actually Mum,' Kit offered as she slid her Current/Elliotts up her legs and gave a little sigh as the well-moulded denim cupped her bottom. 'I agree.'

Outside on the flagstone-and-lawn entry, Annalese turned to Kit. 'Let's look online,' she said. 'I'll purchase, you can try them at home, and we can courier back the ones you don't want.

It's the easiest. I honestly don't know why anyone bothers with stores, I mean the *lighting* for God's sake. Your *dimples*.'

In the countryside, the soft hills and open landscape absorbed some of Annalese's severity. But here, in the city, her mother's savagery reverberated, revisiting Kit on endless loop.

Annalese put the toes of her kitten-heel booties together and slid on her sunglasses. 'And over lunch,' she said, without querying whether Kit wanted lunch, 'while we're eating we can begin talking about the schedule. I know you and Scott haven't set a date, but it will be easier for you to choose a dress if you know when it's going to be, morning, afternoon or evening. Yes?'

'Yes,' Kit said and felt something die inside.

❧

'Kit?' Scott said. He'd said it twice.

They were in the kitchen cooking after Kit's day with Annalese.

'Kit,' he said again. 'How'd it go?'

Kit continued to move onion around in a pan and finally replied, 'Scott. Please don't ask favours of Annalese. When she thinks she's helping, she thinks she can do and say whatever she likes.'

'Come on, Kit, she's fine.'

'She isn't fine. She asked me if I was planning to lose some weight before the wedding.'

Scott opened his mouth to speak then closed it again and made a *pfff* sound.

'Do you even care what she thinks?' he said. 'I don't. All I care about is that she has a clearer head than you *and* your brother, *and* cares more about us getting married than Piper or anyone else. I value that, as should you.'

Kit watched as the onion turned glassy. She heard Scott say her name, like a question, and after a while she heard herself say, 'You're right,' like he wanted her to.

He kissed the top of her head like a handshake at the end of a business transaction.

Later, after Scott was in bed, Kit sat at her computer.

She hadn't seen the vineyard photos yet so ejected the card from her camera, slid it into her laptop, and images filled the screen.

His head was cropped.

The muscles in his neck were ropy, hands dirty.

The grapes seemed to melt in his grasp and his shirt had become soiled and sheer with the fruit's juice.

Kit uploaded Raph into her online magazine, then captioned, flicked back, flicked forward, captioned. Then she remembered.

She reached for her bag, slid her hand slowly in and her fingers found it. Wet from the day before and unclean in every sense of the word, she cupped the T-shirt in her hands and put her face to the crumpled cotton.

There she stayed, felt the wounds of the day slowly knit themselves closed, and when her soul had reassembled itself, she inhaled, and it appeared.

The feeling and the word came and she reached for the keyboard, typing the word into the blank title space on the cover page of the magazine.

Hunger.

On page five of *Hamper*, Jimmy Hillinger's industry column reported the month's new product releases.

'Oh just shut the fuck up,' Kit said from the passenger seat. The magazine was the only reading material Piper had in her car.

Piper glanced over.

'Jimmy's article,' Kit said. 'Have you read his latest? In the new issue?'

'Not yet.'

'He includes Gossard in his boutique products report, saying: *"Industry darlings and long-time family-owned Gossard Range have been future planning. Just this month, restaurants and select purveyors became the first to sample the company's premier yield of black truffles, grown – we believe – on the family's Yarra Valley estate. Reports from Gossard insiders, however, say that this is just the beginning of diversification for the brand, rumours hinting at the release of a new Gossard beverage, one that may diverge from their current popular viticulture lines. But with veteran director Connor Gossard giving nothing away, all one can do – is wait."* '

Kit dropped the magazine and texted Marc. '*Did u see Jimmy Hillinger's scribble in this month's* Hamper? *If not: read. Copy in Dad's office.*'

Marc texted back. '*Not a "bad" mention but can we gag that fuck? Where's he getting this from? We're not even near ready to announce. Arenberg & Gossard will b on our arse if he leaks, Dad'll kill someone. Jimmy's ur fault, u can never ever harangue me about my hook-ups again.*'

'Who's that?' Piper asked.

'Marc,' Kit replied. Piper failed to hide the smile that appeared with his name.

'No,' Kit said, but Piper's smile remained.

Ten minutes later, they turned into Cannock Chase.

'So this *isn't* your place?' Piper said.

'No,' Kit replied, 'just our neighbour's … for now.'

They drove past the orchards and up onto the rail line.

'Wow,' Piper said when they reached the rail tunnel. 'What's this?'

Kit herself was still in awe of the strange, grand place. 'It's a disused railway tunnel,' she said. 'Dad's been using it to cellar cider. The conditions are perfect, apparently.'

Piper brought the car to a standstill by the tunnel doors.

'What are you holding?' she asked, peering down at Kit's hands.

'It's a rag.' Kit started to get out of the car.

Piper grabbed the thing.

Kit let her have it and walked as if unperturbed towards the tunnel.

Piper got out of the car.

'It's not a rag,' she said. 'It's a T-shirt. Of a man.'

Kit walked back towards her friend and put out her hand.

Piper didn't respond.

Kit cocked her head, gestured again, and because her friend remained unwilling, she grabbed at the T-shirt.

Piper giggled, resisting, Kit tugged, won, and carried the spoils with her into the tunnel.

Inside was dark, smelling of yeast and moss, and Kit groped forward until she found the makeshift desk by the wall with the lamp. She heard the generator running, the lamp switch worked, and in the glow she tore a piece of paper from a roll and scrawled 'Raph' on it.

She laid the folded T-shirt on the desk and put the note on top.

'Whose was that?' Piper asked as Kit walked outside. 'Raph's? Was it Raph's?'

'Yes.'

Piper eyed her. 'Have you been meeting here? In secret?'

Kit got back into the car.

Piper followed. She hid the car keys under her leg to show they wouldn't be leaving.

Kit rolled her eyes. 'It's nothing. I was too embarrassed to give it back to him so I left it there, where he works.'

'"It's nothing,"' Piper mocked. 'Why did you have it in the first place?'

'I laundered it.'

'*Why?*'

'There was a photo shoot, the shirt got dirty. I offered to launder it because he doesn't have a washing machine.'

'Sex dirty? Dirty from sex?'

'You think I'm fucking cheating?'

'I don't know! Hopefully!' Piper's words echoed in the small, motionless car.

There was silence.

Finally, Piper removed the keys from under her leg, started the car and they drove out, on towards Gossard Range.

'Hello!' Annalese was charming and gregarious as she kissed Piper on both cheeks. A Martha Stewart apron was tied around her slim waist and she spanked Kit playfully with a wooden spoon as she pecked her, too. 'Hello darling.'

Piper positioned herself on a barstool. 'I can't believe this is my first visit to Kit's family home. It's beautiful driving in, Annalese.'

Annalese beamed, gratified, and Piper offered to help with dinner.

'Can you cook, Piper?' Annalese replied. 'I always expect people involved in food to be good cooks but our dear Kitten, dear me, despite her photography skill she's a *horrendous* cook. It's our private joke, isn't it sweetie.' She stretched her mouth into a grin that Kit didn't return.

Kit knew that Piper hadn't quite believed her stories about her mother. Now, on Annalese's turf, Kit watched her friend flail. 'Oh, I can pull off a soufflé, but I prefer an omelette,' she blathered. 'And Kit isn't a *bad* cook, but maybe that just gives away my low standards!' Piper glanced at Kit and mouthed hopelessly *'I'm so sorry'* while Annalese's back was turned. Kit waved the apology away. She was used to guests siding with the bully; it was a form of self-defence.

'Slice these,' Annalese said and handed Piper a laden chopping board.

'Of course.' Piper sounded nervous and Kit felt anticipatory pity.

'Oh Piper!' Annalese turned even sooner than Kit had expected. 'You don't use the *green* bits.'

Piper's knife hovered above the whites of the leeks as Annalese proceeded to rant: 'Bitter! Woody! Tough!' When it was over, Kit smiled and offered Piper an I Told You So face.

'Annalese. Of course you're right,' Piper said. 'It's very important that you *don't* use the greens of the leeks, I'm so glad you were *so* quick to remind me. Can I make you a drink? I think we all need one.'

Piper was at the drinks trolley when a text message vibrated in Kit's pocket.

'Holy motherfucker.' Piper's message read.

Kit tried not to laugh. *'Isn't this fun?'* she typed.

'I admire and love you so much more now,' came Piper's reply, and Kit glanced towards the drinks trolley to see Piper pump her fist against her chest, make a peace sign and mouth RESPECT.

One sound had been Kit's favourite growing up as a child: the sound of men, scuffling in the hall. It was a sound that meant her father, her brother or both were home. It was a sound that meant she was saved.

She heard it now.

'What a wonderful couple of days ahead!' Connor's arms were wide, tummy pushing the buttons on his shirt, a wine bottle in each hand. 'Hello daughter and daughter's friend. I'm very excited about our design weekend.'

'As are we,' Piper said with a smile. Marc appeared and she appeared briefly abashed. 'Whisky sours, gents?'

'Yes! I haven't had one of those since college days.' Connor beamed.

Annalese began speaking loudly. 'Entrée of *ajo blanco*, mains of leek, gruyère, potato *en croute* with radicchio salad and your favourite for dessert, Connor darling.'

On Sunday afternoon, as their visit to the estate drew to a close, Kit surveyed the table littered with Piper's sketches, pastry crumbs and stained espresso cups.

'The letterpress.' Connor finally folded his arms. 'Forget the cost, I've decided. The traditionalism of the letterpress will represent the inherited nature of the recipe and the reawakening of Gossard's *cidre bouché*. Letterpress. My mind's set. And yes I like the image, Piper, perfect.'

Piper put down her pen, picked up the letterpress sample, and ran her finger over the textured debossing. 'In that case, I think we're done,' she said.

'Wonderful.' Connor clasped his hands. 'I appreciate your time, Piper, you're a clever cat. Why don't you have your own business? *We'd* be a client.'

'I don't like having clients,' Piper said. 'Their needs are too varied and too many.'

'But wasn't I just a walk in the park?'

'A stroll.' Piper smiled.

Connor spread his arms wide to scrunch both she and Kit into a hug. 'It's all getting very exciting, kids!'

13

Kit watched Scott move.

It was when he was doing what he loved that she found him most attractive and right then – moving carefully back and forward, wrapping a stool in brown paper and tape – was one of those moments.

'So will you?' Scott looked up to see that she'd heard him.

Kit hesitated then picked up her car keys. 'Yes. I will.'

Scott was readying to leave for London, where he'd be presenting his final solution to the stool design brief, and the London Design Festival would soon follow.

He'd just asked Kit to set a wedding date with Annalese and the Barossa staff while he was away. Kit didn't know why she'd agreed. She didn't want to discuss her wedding with anyone other than the one other person who was at the heart of it.

'What time's your flight again?' she asked.

'A car's coming about five.'

Kit glanced at her watch. 'It'll take me an hour to get to the valley … I'll have lunch at the homestead, get the sweater … back by half four.' She started down the stairs and Scott asked her to wait.

'I can't decide which to take, Cutler and Gross?' He put on an ironic, round-framed pair of sunglasses, reminiscent of spectacles, 'or, Thom Browne ...' he replaced them with tortoiseshell and steel aviators.

Kit rested her chin on the balustrade. 'The tortoiseshell.'

'I think the Cutler and Gross.' Scott turned from the mirror to Kit.

She raised a thumb before she kept on down the stairs.

❧

Connor was reading the paper at the homestead dining table when Kit walked in, yawning from the drive.

She'd called from the car to say she was coming and her father rose from the kitchen table 'Hello, darling.' He beamed.

'Mum's still not back?' Kit gave him a hug.

'No.' He scratched his head. He'd mentioned over the phone that Annalese had gone out for a ride and had been gone hours longer than expected. 'Why didn't you phone earlier about Scott's sweater? Marc went into town this morning, he could have brought it to you and saved you the drive.'

'I don't mind. Scott'll be packing all day, I wanted to get out.'

'When does he leave?'

'Tonight.'

'What's so special about this particular sweater that he just can't do without it?'

'It's my fault,' Kit said. 'I borrowed it and left it here last time. It's his favourite for long-haul flights. I didn't mind coming.'

Connor waited before he gave a wry laugh. Her father loved Scott but Kit knew her fiancé's fastidiousness didn't go unnoticed.

'What time did Mum go out?'

Connor studied his watch. 'Let's not get too worried for another … three minutes, when my coffee's percolated.' He sat back down and stabbed the paper. 'Arenberg Gossard Valcourt Mantel have just bought a hotel chain – how boring. That's what you do when you've got nothing left to do.' The percolator began to sputter and Connor stood with a stretch. 'Well, I suppose it's time to be officially concerned. Your mother left four hours ago, said she'd be gone two.'

'That is a bit long,' Kit said, before they heard a knock on the front door that preceded footsteps in the hall.

'I was going to send one of the men out,' Connor said. 'Now you're here, could you ride out with him? You know Mum won't be happy to see *staff* on the weekend …' He made a face. 'If the fourwheeler wasn't being serviced and I wasn't such a clod on horseback I'd go, but–' His head turned to look at the person who'd appeared. 'Raph, great, thanks.'

Raph stood in the mouth of the hall, boots laced, jacket zipped, ready.

'Sorry to bother you on the weekend, mate,' Connor proceeded towards him. 'Marc's in town and I couldn't very well let my wife go missing.'

'It's not a problem,' Raph said and they slapped each other's shoulders.

'Where's Sergeant?' Connor said.

'Outside–'

'Don't leave the poor boy in the cold!' Connor walked the length of the hall and they heard the sound of dog nails on floorboards before Raph's hound joined them in the lounge.

'Good boy, good boy.' Connor stroked the huge animal's neck. 'Quick espresso, Raph?'

'You make a good one,' Raph smiled, and Connor grinned.

They walked together to the kitchen. Kit, watching them lean against the island bench to chat, realised how close they'd become.

Connor chaperoned them to the old sheds between the house and the winery. The stone buildings smelled of hay and leather oil, a smell that reminded Kit of her mother.

'I'll be fine, Dad,' Kit said as Raph strode ahead. 'Send him back, it's his weekend, he shouldn't have to do this.'

'No, no,' Connor said. 'He's here now, he doesn't mind. I don't want to end up with both my girls gone missing. Better if he's out there with you.'

'Dad, don't be silly, it's fine, I'll–'

'He's happy to. He doesn't mind.'

'I don't need him, Dad. I'll be fine.'

'Is there something wrong?' Connor peered at his daughter. 'Is there something wrong with Raph? Do you not like him?'

Kit wanted to shout that *yes* something was *very* wrong.

'Never mind,' she said. 'It's fine, it's fine, we'll go together, it's fine.'

Connor appeared relieved. 'That would put me at ease, thank you.'

Kit let her horse nose her hand before she buckled its bridle. 'Are you a good rider?' she asked Raph, without looking at him.

The reply came with the sound of a saddle being thrown across a horse's back. 'Not bad.'

Connor grinned. 'Bloody renaissance man. What can't you do?'

Raph gave a low laugh. 'I'll make you a list,' he said.

Connor helped Kit onto her pony. 'My guess is that she took the track to the river,' he said. 'Then she would have ridden across, along O'Connell's fence line, and into the State Forest. You won't get reception in there but when you do come into range, call. I'll find Scott's sweater and have it ready for you when you get back.'

Connor gazed up at Kit, Raph wheeled around, and Kit followed.

Lunch. Retrieval of the jumper and lunch with her father.

Those were the reasons she'd come and these activities were acceptable.

Activities that weren't acceptable included watching Raph on horseback … watching Raph's body cock, adjust and right itself … watching Raph's fist grip the rein.

Kit softened her shoulders, stretched, glanced from side to side, let her neck feel long. She thought of Scott at home, packing alone, and knew that that's where she should be.

'Annalese … she's a good rider?' Raph asked, as fern, cutting grass and bracken replaced the European plantings of the estate.

Kit felt their isolation, the lack of anyone else to reply.

'Her horse is a brat but she can ride,' she said.

They crossed the low stream. The muffled, wet clattering of hooves on pebbles ended and the sharp swishing of reeds began as they climbed the low embankment. Sergeant kept pace.

'How are the wedding plans going?' Raph asked. 'They say the Barossa estate.'

Kit felt affronted but didn't know why. 'What else do they say?'

'They?'

'*They*,' Kit said. 'Whoever said that.'

'Your father,' Raph replied.

'Yes …' Kit conceded uncomfortably. 'The Barossa.'

They rode on in silence. Kit rotated her shoulders, inclined her head both ways. Her eyes saw the makings of a photo.

She looked away from it, then back – Raph's boot, soiled and textured as it swung hypnotically on the steel ledge of the tan leather stirrup. She imagined framing the shot, blinked and the image sat imprinted on her mind.

'Are you concerned?' Raph said.

Kit opened her eyes. 'What about?'

'Annalese,' he said.

'No. That woman is in no way vulnerable.'

'Really? I'd disagree.'

'Is that what you thought when we met you on the rise that day? When her horse kicked you in the shin and she glared at you with disdain, like it was your fault?'

Raph thought for a minute. 'I didn't notice the disdain. I was referring to her physicality. I meant she could fall off the horse and break in two.'

'I like the visual.' Kit smiled.

Something was flapping up ahead and the pair cantered forward.

Snagged on a branch, fabric billowed, Annalese's hair entangled.

'Nice scarf.' Raph dislodged it and Kit reddened, ashamed that her mother rode in Saint Laurent. She enjoyed watching Raph stuff the delicate silken square between saddle and horseback.

'Odd that it was just left there,' he said.

Kit glanced around and saw that trail bike marks scored the muddy track.

'Oh,' she said. 'She'll be this way.'

They took the short, steep incline to a parallel trail, narrow but grassy and secluded along the neighbour's fence line. They rode until it became tight, dismounted, and led the horses forward. Soon Kit heard what she'd expected: her mother, up ahead.

Annalese was cursing as she told her skittish horse to calm down. 'Fuck! Calm it. Shush the fuck up, please ...'

Kit knew that the way opened up just ahead and was glad that it would be there, and not on the cloistered narrow path, where they'd meet.

'Hey! Mum!' Kit called out, and a moment later they came upon Annalese, waiting in the clearing.

'Well fuck,' she said when she saw Kit. 'It bloody well happened again.'

Annalese looked like Top Deck chocolate, one half clean, the other brown with mud.

'Are you okay?' Kit asked. Annalese pursed her lips by way of reply. 'Mum, you should ride the other tracks, the trailbikers have equal rights to these ones.'

'Don't be ridiculous. They're fucking outlaws!' Annalese's shrillness made her horse buck. 'They're fucking dirt-biking little shits. I'm going to get Connor to snipe them in their moronic little heads. Then I'm going to call the council. Now this bloody horse won't let me back on.' She swore again.

Raph began to speak but Annalese stepped forward and yanked her scarf from beneath his saddle. 'Thank you *very* much.' She brushed the embedded horsehair. 'Now it will need the drycleaners.'

'Better than not having it at all,' Kit said. 'We're going to take the main track back. It's too late in the day for bikers now.'

Sergeant came bounding up the track and Annalese screamed. Her horse bucked again.

'Mum, Mum, it's Raph's dog.'

'Get it out of here! It's upsetting the horse.'

'No, you're upsetting the horse.' Kit turned and led the way to the main track.

'Now it'll *never* let me back on,' Annalese kept muttering. 'We're *all* walking home,'

They hit the muddy trail and Raph gave his reins to Kit. Slowly, he approached Annalese's horse, yawning and smiling to show the horse he was calm.

As Annalese watched, the horse let him near. When he was close, he raised his hand, and began to gently rub the horse's back. The horse's twitching began to still.

When the horse was completely at ease, Annalese marched forward without invitation and mounted it. She settled into the horse's saddle without acknowledging Raph, and instead leaned forward, stroked the horse's mane, cooed in its ear, and as though this had been the remedy, said, 'All better,' and guided the horse forward.

Raph said nothing.

Kit didn't either.

Each other's silence was the only thing they encountered on the ride home, and when they reached the Gossard boundary, Annalese cantered towards the homestead. Raph went in the other direction up the hill, and Kit followed him.

14

'That's happened before?' Raph said as they tied up their horses by the shearers' quarters.

'Annalese and the trailbikers?' Kit said.

'Yes.'

'At least twice.'

'And she persists?'

'She's stubborn and self-righteous, so yes.'

Raph opened the door to the shearers' quarters. The building was stone to windowsill height and topped by weathered shiplap timber boards that led to an old tin roof.

Sergeant loped ahead. Raph offered Kit a drink but she lingered at the threshold.

Raph glanced back. 'The age of a structure doesn't necessarily equate to rodent, insect or arachnid infestation,' he said, misinterpreting her trepidation. 'I'm yet to see a sizeable spider.'

Kit smiled a little as though he'd addressed her fear. The faded grey boards sounded hollow beneath her boots as she followed him in. She took up a seat in one of two worn chairs and finding a hole in one of the soft leather arms, began to fiddle with it, uneasily.

'These seats weren't always here, were they?' she said for something to say.

'No,' he said, and opened the old gas refrigerator, pale buttermilk with lever handle.

It had been fifteen years at least since Kit had been inside and she glanced about the space – at the incandescent bulbs in rusted wire baskets that lit a tattered Oregon bench, and the worn out butcher's block that sat flush with the counter. Utensils, herbs in jars and bottles of spirits were lined up atop the bench, and a few books and a woodgrain Tivoli radio were all that adorned the improvised lounge.

In the open door to the bedroom, the deerhound lay, watching her.

'A fortified?' Raph lifted a Pedro Ximénez from above the fridge.

He waved the open bottle under Kit's nose and she inhaled the vapours of burnt toffee.

'It's early,' he said, 'but you look cold.'

'I'd like one, thank you,' Kit replied, and Raph poured two measures.

He handed Kit the glass. She didn't meet his eyes, but their fingers touched, his warm, hers cold, and she waited, eyes low until Raph turned his back and she could peer up again.

Kit watched Raph peel back the paper of a soft cheese then sink a knife into it.

The blade penetrated, withdrew, then swept the ooze atop a savoury wafer. Raph tussled with a bunch of dried muscatels, sunk a wizened fruit into the wet cheese, and turned to Kit. She forgot to look away.

His eyes held hers, his hand stretched out, and they met in the middle, Kit aware of the soft cheese overflow that descended onto her fingers as the wafer transferred.

'Thank you.'

Raph lifted his glass and filled his mouth. 'Romate, Spaniards, from Jerez,' he said as he stared into the empty tumbler, then ate a clump of cheese off the back of his knife.

Kit decided that she shouldn't be there.

The wine had begun to warm her mouth. Her body was softening, and fearing the softness, she put the biscuit in her mouth, crunched it to nothing, and stood.

'I'm sorry if you felt like I intruded today,' Raph suddenly said, putting the knife down. 'I came to help Connor but I'm aware that my living here is of use only to him. If I'm overstepping yours or your mother's boundaries, tell me, I can vacate.'

For the first time, Kit saw a flash of vulnerability in this man. It was fleeting, gone as quickly as it had come, but perhaps, she thought, some part of this self-governed man had become invested in Gossard Range.

'Yes …' She slowly began to nod. 'You are an intrusion.'

He dipped his head, knocked back his second drink and straightened as if to see her out but she picked up her camera, pushed past him to the bench and focused the lens on the oily rim left behind in his glass.

'A welcome intrusion,' she said and took the photo. 'I'm hungry.'

Raph lined up seven items: kipfler potatoes, red onion, gorgonzola, flour, butter, eggs and milk.

After Kit's declaration of her appetite, she'd felt him watch her, silent as she took the photos: his glass, the knife in cheese, muscatels, sprigs of thyme in a chipped jar by the sink. Then, without speaking, he'd collected what was now on the counter.

'I hope you can make pastry because I can't.' Kit surveyed the ingredients as Raph leaned against the bench. 'I can't cook generally,' she said, 'I should say that outright before you expect anything.'

Raph folded his arms. 'But you're a food stylist.'

Kit put her camera down and slid her glass forward for a refill. 'So?'

'Surely you have to make pastry for shoots.' He pulled the stopper out of the Pedro Ximénez.

'Not necessarily. I can get someone else to make it. Or I buy a block from a good staple store and roll it out.'

Raph's eyes flickered. His expression matched that of the spider scare day and Kit guessed that like most men, he enjoyed revelations of a woman's weaknesses.

'Pass me that,' he said, nodding to an old slab of marble propped against the wall.

Kit handed it to him and he laid the board on the bench before proceeding to deposit flour and butter into a bowl.

'What next?'

Raph hesitated, wiped his mouth, then beckoned for her to come to the trough. She stood where he told her to. He emptied a bag of potatoes, turned on the tap, positioned himself behind her, then reached around and took her hands.

'Potato washing one-oh-one.' He put a potato in one of her hands, a scrubbing brush in the other.

Kit spun back with a laugh. 'I know how to scrub a fucking potato,' she said. Dirty water dripped from the scrubbing brush down Raph's white front. He gazed at it.

'Sorry,' Kit said. He tugged his T-shirt off. Kit spun to face the trough and pressed her wrists against the cold steel, her heart beating fast.

'Where's my clean one?' she heard him say.

'What do you mean?' Kit stayed facing away.

'My clean T-shirt.'

'You only have two T-shirts?' Kit frowned.

'Yes. Where's my other one?'

Kit swivelled back to face him. 'I left it in the cider vault … in the tunnel.'

'Why?'

'I–' Kit began before she smiled. 'I don't know.'

His eyes flickered, entertained.

'You should buy more,' she said.

'You should have more respect for the ones I have.'

Kit shrugged and returned to the sink.

'Come here,' he said.

Kit glanced back.

'Here.' He was gazing into the pastry bowl. Kit walked towards him and he reached out to take one of her hands. 'Good, cold.'

He guided her hands into the bowl and Kit felt the mixture, fragmented parts that looked nothing like their combined selves should, and wondered if anything of merit could eventually come of something so simple.

'I'm sorry about your shirt,' she said.

'I forgive you. Don't overdo it.'

Kit coughed with a laugh.

'I mean the pastry,' he leaned in. 'Don't overwork it. Quick and gentle.'

'Quick and gentle' felt like an oxymoron. 'This isn't working–' she said.

Raph ignored her. 'Turn it out.'

The dough landed on the floured marble board and a plume of white filled the air.

As Kit bent to retrieve fallen buttered baking parchment, flour settled in the hair of Raph's stomach, and she thought how much Scott would have hated the disorder.

She returned her hands to the smooth ball.

'How does it feel?'

Kit closed her eyes, cupped, squeezed. 'Smooth …' she began. 'Smooth and firm … I think good … a good dough …'

'How do you know?'

'I can tell.'

'Yes,' she heard a smile in his voice. 'You can.'

The lightly baked pastry case sat on the bench.

Raph filled it with par-boiled potatoes, red onion, and thyme.

'Can you please pass me the cheese?' he said.

Kit put down her camera to reach for the gorgonzola then began tearing it into the pastry crust.

One, two, three – chunks fell from her hands – four, Raph suddenly caught her arm.

Kit watched as his hand encircled her wrist. He waited, seemed to assess the soft, white cream that clung to her fingers, then brought them to his mouth.

One minute Kit's hands had been her own and the next they'd become his. Raph was tasting her fingers one by one and Kit felt her eyes begin to close, the world suddenly wet … warm.

She tore her eyes open, managed to pull her hand away and their eyes met.

'I apologise,' he said, but she knew he wasn't at all sorry, just like she wasn't.

She went to the sink and quickly scrubbed at the warm feeling that had begun to spread. It was too late – her whole body had begun to ache with warm.

Raph had seen something he wanted and he'd taken it. He'd seen something that made him hungry and he'd eaten it.

Kit dried her hands. She walked to a chair.

Without words, they'd both somehow agreed that silent withdrawal was the best way to deal with what had just transpired between them.

Raph handed Kit a drink.

She picked up *Monocle* magazine from the floor, thumbed through it, picked up another, and kept on until the oven door screeched and she glanced up to see Raph's bare back twitch as he took the tart from oven to bench.

The full pastry case slid from its mould onto a board and Raph quartered it with a knife.

Melted gorgonzola pooled from broken pastry walls onto Kit's plate; Raph had put the circle of old china on her lap and she nudged the food with her fork.

'Why can you cook?' She peered at him beside her.

'My mother,' Raph took a moment to reply. Kit heard tenderness.

She took a mouthful and waited for him to elaborate. He didn't.

'Well,' she said. 'Mine's my excuse. Annalese's kitchen was off limits. I suppose I never really learned.'

Raph rested his glass on a pile of books that sat between them like a table. He broke a piece of pastry from his tart and chewed it.

'But your pastry ...' he said. 'It's perfect.'

Kit considered the food.

'You don't like it?' he said.

'No, it's–'

'It's flawless.'

'As flawless as your mother's?'

There was no reply and Kit looked up to find Raph watching her, his expression intense, somehow significant. Kit sensed that talk of this person, his mother, had opened a way into him and she found herself wanting to reach out, to have him take her to all the places she knew he kept hidden.

'Yes.' Raph's gaze fell, the way closed, and he smiled a little. 'And that's saying something.'

Kit stared at her plate and took another mouthful.

Raph took a drink, set it down again and Kit followed the movement to the book atop the pile, ringed with watermarks.

'Thoreau.' She reached out and ran her fingers over the cover.

'*Walden*,' he replied.

'Yes. I haven't read it.' Kit gazed at the cover illustration of a shack in the woods. 'But I can imagine why you'd like it. A hymn to solitude, isn't it?' As Kit said the words she grew suddenly aware of the solitude that surrounded them. 'Is there mobile reception up here?' she said.

'No,' Raph replied.

Kit reached for her phone and checked the time.

She blinked, the time blinked, and she swore, twice, three times, stood, covered her mouth, and – 'Fuck, fuck, fuck,' – she turned and ran to the door.

'What?' Raph stood.

'It's seven-thirty,' she yelled. 'Scott – he's left – I forgot him!'

As Kit pushed out the front door, she heard a four-wheel drive roaring up the hill and shielded her eyes from the headlights. The car zoomed towards the shearers' quarters and Annalese's voice rang out from the driver's side as the car drew near.

'Katherine! What the hell are you still doing up here? Scott just phoned from the airport – he's left! You missed him!'

15

Kit decided not to tell the whole truth.

She called Scott on his stopover and told the half-truth, that Annalese had gone off-grid in the forest and that this was the reason she didn't make it back in time with his sweater. That there was no mobile reception in the forest was a full truth and she told him that, too.

She'd never let Scott down before.

For this reason when she told Scott her explanation for not seeing him off, he believed her, and not only believed her, seemed unperturbed, as though he wouldn't consider the truth to be something she would hide.

But she had hidden something. She'd forgotten Scott because she'd forgotten herself – with Raph – and to appease her guilt, she revealed the only other thing that wasn't yet known to Scott. She sent the link via email.

Subject: *New venture*
Main: *Toying with a new project. Your thoughts appreciated as ever: www.hungerbykitgossard.com*
K. xx

Unemotional, she then uploaded her latest collection: moody, under-exposed frames of lush food against the ashen interior of an old building, the lightly floured abdomen of a faceless man, and the silky remnants of a Spanish digestif in two glasses …

Cooking Lessons on Gossard Range.

She titled the entry and closed her laptop before her body had an opportunity to respond.

❧

'Your dad was very excited when I called him.' Piper arrived late to the *Hamper* studios with a box from the letterpress printers in her arms.

'It's so nice you being a part of all this,' Kit said as Piper undid the box and withdrew the first label: die-cut at the top with a hole big enough for a bottleneck.

Gossard Range – Cidre Bouché, it read.

The only graphic was the tiny outline of an apple, printed in gold foil and positioned neatly above the words. 'Dad will be thrilled.'

'Tell him to get *Hamper* to run a product preview just before the cider launch.' Piper put the label back. 'Jimmy will be gagging to do it.'

Someone opened the studio door. Kit squirrelled the lid back on the box. '*Shhh* until then,' she hissed, and Piper nodded knowingly as she tapped the side of her nose.

❧

Whenever Kit saw a black Cayenne, she was reminded of Annalese.

Never having memorised her mother's numberplate however, she was now unsure if the four-wheel drive parked out the front of her apartment was a warning or not.

She climbed the stairs to the front door and by the time she heard her mother's singsong call, was already too far in to turn back.

'Darling!' Annalese darted around the corner. 'Champagne?'

'Mum.' Kit's stomach lurched. 'How are you?'

Annalese led the way to the lounge room and put a glass of champagne in Kit's hand.

'Are you staying for dinner? The night?' Kit steadied the full flute. Her parents' bedroom in the apartment hadn't been opened by anyone but the cleaner in a long time.

'Perhaps.' Annalese smiled. 'Depends how long it takes ...' She turned towards a pile of black, bowed gift boxes that though familiar to Kit, were larger than she'd ever seen. 'I've been shop-ping, I've been shop-ping,' her mother sang.

'Fuck,' Kit said.

Annalese ignored the profanity, went to the bedroom and returned with a dressing mirror.

'I haven't shaved,' Kit said.

'Darling, I'm your mother.'

'I need a shower.'

'After a day in the office? You've hardly been rolling in dirt.' Annalese went to the stereo, put on Keith Jarrett, picked up a box, pulled it onto her lap and patted the space beside her on the lounge.

If there were dirt, Kit would roll in it.

She would throw the champagne all over herself right then and there and thrash around in the filth.

Annalese patted the lounge again.

Kit stepped forward, Annalese took her wrist, and Kit felt herself tugged down to the lounge.

'There.' Annalese put the box on Kit's lap.

Kit's hands felt limp.

'Undo the bow!' Annalese said and Kit fumbled with the fabric ribbon until it fell away, then she slowly lifted the lid.

White tissue and a sea of cream silk lay inside.

'Did you know Net-A-Porter did bridal?' Annalese said. 'I wouldn't have bothered leaving the house the first time if I'd known. Free shipping!'

'Mum.' Kit's voice was uneven as she put the box aside. 'This is very thoughtful but–'

'At least look at it,' Annalese said and reinstated the box on Kit's lap.

Kit shifted her gaze to her mother, Annalese said the words again, and Kit slowly peered down.

'Hurry up!' Annalese poked her, Kit raised reluctant hands and slid them into folds of silk. 'Rochas,' Annalese said as the dress came out of its casing. 'And we have a Lanvin, Temperley, Delpozo ...' she paused '... I can't remember them all. Do *not* tell Connor about this. I was very naughty getting them *all*.'

Kit suddenly felt a tear begin in her eye. She brushed it away. This was her mother–this was her mother being thoughtful.

Annalese pretended not to notice the emotion and asked, 'Do you have the right bra on?'

Kit withdrew the gown and laid it across their laps. 'It's beautiful,' she said, and meant it.

'I know,' Annalese cooed. 'I think we have somewhat similar taste even if we can't *usually* wear the same things. Don't you think? Put it on!'

Kit stood, Annalese began to fuss, and when she was ready, Kit looked in the mirror and ... laughed.

'Oh my God. It looks awful,' she said.

'Oh.' Annalese sucked in air. 'Yes, it's not right is it, I got that *quite* wrong. Next!'

Kit's insides turned as Annalese lifted out a Lanvin. She stood uncomfortably as her mother tugged, zipped, hooked and smoothed, then stood back.

'Now that looks nice,' Annalese said. 'The shortness means it isn't traditional but you've got good legs. Best to flaunt what you've got.'

Kit stared at the white shape in the mirror.

'Or do you *want* traditional?' Annalese cocked her head.

Kit seemed unable to move.

'Kit? Because the winery does look traditional, but what about Scott? Conventional in a tux?'

Kit's hands gravitated numbly to her waist and she watched them smooth down the front of the dress.

'Well you're clearly not excited about this one.' Annalese began to tug Kit out of it and into the next.

When the new garment was halfway on, Kit said, 'Wait.'

'Almost there.' Annalese tugged it further.

'I don't want to do this Mum. Hang on. Please.'

'We've only just *started*, Kit.' Annalese kept going.

Kit tried to pull away.

'Don't being silly, Kit.' Annalese tugged again.

'No you don't, Mum, wait.'

'Don't fight it. Stop, Kit. This is what you want. This is what you want and you need a bloody dress.'

Kit pushed the dress to the floor and leapt out of it. 'I need champagne,' she said. Annalese swore after her daughter as Kit went to the kitchen and found a bottle in the fridge. She poured one, returned to the lounge and stood, sipping it hastily in her underwear.

Annalese flumped back on the couch. 'Be serious, darling.'

The bubbles went up Kit's nose. She walked back to the kitchen, poured a gin and O.J. at the servery, and said, 'Do you want one?'

'You're wasting good Hendrick's with bloody O.J., Kit.'

'Tonic?'

'Kit, you're working yourself into a needless state.'

Kit took a shot of gin from the lid, poured a G&T and handed it to Annalese.

'They're just dresses for God's sake, Kit. What's wrong with you?'

Kit gulped her gin and juice, surveyed the pile of boxes and her semi-naked body in the mirror and wondered what *was* wrong with her. What was *wrong* with her?

Someone started decoding the front door. Annalese frowned at the sound, and Kit frowned back at her.

Marc strode in with a boombox on his shoulder, eighties hip-hop grinding from a cassette.

'Why–are–you–nak–ed?' he rapped, before turning off the music. 'And why's our mother here?' His hand disappeared behind him into the entry vestibule to block entry to someone in tow. 'Hold up. Family member insufficiently clad.'

Kit scuffled for her long knit. When it had fallen down her torso, Marc said, 'All clear.'

Raph appeared.

He took in the women, glanced down, and leaned quietly against the wall. Kit considered crumpling. She stiffened and inhaled, showing no emotion beyond a tic of her little finger.

Annalese folded her arms and stared at Marc.

'Will you be staying, mother?' Marc said. 'You're more than welcome to join us.'

'I didn't realise you were coming in to town tonight,' Annalese said.

'Nor did I know that I would be stumbling across your lovely face.'

Annalese scowled then skolled her gin.

Kit smiled and did the same.

'What are we drinking?' Marc asked.

'Can I speak with you?' Annalese said.

'Can it wait?' Marc grinned, not needing to speak with his mother to know what she wished to say.

Annalese glanced at Kit, then at the boxes. She began to stuff white fabric into black cardboard then stacked them to one side.

'I'm leaving, Kit,' she said, 'and whatever you do, do not let *anyone* touch those.' She picked up her keys and let the door slam as she went out.

'Shall I apologise for something?' Marc said. 'I'd just thought it would be nice to have a night kicking it with you while Fifi is away. Was that wrong?'

Kit went to the kitchen drawer, got two straws, made them into one long straw then threaded it into the half-full bottle of champagne.

'That's the spirit,' Marc said. 'Hey, did you know this is the first mixtape you ever made me?'

'No,' Kit said.

Marc tried to make her dance. 'Want to invite Piper over?'

'No.' Kit pulled away.

'Even though I brought Raph for you …?'

'Don't be ridiculous.' Kit gripped the neck of the champagne bottle, walked into her bedroom and fell forward onto the bed.

Someone soon appeared in the doorway.

Kit could sense who it was and didn't care that she was face down or that her short knit dress had slithered too high.

Raph walked over and took the bottle out of her hand. 'Are you alright?' he said.

'What are you doing here?' Kit replied.

'Marc invited me.'

'Why?'

'I don't know. Shall I leave?'

Kit let the duvet swallow her face. She stayed there in the darkness until she felt Raph grip her shoulder, flip her over, and the contact made her heart speed.

'Has something happened?' he said.

Kit hadn't seen or spoken to Raph since she'd ran from the shearers' quarters, ran and left behind her half-eaten dinner and other things that had no name.

She levered herself up and held his gaze. 'I've just now been trying on wedding dresses,' she said.

Raph's eyes stayed steady, then he blinked, reached out and took the champagne.

'I'll make you a proper drink,' he said as he walked out. Kit rolled off the bed, lay on the floor for a while, then crawled after him.

Hendrick's, orange juice and a bottle of Lillet stood on the bench in the kitchen.

'You found a clean T-shirt.' Kit looked Raph up and down, and because her head suddenly felt too heavy, she rested it on the counter and added, 'Well done you.'

'Yes, well done me,' Raph said and Kit raised her head slightly so she could see his torso move with the activity of his hands.

'Where's Sergeant?' she said.

'At the homestead. With the other dogs.'

'My mother let him stay at the house?'

'No. She was out … obviously.'

Kit put her head back on the counter and Raph scooped ice from the icemaker.

'For me?' Marc appeared and skolled Raph's cocktail. 'A Bronx?'

'Basically,' Raph said.

'You're a fucking show-off,' Marc said as he wiped his mouth, 'but cocktail hour's over. The eight-oh-eight tram is en route.'

Kit followed Marc into the lounge and found the room was now filled with his friends. She located her heeled sandals by the couch and fumbled with the ankle strap as she hopped with the others towards the front door.

It was winter time, Kit had forgotten.

She'd snatched a felt hat from a hook as they'd left, but only because she liked how the equestrian-esque cap framed her face, not because she'd remembered it was cold out. The alcohol had made her both warm and tipsy, but not warm enough to negate the tipsiness that had made her forget the season and her coat.

Cold wind gusted up Collins Street and Kit pulled the domed cap over her head as cold air moved through her loosely woven knit, plucked warmth from her body, and continued on.

The group turned down a lane and the wind dropped. Kit took the opportunity to heed her problem, the one Marc had brought with him into town that night, the one Kit hadn't yet encountered in any place other than a vineyard.

Now she stared at it, watched the problem stride over cobbles and past brick walls, and felt confused by seeing this wild creature, Raph, amid drainpipes and graffiti.

An illuminated sign, mounted high on brickwork, indicated that they'd reached their destination. Presgrave Place was tucked deep in the neglected heart of a central city block, an alley that serviced the back ends of hospitality tenancies. The way was littered with rubbish bins and kitchen detritus, but at the end sat their reward: a tiny wine and coffee bar that served Euro snacks and crafted cocktails.

The space was standing room only, and with twelve people inside, already at capacity.

Marc's group hung back outside, against the brick wall and Kit quietly held onto her brother's arm, wanting to sit but seeing nothing fit for the purpose. She wished the alcohol would wear off.

Six people soon left and because they were nearest the entry, Marc's five friends went ahead.

'Do you want to go in?' Marc offered Kit or Raph the last space.

'They're your friends, you go,' Raph said. Kit let go of her brother's arm and watched him disappear inside.

She stared at the cobblestones beneath her feet, head light, body seeming to sway though it wasn't, sensed the sleeve of Raph's jacket against her arm and imagined the warmth that its thickness enclosed. She liked the jacket. It had a fine, flecked, grey quilted wool shell that looked light and thick with down. A tall, ribbed collar grazed his chin.

'Here.' Raph began unpopping the jacket's studs.

'No,' Kit said, though desperate for the thing. 'No.' She felt proud for no reason.

'I don't need it.' Raph unhooked the zipper, the shell swung open, and like it was only right and fair, Kit turned towards him and despite Raph still being inside it, she slid beneath the open flaps of the jacket. She tucked her arms around his waist, pressed her face into the nook below his collarbone, and a quiet sigh came unbidden as she gloried in the primal satiation that came with relief from great hunger or discomfort.

Raph stood for a moment, motionless, apparently taken aback, then he pulled her against him. Kit felt the jacket tugged around them, and the moisture from her breath began to dampen her face.

The door to the bar suddenly opened, and a couple meandered out, talking. Kit waited for Raph to release her so that they could go inside. He didn't. They both stood unmoving, Kit moulded to him, his jacket moulded to her, his arms around the layers, holding it together.

A drop of moisture landed on Kit's toe. She shook it away.

Another was followed by another, and when it was raining, Raph's arms fell away, his hand encircled hers and they ran inside.

The space was a dim, four-by-four-metre box with high ceilings and dark timber wainscoting. A high bench ran the length of one wall, a brass footrest ran parallel below, and a small plaque read NO PHOTOS.

'What would you like to drink?' Raph said as they leaned against the bar. The cocktail station behind was lined in subway tiles and Kit ran her eyes over the list on a pegboard.

'I'll have an Americano with … Fever Tree.'

'Vermouth and soda,' Raph said. The bartender got busy.

'Huzzah! You're in!' Marc took a mouthful of drink then smacked his lips. 'Nice to see you outside of work for once,' he said.

'Yes,' Raph replied.

The sight of Raph in a place like this felt strange – his wildness muted by the white noise of urbanity. Kit wondered if he felt discomfort being there.

'I tell you, this guy, Kit, this guy – for want of a better word – is a fucking genius. How was that call you made about the cider the other day? Time saver.'

'Glad it helped,' Raph said.

'Your *help* is making me look bad. Kit, this guy makes me look bad.' Marc punched Raph playfully in the shoulder.

Kit turned towards the bar and stared into her glass, watching the volume descend as she sucked on her straw and the men tussled.

'So how long are you planning on staying?' Marc said. 'At Gossard?'

Kit glanced at Raph.

'As long as I'm wanted.' His eyes met hers and Kit felt goosebumps.

'Well as long as you're here, I'm fucked,' Marc said. 'You outdo me on all fronts. You're after my inheritance.'

'I wouldn't turn it down.' Raph smiled as he took a sip of his vermouth.

'Get him out of here, Kit, the man needs to go.'

Kit knew she was supposed to joke 'yes, the man has to go', but the words wouldn't form in her mouth.

'I'm glad–' she said instead. 'I'm glad Dad has you.'

Raph's eye twitched and he replied, 'I'm glad I can be of assistance.' Then his hand rose, and Kit felt his finger smooth a droplet from her lip.

'Let's go, Marc,' she suddenly said. 'It, it feels crowded.'

Marc drained his drink.

Outside, the rain had stopped. Kit took the arm of one of Marc's friends and hurried ahead with her down the lane, not wanting to be caught alone with Raph.

'How've you been?' the woman said.

'Good,' Kit replied. 'You?'

'Well, thank you, I–'

'Fucking hookers.' A man and his friend lurched along the lane.

Kit moved forward but one slurred, 'Wanna fuck?'

'Piss off,' Marc's friend replied but the man grabbed at Kit's purse.

Kit stumbled back, felt someone catch her, then saw one of the men thrown against the wall.

'You. And you. Fuck. Off.' Raph spoke with an assured authority that Kit had never discerned in him before. Something about his tone and stance implied that he could deliver swift retribution, to anyone, any time. Heeding it, the drunks stumbled away.

'What the hell?' Marc was there.

Raph picked up Kit's purse and handed it to her.

'Just some arseholes,' Marc's friend said.

'Thank you,' Kit said to Raph and his eyes flicked over her, checking she was unharmed. When his gaze returned to her face, he cocked his head towards the mouth of the lane.

Back on the main street, Kit turned to Marc. 'I think I'm going to go home,' she said.

'Really?' Marc sounded disappointed but Kit nodded and raised her hand for a cab. 'I can come back with you ...'

'No, I'm fine,' Kit said as the cab pulled in. 'The night's young. Go have fun.'

She opened the cab door, waved, and the car drove away.

❧

'So they were just two random arseholes?' Piper said down the phone when Kit told her.

Kit could still see it – Raph's silhouette in the alley.

'At least Raph was there, I mean if it was just *you* ...'

'Yes,' Kit said, 'I know.' She was on the lounge in the Gossard's apartment, a bowl of spaghetti on her lap.

'I'm sick of that kind of shit,' Piper said. 'It's just bullshit.'

'I know.'

'What did you say to him?'

'Who?'

'Raph.'

Kit tried to remember. 'Thanks … I think.'

'That's it? You just said thanks?'

Kit replayed the scene once more in her mind. 'What else was there to say?'

'I don't know,' Piper said. 'Surely something …'

16

'He better not have stayed in the apartment.' The bunch of bulbs in Annalese's hand quivered as she folded her arms, knocking their flowering heads.

She and Kit stood by the winery building, watching the muted green of Connor's Jag come towards them, Connor in the passenger seat.

'I cannot abide that Connor would buy such a car then let someone like that behind the wheel. I swear that winery hand's a drug dealer ... and that dog that follows him around is like a ghost covered in hair. You and Marc better not have let him stay in our apartment last Friday, Kit.'

Kit said that he hadn't stayed and it was true. She didn't know where he'd slept.

The Jag drew near and finally came to a halt.

The two men remained in the cab and Kit could see her father and Raph talking, gesturing towards the dash as Connor leaned in. Then there was a crack as the hood popped. Connor climbed from the passenger side and rested his arms on the open driver's window.

'So you can't just push it like you normally would,' Kit heard

Raph say, 'when the clutch is down, you have to slap it, slap the shifter hard.'

'Yeah, yeah …' Connor said.

'Let's take a look at that butterfly valve, the choke's definitely sticky.'

'Bloody temperamental …'

Raph climbed from the car and they went to peer at the engine.

'See?' Annalese said. 'He deals in drugs and stolen cars. How else would he know what he's doing? Your father's a soft touch, Kit, he'd let any creep wander in off the street.'

'Raph's not a creep.'

'How would you know?' Annalese eyed her. Kit looked away.

Connor was wiping his hands on his pants as he came towards them. He pecked his wife's cheek.

'Hello, sweetie,' he said to Kit. 'Raph's just schooling me.' He glanced back towards the car, hand like a sun visor on his face as he watched Raph lower the hood. 'Raph!' he called. 'Take it for a spin, see if that's helped. Kit, you've only been out once, go on.'

'No,' Annalese said.

'Yes.' Kit walked to the car.

Raph was in the driver's seat. A half-eaten sandwich was on the dash and he picked it up as he pulled the car around. They coasted away down the drive, Annalese's voice faded, and when there was no other sound than the hum of the engine, Kit turned to him.

'Thank you for the other night. I didn't expect you to do that … to look out for–stand up for–me, or whatever.'

Raph changed speed with a slap of the gearstick then wrapped his fist around the leather arc of the E-Type's steering wheel. 'It was nothing.'

Kit watched him then fiddled with the settings on her camera.

When she looked up, Raph was raising his hand to his mouth, a cold-cut lolling out of his sandwich. She took the shot.

'You know about old cars?' she said.

Raph squinted ahead. 'Not really.'

'That's not how it seemed.'

'My father likes them … something rubbed off,' he said.

'Are you like him?' she said.

'Who?'

'Your father?'

Raph paused and there was discomfort in his voice when he replied, 'At times.'

Kit raised her camera and took another photo.

'What are those for?' Raph glanced at her.

Kit knew that he meant the photos but didn't respond.

'What are the photos for?' he said.

Kit gazed out the window. 'My journal.'

Raph frowned.

'A journal?' he finally said.

'It's a … magazine … thing.'

Raph stared ahead, then took two quick bites of the sandwich. Kit framed his mouth, crumbs, the canvas of the soft-top overhead, daylight edging in.

'What's it called?' Raph said.

Kit shifted in her seat. 'Pardon?'

'The name. Of your magazine.'

Kit's tongue roamed her lips. The word would have been all too easy to say because it was no longer just a word, it was becoming her.

She ran her tongue along the underside of her lip and the word said itself. '*Hunger.*'

Raph adjusted his grip on the wheel.

Kit waited.

'Hunger?' he said.

Kit said the word again and turned to see his mouth move into a small smile.

'I know the feeling,' he said.

There was an unfamiliar car at the winery building when they returned.

They'd been silent for the rest of the short drive and when Kit got out, someone appeared by the cellar door.

'Little Gossard!' She recognised Jimmy Hillinger's voice before she recognised him. He waved, phone in his hand.

'Who's that?' Raph asked.

'Just some fanatical food journo,' Kit said. Raph locked the car and headed towards the winery building. Jimmy gave him a curious once-over as he passed.

'What are you doing here?' Kit said.

Jimmy put his hands on his hips, strode forward, and took his time gazing around. 'There's a general air of busyness and anticipation around Gossard.' He breathed in and out. 'I feel like there's a lot going on that you're not telling me. I was just doing a story at the new distillery down the road and thought: why not drop in on Gossard? Why not have a chinwag on my way home? I'm glad I saw you because I couldn't find a soul in the offices!'

'No thanks,' Kit said. 'See you.'

'What? Come on. Let's get a coffee at the cellar door.'

Kit turned and walked away. She expected him to follow or insist and didn't know what to make of it when he didn't.

At the homestead, she found her brother and father where she'd expected they'd be, taking lunch in the kitchen.

'Has he gone?' Marc said.

'Jimmy?' Kit replied.

Marc nodded. 'He drove up just as Dad and I came in. We've been hiding up here until he buggered off.'

Connor pulled his gaze from his newspaper and removed his glasses. 'What did he want?' He rubbed his eyes.

'I'm guessing details about the new ventures.'

'Well he won't find the news he wants here.' Connor looked smug. 'The staff know next to nothing. My money's on his still chasing *you*, sweetie.'

'I actually heard recently that he might be in the closet ...' Kit said. 'I think all I ever was to him was a beard.'

Marc laughed and bumped his forehead with his hand. 'That makes so much sense. Condolences, Kitten.'

17

Marc had cooked Kit dinner in his cottage and now they sat in front of their empty bowls and his open laptop. In reference to the screen display, he said, 'Care to explain?'

Kit swirled her wine. 'What's to explain?'

'Explain why,' Marc said, 'when I googled Gossard Range this afternoon, link six in the search results was a *pornographic magazine* curated by my *sister*.'

Kit leaned in. The typography Piper had crafted was perfect: the word small enough to be positioned wherever the cover image dictated. Still, she hadn't expected the page to appear in a search for Gossard Range, she shouldn't have tagged the photo, that was a mistake.

'It's very narcissistic to google Gossard Range.' Kit put her glass on the table and crossed her feet underneath.

'I was keeping Arenberg off our back,' Marc said. 'I was checking that the cider hadn't been leaked. I found nothing about that, but this–' he gestured towards the screen '–this I did find.'

Raph with his sandwich. Kit had unexpectedly taken the cover photo that day. She'd uploaded that afternoon, Issue 1 of *Hunger* had gone live, and already her brother had found it.

'Kit. These photos are fucking raunchy.'

'It's just a food magazine, Marc.'

'It's not *just* a food magazine.'

'It is.'

'What it *is*,' Marc said, 'is an intoxicating, lusty collation of photos that are *vaguely* food-centric. It's food porn, or just plain porn, I can't say for sure.'

Kit laughed quietly.

'Well aren't you going to ask me what I think?' Marc said.

'Didn't you just tell me?'

Her brother's mouth made huffing sounds that meant 'no'. He leaned back and put his hands behind his head. 'It may be sex-soaked, but I have a sneaking suspicion it may also be groundbreaking. I'm annoyed you've been keeping it from me,' he said.

Kit took up her glass and gazed into the swirl of crimson that was her family's lifeblood.

This corner of the internet she'd created wasn't there to be approved of. It was a place she'd built only to house the ideas and images that couldn't live elsewhere.

She patted Marc's hand. 'Well, I'm glad you like it,' she said.

'Of course I fucking *like it*.' Marc tugged his hand away. 'It gives me hope. I thought my sister had faded into folds of wedding dresses and faffy-Fifi-furniture. But this is *hot*, the fucking opposite to what I'd expected of you since you began your new *Hamper* "career" ...'

Kit looked at her brother and realised how little she revealed of herself, even to those nearest.

'Is it Scott being away? Are you unhinged? Off the leash? This kind of output takes me back to young Kit … Kit before Fifi tied you to one of his chairs and told you to stay.'

Something stirred inside but Kit shut it down.

'Not that I'm bad-mouthing Scott …' Marc got up and cleared the plates. 'I mean I like Scott, he's fine–'

'*Fine?*' Kit's gaze followed Marc to the kitchen. 'We're getting married!'

'I know, I know. Of course I didn't mean just "fine". You two have a special, reciprocal creative thing going on that I don't understand and I know that he's really good at what he does, he wouldn't do wrong by you and … yeah, he's surely *beyond* fine, he's hopefully mind-blowing.'

Kit's head swung to stare straight ahead again, and Marc sat down beside her as he refilled their glasses. 'Anyway, forget I mentioned Scott. This has nothing to do with anyone else. It's about you. You're going to have to launch whatever this is, make it a "main" not just "side" thing.'

Kit gazed at the digital cover: the canvas roof of the Jag, the meat of Raph's sandwich, his mouth, the dash, crumbs, hands dirty on white bread, face cropped but for a freckle atop his lip …

The petite word sat below his thumb: *Hunger.*

Marc was staring at it too. Suddenly he leaned forward and his finger skated on the trackpad.

He scanned through the photos and Kit saw it all: a man and truffle hunting, a man with wet grapes in the vineyard, a man eating, a man with a drink and flour in the shearers' quarters, a man in a car with food in his hand …

'Are most of these …' Marc's words were slow as he peeled backward through the animated pages. 'Fuck, who *is* that?'

'Who?'

Marc turned to study her face. 'Who's that man?'

Kit stood. Marc grabbed her hand.

'Does it matter?'

'Who *is* it?'

'Didn't we just get through saying that this wasn't about someone else?'

'It's the same fucking person in every photo, Kit!'

Kit tugged her hand away and walked to the kitchen.

'It's Raph!' Marc called after her. 'It's fucking well Raph!'

'You're radiating like a furnace,' Piper called over chant vibrations. 'It's making me sweat.'

Kit curled her tongue and breathed through it, a 'cooling breath' that she quickly deemed ineffectual.

Back to back with Piper in a partner pose, she was already down to her sports bra when small beads of sweat began to roll down her cleavage and she took her hands from prayer to mop them away.

It was Marc's fault.

'Whatever you're thinking, stop,' Piper said.

It was Marc. It was his fault.

'Channel your energy,' the yoga instructor incanted. 'Whatever your emotion, whatever you're feeling – *channel it*. Harvest it for higher use.'

Kit scrunched her eyes shut and wondered what the fuck 'higher use' meant.

She'd tried to keep it under her control but now Marc had smashed the walls down. She'd tried to put Raph in a box, contain him, tuck him within the walls of *Hunger* but Marc had dropped the drawbridge, broken the dam, and now Raph streamed out.

Raph. Freedom. The essence of a man.

Kit wanted to consume him and be consumed. She wanted out of her world and into his and the worst part was … now Marc knew it.

ॐ

Kit's phone rang halfway through a shoot.

She tried to answer it, but her wrist tangled in the strap of her DSLR. She knocked props over before finally stuffing the phone under her ear.

'Are you there?' she said.

'Can you talk?' Marc replied.

'Is it urgent?'

'Fairly.'

Kit signalled 'time-out' to her assistant, bumped into a staffer who came through from *Hamper*'s editorial suites, and made for the neon exit sign. The morning's yoga class hadn't channelled any energy. It had scattered it, and now chaos had become her. Kit stumbled into the fire escape. The door closed and she inhaled, absorbing the cool silence.

'If you're calling to talk about my magazine again and what–'

'No, Selfish,' Marc said, 'I'm not. Are you on your iPhone? Put it on speaker.'

Kit tapped the phone. 'Yeah?'

'Now go to *thegastronome.com*.'

'Why?' Kit said as she typed the URL.

'Jimmy Hillinger's blog.'

'He has a blog?'

'You haven't read it? It's popular.'

'Why the hell would I?' Kit said, and watched as a headline loaded with the beginnings of a photo. 'What? Is that–'

'Yes,' Marc said. 'He stole it from the offices. When he was here.'

On the screen was a photo of Gossard Range's *cidre bouché* label and below it, Jimmy's post read:

After months of speculation, I was delighted to take this pretty little teaser away from a recent meeting with my friends at Gossard Range. My guess is that this new introduction to their loyally followed brand will be an homage to their Gallic roots, cidre bouché *denoting a well-bred French-style cider under cork.*

Will the product live up to the name's implied distinction?

We wait with appetites whetted …

'Fuck,' Kit said.

'He's a fucking twit.'

'Does Dad know?'

'Yup.'

'Is he okay?'

'Well forgetting the obvious implications, he's pretty disappointed that he couldn't break the news on his own terms, detail the cider's exclusivity, and all that.'

'Shit.'

'The cider's still meant to be on lees. It's not ready.'

'I know.'

'But now Arenberg & Gossard will find a bloody cleanskin cider somewhere, smear their own label on it, and call it *cidre bouché* for no other reason than to stay neck and neck. We'll have to expedite if we want even a chance.'

'Surely Jimmy's blog isn't on AGVM's radar.'

'Probably not, but he's dropped a big bit of news. Gossard Range hasn't launched a new product since founding. It's only a matter of time before AGVM copy ... undercut ... fuck knows.'

'They can't muster anything overnight. The Cannock Chase orchards, the heirloom recipe, they're all rare – can't be imitated. Jimmy doesn't know anything about either, nor does AGVM.'

'I hope so.'

'I'll come and see Dad soon. Poor man, he–'

'No,' Marc said.

'I'll come when–' Kit began again but Marc interrupted again.

'No, it's fine.'

'What? Why?'

'You know why.'

'What?'

Marc laughed.

'Marc?'

'Kit, I can't believe I'm saying this but ... I think you should keep away from Raph.'

'Marc, come on, that's ridic–'

'Have you looked at your photos? Do you not see what's in them?'

'You think that's what my photos were about? Him?'

'No. They're about you. They're your work, they're about you, and they're incredible, but to me, your "inspiration" is plain.'

'Yes. That's exactly all it is. Inspiration.'

'Is it?'

'Why do you even care?'

'Well usually I wouldn't! You know I'm all for you exploring your options but unfortunately we're at a really critical moment with the cider. I need to put Dad first. Raph's indispensable right now. He's the only one Dad's let in on it all and we need him, a lot. If you and Raph … if you … it's just too much of a risk, especially with Mum, if she knew that you and a staffer were–'

'Nothing is happening, nothing's going to happen.'

'Then you shouldn't have a problem keeping away.'

'That makes me sound pathetic.'

'No. I just know that you're a passionate person. You're human … like me.'

'I'm nothing like you,' Kit said, immediately wishing she hadn't. There was silence. She felt bad, and murmured, 'I will.'

'What?' Marc said.

'I *will* keep away.'

Kit didn't want to keep away. Marc saying no made her want to say yes. Satisfaction with expression through art alone seemed suddenly alike to being satisfied with seeing the tip of an iceberg. Only a fool didn't wonder what lay beneath.

She wanted so badly to say yes and knowing there was only 'no', she called Scott.

While his phone rang, she scanned his Instagram feed – designers, studios, prototypes, exhibitions – and was instantly up to speed and ready to converse.

'Kitten,' he answered. 'How are you?'

'Hi! Good, you?'

'Great, it's going well.'

Kit heard music. 'Are you out?'

'Just a party,' Scott replied, sounding like he was enjoying it. It was the first thing she thought of so she began telling him about the cider label and Jimmy.

'What's that about, sorry?' he replied.

'The Gossard cider. A journo leaked it online today, before we were ready.'

Someone in the background spoke to Scott and it was a moment before he responded. 'Is that a big problem?' he finally said.

Kit stood in the middle of the lounge room in the Gossards' apartment, eyes square to the array of wedding dress boxes arranged carefully against one wall. 'It just means there's a chance Arenberg & Gossard will leapfrog us with a matching product before ours is off the ground.' She paused. 'It's just pressure that Dad's not well placed for, and I guess disappointing considering everything he hoped.'

The person kept talking to Scott.

'Hello?' Kit said.

'Sorry, sorry, here's hectic, every second feels–' Scott faltered with a laugh. 'I need to get around to everyone … there's some

162

fantastic photographers here too, Kit, you'd love it. Do you mind if I get off the phone? Connor will be fine, he's a big boy. Speak more later?'

'Yes, sorry, of course. Have fun.'

'Thanks. Bye.'

The phone went dead. Kit marched over to the dress boxes.

&

It had rained. The potholes along the Gossard Range drive had become puddles that the Defender's tyres now emptied.

Kit glanced in the rear-view mirror, saw that the last corner had capsized her stack, and was glad that the homestead was visible in the distance.

She pulled up and was relieved to find that the boxes' lids remained in place. She stacked two piles and carried the first in a beeline towards the homestead.

Her mother's car wasn't there and Kit felt grateful that Annalese wouldn't be inside to question her.

She snapped her head around. She'd heard an engine but it was just a tractor down by the winery building. She took a couple more steps, glanced back to be sure, but what she feared – Annalese driving up the drive – was absent.

She hurried on and the heel of her boot suddenly found a stone, she swayed. She stumbled, righted herself, but the middle container began to slide. The box fell forward, the others followed, and suddenly there was only one box in her hands – the rest on the watery drive.

She swore and crouched.

'Are you okay?'

Kit glanced behind her and saw Raph carrying an armload of vine cuttings towards the house.

'Fuck.' She began to sweat as she tried to reassemble the pile.

'Can I help?' he said.

She glanced back. 'What are you doing?'

He looked down at the load in his arms. 'Wicker,' he said. 'Your mother's garden.'

Kit swore again and he dumped the greenery and came forward.

'Thank you, but I'm fine,' she said. He nudged her aside, tugged the dripping boxes up by their bows, and strode towards the car.

'They're for the house,' she called, but he continued on to the boot, collected the remainder, and carried them all towards the homestead. As he passed her, Kit watched his muscles twist, arms littered with vine debris. 'Stop,' she said.

He paused on the entry ramp, and she walked towards him with a small crease in her forehead that he began to mirror.

'Yes?' he queried, and Kit came to a stop in front of him, heart thudding no, no, no …

He lowered the boxes as if knowing he'd need his hands and she watched the shapes settle on the ground before he flexed his fingers and no, no, no …

'Yes?' he said again, searchingly, as she stood on her tiptoes.

When her head was in line with his she said, 'Yes,' and kissed him.

'*Katherine!*'

Kit fell back onto flat feet and looked towards her mother's voice.

18

Raph didn't look at Annalese.

He gazed at Kit, eyes on hers, until she glanced down. Then he bent, lifted the boxes and walked to place them on the decking before Annalese's feet.

He had made her feel safe. The boxes had been their fortress, and now Kit stood exposed and unfortified. He went to say something to Annalese, seemed to think better of it, then collected his clippings and walked out of sight around the side of the house.

Kit looked at her mother. Annalese looked at Kit, then at the boxes.

Kit tried to gather them in the way Raph had but her hands were too small. Annalese powered over and dragged them into the house.

Annalese stood with her arms folded, back to Kit.

The living room window was large; it framed the back garden and Raph, laying down his vines.

'You've got to be joking, Kit.'

Kit didn't reply.

'What did I do to you children to give you such lowly opinions of yourselves?'

'I assume that your question is rhetorical and that you don't want an inventory?' Kit said. Annalese's bony shoulders twitched beneath her fine silk top.

'Nothing,' Annalese said. 'I've done nothing and this is how you behave.'

'I'm sorry about the dresses.' Kit watched Raph. 'That you bought them all for me was extremely ... thoughtful, very thoughtful. You meant well and–'

'I wouldn't have bothered had I known you were flapping your fanny at the creepy gardener!'

A curl of hysteria unfurled in Kit's chest and she put her hand to her mouth, and waited for it to recede before she replied.

'Mum,' she said. 'I came up to drop off the dresses so you could return them. They were bought on your account, so would you mind?'

'You've chosen one, I assume?'

'I haven't, no. I want you to send them back.'

'And by that you mean Scott knows you're having an affair?' Annalese turned to face her.

Kit spat a laugh. 'Mum, I'm not having an affair.'

'Don't patronise me, Katherine, you're clearly fucking the fucking gardener.'

'Raph is not a gardener and I'm not fucking him.'

'It's cliché and rank. You need to stop it.'

'There's nothing to stop.'

Annalese gave Kit a once-over then turned back to the window. 'I won't be surprised if Scott never comes back,' she said.

'I told you he wouldn't last long here and now he has nothing to come back for.'

Kit's eyes left Annalese and returned to the man beyond the glass. 'Thank you,' she said before she left. 'Thank you for returning the dresses.'

☙

Kit gazed at Piper.

Her friend's red hair was flung out across Kit's pillow – eyes smiling.

'Just laugh already,' Kit said.

'I'm sorry!' Piper burst into laughter, eyes watery. 'I'm sorry. It's just … it's funny.'

Kit's face was stony.

'Here.' Piper wiped a tear away. 'Try the lemon curd.'

A row of pastel macarons was lined up on Kit's doona. Piper passed her a yellow one.

'I just can't stop thinking about the scene,' Piper said. 'Uptight Annalese opening the door to find you necking the grubby help, soggy couture at your feet. It's cinematic brilliance.'

'It wasn't.'

'And *flapping your fanny*?'

'Don't imagine that. Don't you dare.'

'I'm not imagining *your* flapping fanny, just *a* flapping fanny …'

Kit's phone rang. 'What?' she answered.

'Kit,' Marc said. 'Really?'

'It was an accident,' Kit said.

'Oh Kitten. *Kitten.*'

'Don't, Marc. I had no choice. I had to go up there. I had to get those dresses out of the apartment. I was just going to drop and leave. Delivery was the only reason I went.'

'Don't fib, Kit. It's me, Marc.'

'I'm hanging up.'

'I'm sorry, I'm sorry,' he laughed. 'You couldn't control yourself. It's okay, I understand, I know the feeling.'

It was true. She couldn't control herself.

Piper took the phone and turned on the speaker. 'It was just a kiss, Marc,' she said.

'Who's that?'

'Piper,' Kit said.

'Hi Marc,' Piper sounded coy.

Marc went on despite a change in his tone. 'I just mean it's cute, Kit. It's cute that you're always on my back about where I can and can't put my junk and here you are, completely unable to keep it in your pants.'

'Lady junk is immobile,' Piper said, 'it's always in our pants.'

Marc laughed, Kit didn't.

'Anyway,' he said, 'despite the rant we endured earlier from Annalese, Dad and I managed to prevent Raph from being both castrated and banished, as well as ever finding out that he might have been castrated and banished. Are you thankful?'

'Thank you,' Kit said, unwillingly.

'You're welcome. Now repeat: I will not make out with staff. I am engaged to be married and I will not make out with staff in front of my mother for fear of dead men racking up in the vineyard.'

'I'm hanging up now, bye.'

168

'Bye!'

'Bye Marc,' Piper said. When the phone went silent, Kit found Piper watching her, face aglow.

'You're happy about this,' Kit said.

Piper didn't answer.

'Why?' Kit asked.

Piper gazed at her before her eyes shifted to search the ceiling. 'I don't know,' she said. 'I like that you let yourself be governed by instinct rather than reason, perhaps.'

Kit covered her eyes so she could consider the words, undistracted in the dark.

'Fuck,' she finally said and met Piper's gaze.

'Scott?' Piper said.

'I love him, he's good for me, he's an amazing person, I just wish–'

'That you felt something.'

Kit stared.

'You just wish you *felt* something,' Piper elaborated.

'I *do* feel something.'

'No I think you're afraid to feel, Kit. What you're doing is thinking. Stop. You're using logic when the world isn't logical. Being with Scott isn't actually logical, for you. Stop thinking, stop reasoning …'

Kit stared at the bright row of biscuits on the pillow then rolled off the bed.

'What are you doing?' Piper stared at her.

Kit began putting on her jacket. Piper frowned. 'I thought we were having dinner,' she said.

'Order something, stay if you want.' Kit picked up her car keys. 'I'll see you tomorrow.'

The drive always seemed longer at night.

The view was gone; there was only the roadside grass and the reflectors, lit by her headlights. An hour out of town, Kit turned down the laneway with the tourist sign that pointed to Gossard Range.

She passed the usual turnoff to the homestead, squinting to find what she sought: the track that led into the old sheep paddocks. She found it. She opened the gate and drove through without bothering to close it behind her.

Small, grubby windows glowed. Someone was inside.

Kit opened the car door and clipped her toe on the running board of the Defender. She steadied herself. The air was cold.

She stood with the car door open. Apprehension began flooding in.

The vague lights of the Gossard homestead were way away in the distance and seemed to blink as trees swayed … in front then away, in front then away. The wind lifted Kit's hair. Her eyes turned back to the shearers' quarters. Her fingers found each other and fidgeted.

She pried them apart, wondered what underwear she had on, turned back to the car, fossicked, and found mints. She crushed white peppermint pellets between her teeth and reached for lip balm. She wasn't ready, but her feet carried her forward.

She felt anything but in charge. Hunger. It was that and that alone that drove her and she kept on, body leading her mind.

Nearing the front door, she glimpsed Raph through the window and stepped back. Music played inside. He sat in one of his chairs, his back bare, and he reached for his glass and kicked back his head. She'd arrived unheard.

The puddle of brown spirits was gone when he returned the tumbler to the arm of his chair. He turned the page of a book.

Kit had stopped breathing. She inhaled, felt hot. She pulled off her jacket, hurried back towards the car, threw the jacket in through the open window and felt suddenly cold again.

She stepped forward, back, forward, back, then wrenched herself towards the front door, and knocked.

The music cut. She shivered.

There were footsteps on the hollow-sounding boards. The door opened, opened wide. Raph stood there.

He shifted his footing, one, two, primed for something wild coming at him in the night but perhaps not prepared for what he found … nothing was as wild and unpredictable as a woman.

He stepped over the threshold.

Kit raised her hands – to halt or draw him in she wasn't sure – and bumps spread across his skin where her hands landed, on his chest.

'Are you okay?' His accent surprised her, as though she'd forgotten he had one.

'I …' she began, 'I just needed to ask …' She sounded formal, like she had actually driven here late at night with nothing more than a question that needed an answer.

'Kit?' he prompted. Something about the way he stood told her the only thing stopping him from touching her was respect, and she knew words were no longer necessary. She took her top off.

He looked at what she'd revealed, back at her face, then down again.

'I want you,' she said, but her voice lacked desire. She sounded stretched and anxious, exactly how she felt, because despite her desperation to be there, she shouldn't be.

Raph's eye searched hers. He pushed his hands back through his hair as if her revelation distressed him. He turned towards the door then back again.

His chest flexed, and Kit's breath caught as he swung her onto the firewood hatch. She felt the tin cold through her jeans and the shiplap boards hard against her back.

Raph kissed her. Kit kissed back and the hunger didn't diminish, it grew. She kissed, grappled, grabbed and still didn't feel she was getting enough.

Her chest arced to meet his mouth and she caught the scent of weathered timber, paddocks, whisky, sweat, and in the silence she cried out.

Raph pulled back. He stared at her face then punched his fist into the boards behind her head. He turned away, breath heavy in the darkness.

Kit panted, bewildered, and reached for him, clutching air.

Raph turned slowly back to face her and wiped his forehead on the back of his arm. 'I'm sorry.' He smoothed his hand through his hair a second time.

Kit's mouth was open but no words came.

He stepped towards her, cupped her back and she felt like a limp doll as he lifted her to stand.

'You–' he paused to take her top from the ground and handed it to her, face pained. 'You too have made me want things I

172

shouldn't.' His eyes searched her face before they glanced away. 'No …' he said quietly, 'no.'

Kit took her top without speaking then watched as he stepped back over the threshold and closed the door.

19

Kit leaned over the pristine white *Hamper* set. Ten salad leaves, ten mismatched jam jars.

Piper punched out vintage labels on Kit's white-on-black Dymo tape dispenser and stuck them to the glass. 'Radicchio. Kale. Beet leaf. Betel leaf. Pak choy and …?'

'Belgian endive,' Kit said.

Piper broke off three leaves and handed them to her. 'Never be ashamed,' she said.

Kit hadn't said she was ashamed, but Piper knew where Kit had gone the night before and her demeanour all but told Piper what had happened.

She stuffed the endive into a slim-necked jar, made it stand tight and tall, and stared. She felt sick. She'd turned the sequence round and round like a figurine in a jewellery box and now she felt sick.

She'd been careless.

She'd been impulsive and over-eager. She'd risked everything, including a good man's job.

She was engaged to be married. She 'had it all' and wanted more. She was selfish, spoiled, felt disgusting and excessive, and now Raph thought this of her, too.

She'd ruined everything. Raph made her feel free, gave her life mystery and hope, and she needed him to be there, even if just as a friend … an acquaintance. Now, somehow, she had to rebuild a friendship with the man in the shearers' quarters. She had to return him to what he once was, a switch for her imagination and nothing more. Wanting in excess of this had been greedy and a mistake.

'Watercress,' Piper read the Dymo sticker as she made it. 'Ten Salad Leaves You Should Know and How to Use Them.'

❧

'It's Dad,' Marc said a second time.

Kit sat in the car. Something like this wasn't something that happened. She'd pulled herself together that day, decided to walk tall and now Marc was – intentionally or not – tearing her down.

'Meaning …?' She shook her head.

'What I said,' Marc replied. 'His heart, there was a cardiac episode.'

They'd finished the Ten Salad Leaves shoot and the day had proceeded as usual. Now, as usual, she and Piper were on their way home, but what wasn't usual was having to pull over in the bike lane … what wasn't usual was Piper swearing at an angry cyclist from the passenger's seat …

'Is he–' Kit began.

'He's okay,' Marc said. 'They stopped a heart attack.'

'Where? Are you–'

'I'm at the hospital.'

'I'm coming.' The adrenaline began.

175

Marc was waiting for her in Coronary Care. They held each other, Kit staring over his shoulder at the door to the room that contained their father.

Finally she stepped inside and found him asleep, skin grey in the poor lighting.

A machine beeped. Connor wore a thin, pale gown, a breathing mask, and the blanket over him appeared cheap and inadequate.

'Oh, Dad,' she whispered and closed the door behind her.

Colourful soft toys. Metallic heart-shaped balloons on sticks. Wilted flowers, unimaginatively arranged. Sitting across from her brother in the hospital's giftshop-café, Kit could only think of how alive he seemed, and she reached across the table to hold his hand.

Connor had stirred enough to share a few words but had then faded back to sleep. Now, Kit meditated on the rough patches of her brother's hand before she spoke.

'What happened?'

Marc's free hand rubbed his eye. 'We'd been waiting all week for Earl to send back the contracts for the Cannock Chase sale,' he said. 'Dad finally got a call from him this morning.'

He took his other hand from Kit and used it to tear at a dry muffin.

'And?' Kit said as she watched him chew.

'It's been sold.'

Small crumbs gathered on the table as Kit leaned forward. 'What do you mean?'

'AGVM,' Marc said. 'They've bought it.'

Kit frowned. Marc put some muffin in his mouth.

'I don't get it.'

'There's nothing to get,' he said. 'We missed out. Arenberg & Gossard, AGVM, they bought Cannock Chase from Earl a week ago.'

Kit shook her head. 'I don't get it, Marc,' she said again.

'AGVM,' Marc said loudly. 'They bought Cannock Chase.'

'What? *How?*' Kit said. 'How is this possible? How was Cannock Chase even on their radar? It wasn't even on the market.'

'I don't know how it–'

'And it's Dad's!' Kit's voice rose. 'He's already–'

'There's never been a fucking contract, Kit,' Marc said. 'Dad was relying on his thirty years of *mateship* with that old fuck. It was handshake shit.'

'I know!' Kit said. 'But why didn't Earl even talk to Dad? He wouldn't go behind his back.'

'Arenberg's offer was unprecedented.'

'But why didn't he talk to Dad first?'

'The offer was at least double what he and Dad had agreed and had a twenty-four-hour expiry. Dad could never have matched it and Earl said he didn't want to draw him into some protracted bunfight.'

Kit put a hand over her eyes. 'Are you sure it's over? Deal done? Definitely? This is too crazy.'

'Yup.' Marc scuffed the table leg with his shoe and scrunched the muffin bag.

Kit pushed her hand through her hair. 'Fuck, fuck. *Poor Dad.*'

'I know.'

'Do you know how AGVM found out?'

'Nup, haven't had time to look into it. Dad's heart attack symptoms started soon after, then the ambulance came and the ECG said his heart wasn't getting enough oxygen. It was fucking scary.'

'The stress ...'

'I know.'

There was silence.

'Where's Mum?'

'Back at the apartment. Getting Dad some things.'

Kit unlocked the door and climbed the stairs two at a time, her heart pounding as she debated which kind of monster she'd find at the top.

It hadn't taken long to get to the apartment. Annalese's four-wheel drive had been parked badly out the front, tyres skewed and half up on the kerb as it straddled two parking bays.

Kit gently opened the apartment door and heard nothing.

The loaf of sourdough she'd left on the kitchen bench that morning had been sliced and left out to go dry.

'Mum?'

There was silence.

Kit called out again, walked down the hall, then heard a sound in her parents' bedroom.

She waited by the door.

'Hello?' She knocked.

'What?'

Kit pushed the door wide and found Annalese on the far side of the room, back to her, face to the built-in robe.

'Mum?'

'What!' Annalese didn't turn as she tugged clothes from the robe and dropped them on the floor.

'What are you doing?'

'What does it fucking look like, darling?'

Kit hung back.

'All this old fucking junk!' Annalese shouted as a handful of scarves floated to the floor.

Kit closed the door and walked carefully forward. 'I can't believe it about Dad …' she said, slowly. 'I was so shocked … how are you?'

Her mother silently tugged, dropped, tugged and dropped. Annalese didn't care to feel. She refused to have or show feelings and now that an army of feelings had arrived, she was without the skill and strength to direct them.

'Mum?'

'What!' Annalese shouted again and suddenly tipped forward like a post. She crashed into the hanging clothes and slithered down, hands gripping, body convulsing until she was on all fours, sobbing into hems.

Kit stepped over the clothes. She crouched and placed her hand on her mother's rocking back.

'Arrrggh!' Annalese wailed. She reached to yank at the clothing again but Kit grasped her hand.

'Don't stop me! I'm getting rid of this old junk! I want to get rid of it!' Annalese yelled as she buried her face in the footwear.

Kit's hand stayed on her back until a fit took over and Annalese kicked the shoes across the floor.

Kit grabbed her mother's arm and the woman flumped against the back of the robe, her hand tearing at the hair that hung over her damp, mottled face. Kit sat flat on the carpet, facing her.

'Are you okay?' Kit touched her mother's shin. Annalese lolled her head back and stared at the clothes overhead.

'I remember …' Her voice was faded. 'I remember the first time I met Connor. He was so cool … *God* he was assured, and sexy.' Her hand batted at the fabric above.

'You both were. You both *are*.'

Annalese scoffed and tugged a loose thread. 'I was a model, I dazzled him … but really, *really* I didn't have much to offer, he was the one with it all.'

Kit had often wondered what it would be like to have a mother who felt … She guessed it might look something like this.

'Then, when I had you and Marc, all I wanted was for you to have a good life, a *great* life, a life like I never had until Connor.'

Annalese found a shoe on the floor. She turned it over as a tear ran down the side of her face and Kit smiled at her mother's fundamental simplicity.

'Mum,' she said, 'you don't need to do this. Everything's fine. Dad's going to be fine. We all have great lives. We're all going to be fine.'

Annalese laughed desperately then covered her face with her hands. There was a beat and Kit wondered if her mother had passed out. She leaned forward.

'I know we're *fine*.' Annalese pushed a hand back through her hair, tone familiarly clipped. She sniffed and wiped her face. 'The only thing that isn't fine is that you've been fucking the fucking gardener. Your father was horrified when I told him.'

Kit was speechless for a moment. Then she smiled. Her real mother had returned.

'You may not have inherited my daintiness and decorum darling, but my shoe size you do have.' She pitched the shoe she held at Kit. 'Vintage Prada, you're welcome.'

That night, they shared takeaway in Connor's hospital room. Afterwards, Annalese and Marc went back to the apartment and Kit went to Scott's.

'Why are you going over there?' Marc asked before she left.

'I feel like being alone,' Kit said, and it was the truth.

The mains power had been switched off in Scott's apartment and Kit tripped on the stairs, hurting her knee. The living room smelled like stale cologne. By the light of her phone, she found her way to the bedroom and sat on the bare mattress.

Kit rubbed her knee as the phone's torch glowed and she scrolled through her contacts, passed Scott's number, reversed, and gazed at it. She waited, then tapped.

It rang, rang out, and disconnected. Kit lowered the phone, lifted the doona from the floor, lay back on a bare pillow, and thought of Connor, alone in the hospital bed.

Her phone jingled. Scott's photo flashed up, and her finger hovered over the screen before it pressed.

'Hi.' She put the phone to her ear.

'Babe!' His tone was elevated.

'Hey …' she said and his reply came at once.

'We did it.'

Kit faltered. 'What?'

'Fermi,' Scott said.

Kit was struggling to think straight.

'Fermi,' Scott said again. 'They bought the licence. I was literally just on the phone to Alexi. They sent through the contract today.'

'Fermi?' Kit said. 'They've licensed your light fitting?'

'They've licensed the Hutch dome as well as a *whole* Hutch family. They've licensed a set, would you believe.'

Scott's agent had begun talks with the large Italian design house, Fermi, some months earlier. Fermi's interest had been in a light fitting of Scott's design, but he'd muzzled any excitement. To license a product to a company of Fermi's fame was rare and career changing, follow-through had seemed unlikely, and so this news was huge. Kit wished she could feel it.

'Scott Baldwin for Fermi,' Scott said.

'Wow. Amazing.'

'Do you want to come to Milan?'

'What?'

'I have to meet with Fermi as soon as this all wraps up in London,' Scott said. 'You should come and meet me.'

Kit began to tell Scott about Connor, but he cut in.

'Can we talk more later? Tomorrow perhaps? I'm out the front of an event, I'm late, and I need to call Alexi back. Oh,' he paused. 'Were you going to ask about your email last week? I'm sorry I didn't get a chance to reply, but in short, I wasn't a fan. The tone felt too ... offbeat, not like a proper food ... thing. I can't think of more to say off the cuff, but I hope that helps, I really should get inside.'

Kit had forgotten she'd done that, sent him a link to *Hunger*.

'Oh yes … thanks … that helps,' Kit lied, numb and fast.

'Great, talk soon.'

The phone went dead and Kit lay, searching the darkness.

20

Kit woke early, feeling unusually calm. She opened Scott's robe and found an Acne sweater and jeans that belonged to her, as well as shoes.

In the bathroom she gathered her Aēsop products and in the kitchen, her Microplane and a casserole dish.

She put them all in her market basket and left.

Kit sat in her father's office at Gossard Range. She'd been to see the neighbour, Earl. She wished she hadn't.

She'd sat while Earl's wife brought them tea, and broken by the news of Connor's health, Earl had asked repeatedly how his friend was doing. 'I misjudged the situation, I can see now that it was a very poor decision,' he'd kept saying.

Kit had overcompensated for his discomfort by saying how happy she and the Gossards were that he'd done so well with AGVM. Then she went back to Gossard Range, and sat in the office alone.

On the phone to Marc, she conceded: 'You're right, there's no going back, the sale's done.'

'Fucking Earl,' Marc said. 'He sought Arenberg, he'd have known they'd pay big for something that was ours – virtually.'

'I don't think so. He was reeling. Arenberg approached him and he just went guilelessly along. I don't think he understood what it would mean for Dad.'

'Why would Arenberg have looked his way otherwise? Earl's a sad, money-hungry old scumbag. Screw him and screw Arenberg.'

Kit stared at a letterpressed *cidre bouché* label on the desk. More sat atop crates of elegantly tapered bottles by the door, corked, caged, almost ready, and she thought of the Cannock Chase tunnel: its smell of moss, fermentation and anticipation.

'How's Dad doing this morning?'

'Fine, they haven't found any blockages, blood tests were promising. He's just desperate to get home.'

Kit stared at the mug of cold coffee by Connor's still-on computer. She leaned over and switched it off. The place felt ghostly.

He wasn't in the machinery sheds.

The men said he'd be in the vineyard. Kit eyed them as they spoke. Had Raph told them what she'd done and if so, would her asking about him fuel speculation? If he'd told just one person about her visit to the shearers' quarters late that night, the whole winery would know by now.

The men's responses were indifferent. Kit left them to climb the hill.

Raph was the only one beyond the family who knew Connor like they did. To talk to him about the sale felt like the right thing to do. Connor's workers loved him but none shared the easy affinity and mutual trust that Raph had achieved. If Marc was Connor's right-hand man, Raph had become his left. Surely, for no one to make contact would be inconsiderate and alienating.

She zigzagged through the vines, trying not to think of the way he'd said: 'No'.

She encountered no one in the vineyard, kept on to the shearers' quarters, and came to a standstill in the place where he'd returned her top to her: 'No.'

She steeled herself and knocked. This was about Connor, nothing more. The shearers' quarters were silent and she waited, then knocked again, had no reply, knocked one last time, then jiggled the door handle before opening the door.

The small windows offered minimal light and Kit let her eyes adjust before she called out ...

On her way back to the winery, she took a different route through the vineyard, glad that if she found him now, at least he wouldn't know it was intended.

Back at the cellar door, Kit leaned against the bar inside. The return walk had turned up nothing.

She stood with a too-early glass of wine by one hand, an old issue of *Hamper* by the other, and wondered if Marc had maybe spoken to Raph about Connor already.

She took a sip of wine, skimmed past advertisements, passed Jimmy Hillinger's monthly *Hamper* column, and paused.

She flicked back.

Jimmy smiled up from the page. Kit stared at him, then turned and jogged up the stairs to the offices.

Marc answered after one ring.

'I just realised,' Kit said.

'What?'

'Jimmy Hillinger. I think he sold out to AGVM about Cannock Chase.'

Marc was silent before he spoke. 'Are you sure?' he said.

'If he got the cider label from the offices surely he helped himself to whatever else he found.'

Marc paused again. 'Fuck,' he began. 'Shit. No … Do you think? He could have. Shit. Do you think he would?'

'I'm going to call him.'

'No. I'll call.'

'I will.'

'Keep it together. He's a journo, he could use it.'

Kit hung up and found Jimmy's number in her phone.

'Fuck, Jimmy,' she said when he answered.

'Kit Gossard,' his voice was smug and lilting, as if he'd been expecting her. 'How are you?'

'Dad almost had a heart attack yesterday so you can probably guess.'

'God,' Jimmy sounded legitimately surprised and concerned. 'Is he okay?'

Kit wondered if she'd already said too much. 'He's absolutely fine. I–'

'Good, because I can't resist asking, was it your news? Did it shock him? Sorry, too soon?' He had a smirk in his voice.

Kit didn't know what he was talking about. 'Jimmy, did you sell private Gossard Range trade information to Arenberg & Gossard?'

He was silent, then he laughed.

'This is not a fucking joke.'

Jimmy paused. 'What is this in relation to?'

'You know.'

'No, I don't.'

'This is about AGVM purchasing Cannock Chase! Do you have any concept of the implications? Why'd you do it? Do you want us to fail? Does this entertain you?'

'You're very quick to blame.'

'Don't ever come here again.' Kit decided that she didn't want to hear his voice anymore. 'Don't ever speak to my family or me again, and if you ever come across me at *Hamper*, walk the other fucking way.'

'Read my blog before you go pointing fingers.'

'Fuck you.' Kit put the phone down and stared at the wall.

Adrenaline ebbed and hate bloomed. Her phone beeped, a message from Piper. '*Um … do u read Jimmy Hillinger's blog??*'

Kit had sat a while, staring at Piper's message. It was too uncanny.

'*Piper, is that you?*' she typed.

'*Of course it's me! Read. NOW. Thegastronome.com.*'

Kit rebooted Connor's desktop. She loaded Jimmy's blog, scrolled to the latest post and the headline – *Sweet or Sour?* – and saw the photo. Of her.

The photo was of her and a man, Kit with a man who was Raph, climbing out of Connor's car at the winery the day Jimmy had visited.

Below was a caption: their names. Kit read the caption twice, then a third time.

Kit Gossard and …

She read it again.

Kit Gossard and Raphaël Arenberg.

Something wet touched Kit's hand and she looked down to see one of the lagotto dogs licking her fingers, Raph's deerhound in the doorway. She tugged her hand away and snapped her gaze back to the screen. The names hadn't changed.

Kit Gossard and … Raphaël. Arenberg.

She made her hands work. Typed the words into Google. Said them aloud.

'Raph … Arenberg.'

Images began to load and the first word she said was, 'No.'

Raph in a tux.

'No.'

Raph in a collegiate rowing jersey.

'No.'

Raph at Paris Fashion Week.

Raph at the Venice Biennale.

Raph at Cannes.

Raph at the Met Gala.

Raph with Elliott Arenberg …

Kit toggled the view back to Jimmy's blog.

Sweet or Sour?

   Kit Gossard hosts French-American playboy Raphaël Arenberg at Gossard Range, and one can't help wondering – is this a culinary case of Capulet and Montague?

   Kit, of local Gossard Range, and Raphaël, of Arenberg & Gossard (AGVM), certainly seem unlikely friends. Despite their ancestors being known trade partners, a modern-day relationship between Gossard Range and Arenberg & Gossard has not only never existed, but the competition between the brands is known to even the most lay wine enthusiast.

With recent reports perpetuating this lore, an amicable Gossard–Arenberg sighting fascinates!

Firstly, prominent valley property, Cannock Chase (rumoured to be the providore and intended launch setting for Gossard Range's new cidre bouché *as well as the source of their recent sell-out truffles), has just been added to AGVM's renowned consortium. Long-time owner of Cannock Chase, Earl Howard, confirms the property's calibre, asserting acres of certified organic soil, prolific truffle, fruit and nut production, double river frontage and a heritage-listed in-situ antique: the 120-year-old once-was valley railway that links the grounds to Gossard Range and notable properties in the region.*

With this sale to AGVM reported, we can only assume Gossard Range has been hung out to dry, which makes a seemingly civil meeting of these two young heirs a bit of a riddle …

Was the meeting for business or pleasure? Cooperative, hostile or secreted? Forbidden, celebrated or now terminated? Whatever the case, a real-life Gossard–Arenberg blend has spicy undertones and we hope for another taste.

Kit's eyes fell to the dog at her feet and the animal stared back at her.

In the G-Wagen outside, the deerhound and lagotto clambered over Kit, and she reversed the car, thinking about the time she'd reversed into him.

Raphaël. Arenberg.

The four-wheel drive careered up the Gossard Range hill, past staff in soiled boots, and on the rocky outcrop Kit jumped out, engine running, dogs in tow.

The old door of the shearers' quarters rattled on its hinges, but the room appeared the same as it had an hour ago – only now, unlike then, it was obvious. The place had been deserted.

Kit could hear the Merc idling outside as she entered the bedroom. The rusted steel bed-base had a new mattress on top and, like the room, was bare.

She turned to go, then saw something.

The dogs nosed the steel men's bracelet watch as Kit slid it from the dust under the bed. The back was engraved.

For Raphaël, from your dad, Elliott.

❧

Kit tried to find the way to Connor's hospital room ... got lost. She backtracked to the main foyer, checked the number, floundered through the maze ... got lost a second time.

She crouched against a wall.

A nurse asked if she needed help. She wanted to ask for a stretcher and to be carried away.

The nurse gave her two rights and three lefts. Kit found Connor, sitting up, smiling, looking very much like the dad she was used to. Marc was there too. At least that meant she'd only have to say it once.

'Raph is an Arenberg,' she said.

Marc rubbed his ear as if waiting for her to get to the point. Connor coughed and folded down the top of his blanket.

'You know Raph?' Kit's mouth was dry. 'Raph from back home?'

'Yeah.' Marc glanced at his phone.

'And you know Arenberg & Gossard? AGVM?'

Marc nodded.

'Raph,' Kit said slowly, 'is an *Arenberg*.'

Connor frowned.

'What?' Marc looked up.

'*Raph* is Raphaël Arenberg.'

'I don't follow ...' Marc said and Kit laughed, desperately.

'Start again,' Connor sat up.

Kit studied his pale face above his white gown. 'I won't, I won't go into it now,' she said, 'I just–'

'No, no, what did you say?'

'Dad, lie down and–'

'Darling!' Connor held up his hands. 'I'm fine. What are you talking about?'

Kit glanced at Marc. 'Let's talk outside.'

'Neither of you are to leave this room,' Connor said. 'If anyone leaves, I'm getting up and I am *running* after you.'

Marc turned to Kit.

Kit had nothing left.

'You're a pain in the arse,' Marc told his dad.

'Good,' Connor replied. 'Now, I'm sorry? Raph? Arenberg? What's going on, Kit?'

'I assume you've heard of Raphaël Arenberg? Elliott Arenberg's son?' Kit said.

'Yes … at some time.' Connor frowned.

'Well Raph *is* Raphaël Arenberg.'

'What?'

'Raph *is* Raphaël Arenberg.'

'I don't get it,' Marc said.

'There's nothing to get! That's it! Raph is an Arenberg! He's Elliott's son!'

'That's absurd.'

'It's true. It's actually fucking true. Jimmy Hillinger's blog–'

'That weird *reporter* said it? That's just–'

'Kit–'

'Use the fucking internet!' Kit said and there was a wait as Marc's fingers danced across his phone.

'Whathefuck?'

Kit waited.

'Sorry, WHAT THE FUCK?'

'Marc?' Connor craned his neck. 'What?'

'No …' Marc glanced at Kit. 'No way.'

'Where are you looking?'

'On Wikipedia. It says, "Raphaël Arenberg, son of American Elliott Arenberg, currently holds successive position in family conglomerate Arenberg Gossard Valcourt Mantel …" What fucking name did he give you, Dad?'

Connor stared.

'Dad? Raph's *full* name?'

'I … he …' Connor managed. 'He was Jones, I think. Raph Jones?'

Marc half laughed, half swore.

'I thought he was just some itinerant worker!' Connor's voice rose. 'He was so good! Are you sure, Marc? Show me, is there a photo?'

'There's a hundred fucking photos. Did you show him everything Gossard Range is working on?'

'Of course! He was the best worker I've ever had!'

Marc laughed again. 'Yes he's the most experienced fucking *worker* that's ever set foot on Gossard Range! He's an Ivy-fucking-League-fucking-educated-son of one of the most powerful fucking men in the lifestyle sector!'

Connor's face was taut.

Marc stood up and raked his hands through his hair. 'Holy fucking shit we've been played.'

'Jesus ...' Connor said, quietly. 'The more I think about it, the more I think back, it makes so much more sense. It seems almost obvious now, everything he knew, everything he did, he–'

'This is horrific.' Marc stared. 'All that humble, quiet shit? That was all an act? And that dog? That couriered purebred? It's fucking obvious. I can't believe this.'

'He left the dog,' Kit said. 'He took his other stuff, left that. It's roaming around at Gossard Range with the other dogs.'

'What a brat! What a piece of shit. What a careless, spoiled–' Marc pounded his lips with his fist.

'What then?' Connor stared. 'What's the story? That he's been scouting us out? That this whole time he was scouting us out for AGVM? I mean, I wouldn't put it past that cankerous bloodline but I just, I don't ...' He held himself rigid then sunk into his pillows. 'And now what? Do we wait? Do we wait and watch them pilfer everything we've worked for? A second time?'

You too have made me want things I shouldn't. No.

Kit had offered herself up, pathetically, guilelessly.

He had been so near to taking everything she'd wanted to give him. He'd been so near to taking everything she had.

'I have to go,' she said.

Kit stood in her apartment.

She lay down, draped her body across the couch, and hung her head off the side to breathe and be sick if she needed to.

He was nothing she'd thought he was. Everything that an Arenberg actually was meant nothing she'd seen in Raph was real.

She hid her face in her arm and saw him striding through the hazelnut thicket, the unbound man with a scent of dirt and truffle about him.

Had he lied to her or had she lied to herself? Had he pretended or had she? Maybe she made up the idea of him, made Raph who she wanted him to be.

Steel dug into Kit's thigh.

She pulled the thing free from her pocket and stared at the Rolex Daytona, the neat encapsulation of her misunderstanding. The man she craved wouldn't care for such a thing, but this man wasn't real. The real man wore this.

She pulled herself up and tapped the keys of her laptop.

Her mail program opened and she found the email sent two days earlier from Piper. She re-read it and replied.

Subject: *Re. Hamper shoot in Paris*
Main: *I'm in. K. xo*

21

R aph had almost been her undoing.

Kit had known Scott was her future when they'd met, and Raph was nothing but an inexplicable, fundamentally pointless, almost fatal diversion.

Scott had been the right choice and – Kit told herself – still was.

The air smelled damp, like wet stone. Kit raised her camera and took the shot.

Nothing had really changed, nothing had to.

Scott was many good things: he was accomplished and smart, he understood style and art … her mother liked him. His disinterest in the foodie scene meant he'd be ignorant to all its incestuous tattling and Kit felt grateful.

She leaned forward and adjusted the vintage Mumm Champagne wicker basket, found years earlier at Izzi & Popo, happy to see it coming into its own. She'd packed one case of props, another of clothes, and on Saturday had landed in Paris with Piper.

They'd headed straight to Clignancourt to forage for utensils and linens at the market then trained the next day to

Champagne-Ardenne and their Épernay hotel – a cream stone Louis XIII beauty with a zinc roof and climbing red roses.

Now on the dirty floor of a champagne cave, the wet innards of a cut brie caught red petals in its ooze ... stems stolen by Kit that morning.

She knew the concept had pushed *Hamper* but she'd been their regretful last resort. Their first preference, *Hamper*'s travel photographer, was ill and when they'd forwarded Kit his idea, she'd nearly agreed to it. But she was better than that.

Just because Raph was a lie, she needn't be. She'd scrapped the sanitised *Parisienne High Tea* concept and created a new one, one that *Hamper* hadn't celebrated, but hadn't declined, either. She and Piper had been sent forth and now Kit's *Bluebeard's Picnic* was being realised.

Bluebeard, a fabled French aristocrat who murdered his wives and kept their bodies in his castle dungeons, was a symbol of mercilessness and desolation. Kit felt both desolate and merciless and this made Bluebeard just what she needed.

An antique Moët bottle lay dusty and broken.

Marinated white cheese dripped herbs and oil; roses were brutalised.

A ragged butcher's cleaver was stabbed into the wax of a yellow cheese wheel, the timber handle faded and cracked.

Kit lay forward, upturned an embroidered antique slipper, opened the camera's frame and took the shot. Champagne vaults arched overhead; the batch numbers sketched on stone. Kit knelt, took another shot and heard Piper approve the images that streamed to the laptop.

Kit had toured the caves of Moët & Chandon and Perrier-Jouët on the Avenue de Champagne some years earlier and the dank spaces had come to mind when storyboarding. Now she, Piper, and a freelance writer, Anne, were clothed in layers of wool beneath a lesser-known champagne house, one which had agreed to let them shoot in their caves.

'Darkness, violence, indulgence … it's growing on me,' the writer announced from across the cave as she read *Bluebeard* in a book of old folktales. She smiled and showed them an illustration: plumes of feathers curling from Bluebeard's headdress as he wielded a sabre above his wife's head. 'Who knew sadism could rouse an appetite?'

Day two's locale had been scouted online.

The dim, grey day was perfect but Kit hoped the reality of the site – a decayed castle in Fère-en-Tardenois – didn't fall short of her imagination.

The ruins sat upon a grassy sandstone hill. Beneath the mound, Kit and Piper set up a picnic rug under an arching tree.

Napoleonic dresses were hung from branches, a man's antique overcoat in the fore, and on the rug they scattered ripe blood plums as though fallen. Kit scrunched cherries in the overcoat pocket, bleeding them through the fabric, then littered the rug with elaborate patisserie and boulangerie goods, flowers and curio, in an homage to the still-lifes she loved, by artists like de Heem.

She gazed at a tiny jug overflowing with yellow clotted cream then set it next to a blood-plum *clafoutis*. She slid a slab of bittersweet chocolate into a too-small pocket of a dress, wiped the dark traces from her hand to the skirt, then trailed a skeleton key from the pocket of the man's overcoat.

Everything was as it needed to be – the castle bereft, ominous – but half an hour into the shoot, Kit paused and asked for Anne's book of folktales. She let it fall open on the rug and cocked her head to assess. The scene needed something … human.

'I'll be in it,' Piper offered.

Smiling, Kit took her arm and bloodied the porcelain skin with cherry juice. Piper lay her limb among the stained linens and edible detritus, and Kit positioned a cleaver.

'Grim enough?' Piper said.

'Just about.' Kit raised her lens.

That night they sat in their hotel room, laptops on beds.

'Still doesn't seem like there's any word from The Priory …' Piper scanned her emails.

Kit rolled over. 'Rosamonde Michel's?'

'Yes,' Piper said. 'Urgh, I wanted to get in so badly …'

'Who doesn't?'

'Yes but I really sold the shit out of us in my email. I felt like we'd be a shoo-in.'

'Didn't you only email a few months ago? I thought it took over a year to get in to that place.'

'I know, I know.' Piper sighed and rolled onto her back. 'Plan B?'

'Well I've told Scott I'm coming …' Kit said. 'I fly to Milan Sunday morning after the Guide Alimentaire Internationale Awards tomorrow night. How about you come to Italy with me?'

'Eight days of uninterrupted you, me and Scott time?' Piper appeared amused. 'I might take a cheeky pass.'

'Are you sure?'

'Very. You dally south. I'll curl up on the Left Bank with a book and then I guess I'll see you back in Paris Tuesday-week for our flight home?'

22

The foodies' equivalent of the Oscars, the Guide Alimentaire Internationale Awards partnered the annual release of the *Guide Alimentaire Internationale*, an iconic green paperback that for over a century had reviewed and rated top restaurants internationally. *Hamper*'s editor or on-location travel team attended, and this year it was the latter.

'Thank you,' Kit said as the waiter poured her another Krug.

Seated at a table with other intercontinentals, Kit had taken the requisite shots and now reached into her gusset bag for her telephoto lens. She brought wizened grey stone walls and a vaulted ceiling into frame, then turned the lens on the socialites who decorated the front-most tables. A man stood.

'F-fuck.' The word escaped Kit's mouth.

Piper turned.

'Oh my fuck …' Kit breathed.

'What is it?'

Black and white, tailored and collared, normally unkempt dark hair combed neatly back, Kit raised her lens so she could see him again, the man she'd last seen on Wikipedia. 'Shit.'

Piper wrenched the camera from her friend, aimed it where

Kit had, and when her breath caught, Kit knew Piper had seen. 'Oh God.'

'What's he doing?'

'Moving.' Piper stared and Kit took the camera back and watched through the viewfinder. 'I think he's headed for the restroom. Go.'

Kit's laugh was incredulous.

'I mean it,' Piper said. 'Confront him.'

Kit lowered the camera onto her lap. 'No.'

'You have to.'

'No.'

'Yes! Go! You'll never see him again otherwise!'

'No. Arenberg own half these fucking restaurants. I'm not making a scene.'

'You're right,' Piper said. 'Let him go. Let him think all's well, let him think that his actions have no consequences, let him enjoy himself. A man should be able to enjoy a nice vintage without a bitch getting all up in his face. You stay put.' She gave Kit's knee an inciting pat.

Kit stood, knocking over her seat. The whole table turned to look. She ignored them, navigated tables, chairs, people – then an intermission was suddenly announced and obstacles proliferated. People stood, pushing their chairs out.

Kit dodged, her hair fell from its do, and rattled and disoriented, angry and afraid, she dragged her locks back then tugged at her jacket – composed and in charge: she'd be both when she got to him.

People were amassing. Bodies had begun to propel her forward and suddenly all she wanted to do was go back–

Then Raph returned. He reappeared through the doors, expression confident and at ease, and he looked one way then the other and strode back towards his table, nowhere near hers.

The crowd flowed around her and Kit's gaze followed the strange man, saw him welcomed back by those who knew him, knew him as she never had.

ॐ

Kit sat in the bar of a hotel in Zona Tortona, glad to have a decent espresso again. Milan was warmer than Paris.

Wearing cuffed chinos and a short-sleeve Hawaiian shirt, Scott approached. He removed his sunglasses, slotted them into his pocket, and pulled Kit confidently to stand.

He'd co-opted an Italian swagger, Kit thought, but if it were indeed an Italian kissing her, his mouth would have been wide, his tongue seeking hers like there was no better pastime in the world. But Scott pulled away and Kit's eyes closed as she put her hand to his chest – let it linger there as she reacquainted herself with the feel and shape of the man she was going to marry.

'Have you eaten?' he said.

'Yes. But I'd forgotten how stodgy Italian bread can be, I had a dire salad roll.'

'Their coffee makes us forgive,' Scott smiled. 'Another?'

They sat on the lounge, ordered again, and Scott put his arm across her shoulders.

'How are the family?' he said.

They'd barely spoken in the weeks since he'd left London, but when Kit had emailed, told him she'd soon be on the continent, he'd called straight away, keen to introduce her to the world in which he was currently being celebrated.

She wondered what it meant that she hadn't felt like speaking to him about Connor again. She decided to get it out of the way. 'Dad almost had a heart attack.'

Scott's phone rang.

'Oh, you're joking, Kit, when?' He frowned, trying not to glance at his phone, then gave in. 'Give me two seconds, sorry. Alf,' he answered the call. 'Give me half an hour could you? Yeah. Speak in a bit. Yes!' he laughed then hung up. 'That's terrible … your *dad?* How is he doing now?' Scott took Kit's hand but there was a twitch in his eye that meant his mind was wherever the call had taken it.

'Call Alf back,' Kit said. 'We can talk later.'

'Are you sure? I'll be five minutes.' Without hesitation, Scott got up and walked towards the door.

Their coffees arrived. Kit picked one up, sipping without interest as she gazed at Scott with his phone, by the exit.

He turned and smiled. She smiled back but knew he wasn't really seeing her.

She took his coffee and handed it to him as she passed on her way to the lobby. He followed, shot the espresso from its demitasse and carried on speaking as Kit walked to reception to ask for Scott's room.

Plan drawings and a laptop were on the desk in his suite. Scott followed Kit inside, parked himself by the window and carried on his phone conversation.

Kit sat on the bed. This was what she wanted. She'd arrived, this was what she wanted and this was going to work.

'Sorry,' Scott said. His call had finished and he was coming towards her. 'It's been like this the whole time. Alf wants me to meet someone. Join us?'

Scott's bright pants were like a beacon as Kit followed them down a colourless laneway into a studio-gallery of a local designer.

'Ah! Va-va-voom!' Alf sculpted an hourglass in the air before he kissed Kit's cheeks. 'You did not tell me that you had this one, Scott. Wow!'

Scott bounced his eyebrows and moved forward.

Alf snickered. 'This smug genius is your husband?'

'No,' Kit said.

'Not yet,' Scott called back, as he and Alf accelerated into the depths of the studio and at the same moment, Kit's phone beeped. She leaned in the open doorway of the building and brought up the email from Piper.

Subject: *Small-mindedness*
Main: *Transferred all photos to* Hamper *HQ this morning. Just got reply. Won't forward to you.*

They hated how Bluebeard's Picnic turned out. Hated it. I almost laughed the email was so fucking parochial.

I'm sorry. It's my fault. I should have had my Hamper *Hat on during the shoot.*

Sorry again and sigh,

Pippy Longstocking

Ps. Hope all's sunny for you in Italeeeee xxx

Kit put her phone in her pocket and walked quickly back to the hotel.

23

The door of the hotel suite opened and Scott entered.

'Where'd you go?' he said, sounding less surprised at her rapid departure than she thought he'd be. He came to stand behind her at the desk and she didn't minimise the photo viewer in time.

'What are those?' Scott leaned towards the screen.

Piper's bloodied arm. A food-littered rug. Broken glass, tainted clothes, a desolate fortress looming large …

Hamper hated them.

Kit felt hated, too.

She felt alone and uncertain, and in the alien surrounds of Scott's hotel room, she couldn't find familiar footing. She wanted to remember who and what she was, wanted conviction and belief, and her mind sought something or someone to tell her she was right.

'They're … it's a shoot I did. For *Hamper*,' she told Scott.

'Really?' He took a closer look. 'They're putting those in *Hamper*?'

Kit hesitated. 'No …' she said. 'They're not.'

'I was going to say,' Scott patted her head, 'that's *not* their style.' He gave a quiet laugh and yawned as his patting ceased, but the condescension Kit felt … didn't.

She felt patted and patronised, and when Scott lifted her hair to put his mouth on her neck, she stood, bumping him out of the way. 'I'm having a shower.'

Scott began to follow, but she closed the door behind her.

'I have a surprise for you tomorrow,' he called out, then she heard him walk back to his desk.

☙

Kit's new Phillip Lim loafers rubbed on the thin skin that covered the upper bone of her foot.

Scott kept them walking. Throughout the drive from Milan to Florence, he'd power-talked about the people he'd been meeting and Kit guessed that the reason he didn't ask about her work was because he thought he needed to save her from it. He perhaps sensed that she didn't like what she did and thought the solution was what *he* did. His success was now, by default, hers.

They walked Florence's sepia streets until they reached a windowless shop, where small letters on the door read *Bove e Porcu*.

Scott pressed the brass buzzer. They waited on the cobbles until a man in a white shirt and fine wool cardigan opened the door.

'*Ciao* Scott! I'm Matteo,' he told Kit, kissing them both before he ushered them down a corridor to a studio out the back. '*Tre caffè?*' He continued towards a drinks station.

Concrete benchtops, burners and beakers, anvils and metal-working tools adorned the space. Daylight streamed from an internal courtyard into the lab. Scott reached out, took Kit's hand, and she wondered if Matteo had a bandaid.

'He and his partner are some of the best.' Scott spoke with a kind of self-satisfaction. 'Have you guessed anything, yet?'

'Sorry?' Kit said.

'Have you guessed why we're here?'

Kit glanced at her smarting foot. 'No, I haven't.'

Scott pulled her suddenly towards him. Kit gazed up into his smiling face. 'A ring,' he said. 'I decided a ring was well overdue.'

Kit stared, uncomprehending.

'I was thinking about you organising the wedding, back home, by yourself, without even a ring on your finger, and I thought, *that's not right.*'

They hadn't yet gotten a ring because Scott had wanted to design it. Scott hadn't designed it because he hadn't had time.

'This is the next best thing to me designing one.' He seemed pleased. 'Custom, hand-crafted, one-off ...' He squeezed Kit's shoulder as Matteo reappeared with coffees. 'Your work, too – Matteo?' Scott smoothed his hand along the bronze drinks tray. 'Beautiful.'

'Your fiancée is also beautiful,' Matteo's voice was kind but Kit felt discomfort. Her watch seemed to have grown too tight and she plucked feverishly at it, eyes on the exit door.

'I'm a lucky man.' Scott took Kit's fidgeting hand and squeezed it.

Kit's reply was disproportionately eager. 'No, *I'm* the lucky one!' she sang.

'You're both very lucky.' Matteo took a sip of coffee.

Kit fiddled with the top button of her collar and glanced again at the exit as Matteo gestured towards his shimmering wall display.

'I find creative people often appreciate something innovative …' He unfastened a piece of super-fine steel mesh. 'We, *Bove e Porcu*, are the only ones who use this fine material for jewellery. I haven't made a ring with it yet but I have been looking forward to doing so. Were you wanting a jewel? We would source it if so, we don't keep precious stones on site.'

This *was* what she wanted. This *was* going to work.

'That's incredible.' Scott peered at the jewellery.

'No,' Kit said.

'Pardon?'

'Not the mesh.' Chains, shackles.

'Cast platinum perhaps?'

'Yes,' Scott said and began to absently pat Kit's bottom. Pat. Pat. Pat. Habitual, empty and familiar. Pat. Pat. Pat. She was his prize, a prize he didn't understand, a prize he'd put in a case and left there because he didn't know what else to do with it. Pat. Pat. Pat.

'What sweet little hands you have.' Matteo's fingers positioned Kit's and she felt cold metal, so tiny, so insignificantly placed–

'Oh!' Her voice sounded correctly congenial. 'It's lovely! If you could just take it off again, just for one moment …'

It was gone and so was Kit, into the courtyard, her hands clutching at her phone, dancing around it with a busyness and importance that she hoped the men would interpret as her attending to something that was equally so.

She dialled no one and put her phone to her ear as Scott and Matteo talked inside.

Kit thought of Connor. A wedding would be something he could enjoy.

A wedding would distract him from what had happened, all that Raph had left behind, and Connor liked Scott, or at least had never openly criticised him …

Kit watched as Scott admired a chair. He wasn't a *bad* man. He was a good man. He was nothing to complain about, in fact by anyone's standards this man was a serious catch.

Who did Kit think she was? Who did she think she was to say no to Scott? Who was she to want more, expect more?

'I liked that one.' She strode back into the studio and Matteo picked up the ring and held it to the light.

'It looked beautiful on you.' He slid it back onto her finger and asked Scott what he thought.

'That one was my favourite,' he said.

'Well, I'll make you one to fit–'

'This one fits,' Kit said. 'We'll take it.'

'You could set a stone here if you wish–'

'Yes,' Kit said, 'we'll think about it, get it retrofitted if we need to.'

'Of course.'

'That was easy,' Scott said on the street.

'Very,' Kit replied.

'I think I did well picking the place.'

'You did. Let's get some gelato.'

'I have a meeting in Milan this afternoon. Rain check?'

Kit handed him the ring bag and adjusted her shoe, wishing she'd asked for a bandaid.

❧

Kit sat alone in the hotel. The circle of skin on her right foot had been rubbed raw. She stared at it. She tried not to stare at the *Bove e Porcu* bag on the bed.

Marc had once trapped a large spider in a jar, which he put in his schoolbag. The bag had sat next to Kit all the way to school and every time the bag had jumped, she'd jumped. Now, glancing at the *Bove e Porcu* carrier, Kit was reminded of that spider.

Her phone rang. 'Kit speaking.'

'Hello!' Piper said. 'Guess what?'

Kit took a breath. 'What?'

'I'm on the train ...'

Kit frowned, not following.

'I'm on the train to The *Priory*! We got in! We got into The Priory!'

'You got a place?' Kit said.

'Someone cancelled! I was available at short notice and they liked my email so much that they picked us! *We're* going!'

'You're on your way now?'

'Right now! Get on a plane!'

Kit covered her mouth and was silent.

'Kit?'

'Shit ...'

'Shit! I know! Hurry!'

'*Shit*, Piper, I can't ...'

'What?'

'I can't. I can't come. I'm here with Scott now, I said I'd be here all week.'

Piper laughed. 'You're kidding.'

'No, I'm not.'

'This is French Art of Food at The Priory.'

'I know, I want to, I can't.'

'Tell me you're fucking kidding.'

Kit was silent.

'Kit?'

'I can't, I'm sorry.'

Kit hung up the phone and stared at the raw skin on her foot. She wasn't leaving.

She wasn't going anywhere. She wanted her and Scott to work. She was staying.

An SMS pinged on her phone. Kit picked it up. Piper had sent a picture from the Bluebeard's Picnic shoot.

Below the dark castle and 'bloodied' fabric, Piper's message read, *'Your camera was born for The Priory. Your eye was made for this.'*

As Kit stared at it, another message appeared, this one from Scott. *'Alexi arrives tonight,'* it read. *'I forgot that I'd said we'd all have dinner. Could you host her? I think I'll be late. Cheers xo.'*

Kit gazed up into the room. She saw the ring bag on the bed and felt her heart rate rise.

She picked up a marker and scrawled on the cover of Scott's sketchbook.

So sorry, Piper called with a project back over border. See you when we're all back home. K xx

She put the sketchbook on the bed, turned from the ring bag – back – away – back – then took the bag and put it in her suitcase.

Kit's flight touched down in Bordeaux at 10 pm, an hour and a half after take-off.

Her cab wound through the countryside en route to the Dordogne, then turned off the main highway onto a country lane. The hills outside were dark but for the distant lights of farmhouses.

'The old priory?' the driver confirmed in English.

'*Oui, merci monsieur,*' Kit said.

At a spotlit sign, he turned down a pin-straight drive and the old trunks of trees chaperoned the cab towards a wide, two-storey stone edifice.

Piper opened the front door in her pyjamas. She led Kit up internal stairs to their room on the second storey and Kit fell forward onto one of two little beds.

Piper gazed at her. 'Thank God, Kit,' she finally said. 'Thank God.'

24

The ex-nunnery residence of Rosamonde Michel felt notably underdone.

Kit woke before Piper and lay gazing at the scene of a mounted hunting party that embroidered the room's only cushion.

The cushion rested on the room's only chair, a faded Thonet No. 14, and a thin patterned rug and nightstand were all that lay between her and Piper's narrow beds.

The understated furnishings contradicted the high-status nature of the destination, but Kit had once read that their host despised publicity – had said that accolades created expectation and expectation created disappointment – so this lack of interior detailing was likely crafted to curb guests' expectations.

The *Art Français de l'Alimentation au Prieuré* – French Art of Food at the Priory – was, at its core, a B&B and cooking school. The skill, character, knowledge, provisions and hospitality of its host, however, had made it a school on every foodie's bucket list.

Kit ran her eyes over the faded wallpaper until she reached Piper. Her friend's eyes blinked open. 'Good morning,' she mumbled.

They hunted for breakfast downstairs.

Tall, white, timber-framed French doors ran successively down both sides of the ground floor and folding colonial screens partitioned a small library from the sitting areas. Kit followed Piper through the light-filled space towards the kitchen.

Scott had called while she was getting dressed. She'd let it go to voicemail.

'Kitten,' the message had begun. *'I got your note when I came in. That's a shame. I would have liked you to meet some more people while you were here. Call me when you can. Oh, and I couldn't find the ring. I hope you're wearing it, send me a picture.'* Kit had glimpsed her naked ring finger as she'd deleted the message.

Fellow guests began to descend from the second floor. The only commonality Kit could gauge was that all – bar she and Piper – must have waited a long time to be here. Age, gender and nationality varied but everyone was headed in the same direction: the kitchen.

A thirty-seat farm table, hanging copper pots, enamelled cast iron, drying herbs, chopping blocks, and a wall of crockery and jugs told them they'd arrived. Kit photographed a stack of sourdough bannetons by the wood stove.

Breakfast was served by the housekeeper. When Kit was halfway through a bowl of coffee and a croissant, the scullery door opened and a woman entered. Petite of height, curvaceous of frame, glasses on a cord around her neck, the woman in her late fifties wore a plain, knee-length, black dress with gumboots, and carried a blue plastic bucket of weedy greens that she sat on the table.

'Bonjour les enfants.' She slid her glasses onto her nose. 'Who knows about weeds?'

'*Bonjour*, Rosamonde!' There was a hum of excitement.

'"Rosa" will do *s'il vous plaît*,' Rosa said. On her way to the sink she added, 'There's so much dissident flora in my garden that my whole next cookery book may be titled *L'Herbe*.'

'I love you Rosa!' a woman shouted and everyone laughed.

Rosa dropped the greenery into the chipped porcelain sink. 'How kind. Welcome to The Priory.' She turned on the faucet. 'Are we ready for some cooking?'

Kit had stopped taking photos. She had missed a dozen, and now lifted her lens to frame water that sputtered from a brass tap onto bristling weeds, and Rosa's garden-ravaged hands.

'Soup.' Rosa smiled for the first time, deep and warm. 'Let us put these *délicieux dissidents* into *une soupe*. It will be a nice way to give you a handle on a good basic stock. *Du bouillon de poulet*. Chicken. It's very easy. The garden tells me what's on the menu and the garden looks different every day. So, I'm sorry I can't tell you what else will be on the menu but I promise there will be food and it will be good. *Ça vous va?*'

Everyone beamed. Kit guessed Rosa's style was a surprise to no one.

'I love her,' Piper breathed.

Rosa smoothed oil along her kitchen shears, then sent the group to pull carrots, leeks and celery from the garden. Unkempt boxes overflowed with flowering thyme, rosemary, sage and other aromatics they didn't recognise.

Kit cut leaves from a bay tree then lingered over parsley as geese doddered by. 'Wouldn't that be nice in a chicken stock?' she said, and a woman, who'd introduced herself as Pearl, tutted.

'No, no,' she scolded. 'French cooking is not a let's-add-what-we-feel-like affair.'

'I didn't see a recipe,' Kit said.

'It's in her head!' Pearl chanted like a groupie. 'Only do what Rosa tells you.'

Kit chopped thyme into her carrier and tried not to smile.

Despite the provincial loveliness they'd been given coloured plastic buckets.

'It isn't pretty,' Rosa had said, 'but I'm tired of my nice old baskets rotting out in the wet garden.'

Inside, the kitchen sink was full. They took their harvest into the scullery. When they finally returned, chicken carcasses were waiting for them beside knives and Le Creuset cast-iron casseroles.

'I'm going to put some music on.' Rosa opened a cupboard, fiddled with an old stereo, and settled on a radio station. She hummed her way slowly back to the head of the table and picked up a cleaver.

'These are the carcasses from the chicken you were served on arrival last night,' she said. 'Pre-roasted. If you wish to waste time with a bouquet garni, there's your string. But we're sieving the thing anyhow and I personally can't abide the bother.'

No one reached for string.

'*Vin blanc* must always be used in a white stock.' Rosa tapped the cleanskin in front of her. 'It breaks down the cartilage. Peppercorns of course, *cold* water always, and a little vinegar to leach out the healing potential of the bone.'

She put the chicken carcass into her red Le Creuset, cranked open the door to the cool room and returned with a tray of chicken feet and innards.

'Feet and organ meat,' she said. 'Depth of flavour and nutrition. If you've killed the poor bird you may as well make the most of it, *non*?'

Kit was aware of Piper fidgeting and turned to see her hurry through the door that led to the garden.

'Our first weak stomach for the day,' Rosa said, then continued, 'chop the vegetables. A cross-section is plenty. No *brunoise … julienne*. A stock is no nonsense.'

Kit put down her knife and moved quietly towards the door.

'Don't slink on my account, *ma chère*,' Rosa caught her. 'I don't care for airs and graces, come and go as you please, all of you. You're not here for me, I'm here for you.' A leek fell in two beneath her blade.

Piper was doubled over by the garden tap, the water running.

'Are you okay?' Kit said.

Piper groaned. She cocked her head to suck water from the faucet then sat back on her heels.

'Shit, I felt totally off in there.'

'Did you throw up?' Kit asked.

'Mm.'

Kit smoothed Piper's hair. 'The chicken feet weren't thrilling, I agree.'

Piper put her hand up like she couldn't speak, then managed, 'Arggh.'

'Mint,' Kit put out her hand. 'Let's find some to chew.'

Kit focused and refocused her lens.

She looked back into the space, quickly scanned around for Piper, and when she saw her reading on a cane lounge across the room, she beckoned.

They'd just finished breakfast on day two and were waiting for the day's first lesson. The morning was mild and the old house seemed to breathe, a breeze touching Kit's bare legs.

Piper flumped down onto the window banquette.

'Look.' Kit pointed towards The Priory's heavily wooded back garden.

'That lens is fucking huge.' Piper took the camera. 'Are you spying?'

'Through the woods.' Kit was smiling. 'To your left.'

Piper angled the viewfinder; laughed out loud.

'That they're fucking is certain,' Kit said, 'but I can't tell who that guy is …'

'Well *she* is definitely Rosa, still in her gumboots,' Piper said. '*He* I don't know. Probably her partner. She lives here with some guy, I think.'

Kit squinted but couldn't see without the lens.

'She's very attractive …' Piper said. 'The French have such good skin, it's all kind of tight despite her size and age. Don't you think?'

Kit took the camera and agreed, then commentated as Rosa and the man made for the pond. 'Gumboots off … oh good … a swim. I thought she might come in to cook, marinating in sex.'

'Imagine if she did. What a legend, what a woman!'

219

Something moved out of view and Kit swivelled the camera to catch someone striding from the woodland.

Piper noticed and took over the camera. 'Oh, young and fit!' she said.

He drew nearer, came towards the house, and was soon close enough to see. When Piper lowered the camera, he sensed her movement and turned to look. He saw Piper first, Kit second. He held her gaze, adjusted his grip on a shotgun, swung dead birds over his shoulder, then continued on out of sight around the house.

'*Merci*, Gabriel, *ce sont de beaux canards!*' Rosa was clothed and leading the group in the morning's lesson.

The dead game lay on the bench in the garden.

'When you pluck a duck,' Rosa said, 'save the feathers. Why waste? Make cushions, sell them for fly-fishing, I don't care. Just don't waste.'

Gabriel was yet to speak and Kit guessed that all he spoke was French. His biceps flexed and a bird's body lolled as he tugged each feather from its flesh. His shirt was bloodied. This was the wild flavour of man that Raph had failed to be.

'Once plucked,' Rosa said, 'we'll decapitate, gut and remove the feet. We'll confit the meat today, then the meat will eventually go in to our cassoulet. The duck fat from the confit will be the grease in which we cook our *pommes frites* and – *voilà!* – no waste, *pas de gâchis!*'

They broke for lunch, leaving the butchered duck in the kitchen, salted and marinating in herbs from the garden. Kit went upstairs to the bedroom.

220

'*Bonjour madame*,' Marc answered her call. '*Comment est votre soirée?*'

'It's the middle of the day,' Kit said.

'But aren't you impressed with my French?'

'I am.'

'I seem to miss you, oddly ...' Marc said.

'That is odd.' Kit tucked her phone under her ear, unzipped her suitcase and began rifling through for a sweater.

'What's news?'

Kit's hand hit something and she looked down ... pulled back.

'Kit?'

'Sorry?'

'I asked, what's news?'

'I ...' she stammered, 'I was calling to see how Dad is.'

'He's fine. What was that?' Marc sniggered.

'What?'

'Kit, you're as transparent as fuck.'

'What do you mean?'

'You're not thinking about Dad.'

'Yes, I was thinking about Dad.' Kit stared at the thing in her suitcase.

'You just started thinking about something else and got distracted.'

'No, I didn't.'

'Yes you did and it's clearly quite fucking distracting.'

'It's nothing. Tell me about Dad.'

Marc yawned and was stubbornly silent.

'Marc?'

'Just tell me the thing you don't want to so that we can move on.'

'Stop being a shit.'

'You're being a shit.'

Kit swore, stared at the thing in the suitcase then began chewing a fingernail as she studied the ceiling. 'Do you remember the time you put that spider in your schoolbag?'

'It gave you a month of nightmares.'

'Yes. I have something … here, in a bag… and it's making me feel like that.'

'What is it?' Marc said.

Kit gazed at the *Bove e Porcu* bag, motionless in her suitcase. 'It's … it's a ring.'

'What?' Marc said.

'It's an engagement ring.'

'Say again?'

'It's an engagement ring,' Kit said.

'What do you mean? From who?'

'Scott.'

Marc hesitated. 'Why?'

'What do you mean "why?"'

'Why now? A ring? Now? You can't still be engaged.'

'What do you mean? Of course I am.'

'*Kit.*'

'What?'

'Don't be *silly*, Kit.'

Kit protested.

'Kit. Come on. You fell for someone else.'

'No–'

222

'Yes. He may have turned out to be a complete arsehole-piece-of-shit, but you fell for him – more than you've *ever* fallen for Scott.'

'You don't know anything, Marc.'

Marc laughed.

Kit didn't.

'Marc, I know you want to push me out into that specifically sad and pointless arena of single people who just can't quite get it together, but I'm not going there. I'm telling you now that it's going to work with Scott. We're together, I care for him, and I'm going to make it work.'

'Why is the ring he gave you giving you so much anxiety, then?'

Kit continued to stare at the ceiling. When he spoke again, Marc had softened. 'Look,' he said, 'of course you know that I don't want to see you in any sad arena with any unpalatable breed of single people, but I also don't want to see you in a sad arena of unpalatable married people.'

'I won't be,' Kit said.

Marc was silent. Finally he added, 'Just … just don't do anything dumb. Don't elope, or whatever.'

'I have no plans to.'

'Good.'

There was silence.

'So,' Kit said. 'Home? Your email said that Dad's back in the office? And that Earl's transferred all the cider stores from Cannock Chase? Is Dad going to sell them?'

Marc was quiet before he said, 'Yup. He'll sell off what we have, but that's it in terms of production. I think he needed

Cannock Chase … the farmgate … to really feel inspired about it all.'

'And he's feeling okay?'

'He's pretty flat, but fine physically.'

'I'm glad,' Kit said, and there was another silence.

'We haven't spoken about your other big news,' Marc piped up. 'What are you doing over there now that *Hamper* has let you go?'

'Go? Where?'

'No, I meant now that you're not working for *Hamper*, what are you doing?'

'I don't know what you mean,' Kit said.

'Jimmy's blog? It said you'd left *Hamper*? The premise was ridiculous but–'

Kit asked him again what he meant.

'Which bit?'

'About *Hamper*?'

'It said that you'd left *Hamper*. Haven't you?'

Kit was off the phone, jogging downstairs, outside and down the drive to the entry gate where she and others had found internet signal.

Thegastronome.com loaded a millimetre at a time until eventually Kit's own face came into view. Then Raph's.

They'd been photographed, separately this time but both in cocktail garb: images from the Guide Alimentaire Internationale Awards.

Arenberg & Gossard Heat Up
Euro-bound for Hamper *magazine, photographer Kit Gossard*
of Gossard Range has reportedly ditched her post to party with

playboy Raphaël Arenberg in Paris. Spotted at the prominent Guide Alimentaire Internationale Awards, *no one is surprised that Gossard – who has long been at odds with the* Hamper *brand over its modest style – has swapped employment for enjoyment.*

Hamper *made no comment on the exit of their high-profile photographer (newbie Kate Pike takes her place) but Centigrade or Fahrenheit aside, the heat is only upping for Australian Gossard and American Arenberg. If only the City of Lights could speak!*

25

Piper held her phone skyward as they stood at the end of The Priory's drive.

'The email came the day we arrived,' she said. 'I haven't even read it ...' Her eyes flickered over *Hamper*'s correspondence. 'Jesus, they *have* given me the job of firing you, or "dissolving the bond" as frigid fucking H.R. puts it. That's horrendous form.'

Kit stared.

'And I can't believe they let Jimmy say that pap on his blog!' Piper said. 'I know it's not under *Hamper*'s banner but he's still one of their columnists, blanket professionalism is surely mandatory. Who does he think he is, Perez fucking Hilton?'

Kit may have hated *Hamper* but she realised it was her last vestige of certainty. Home, family, relationships – those foundations had fissured.

Piper still belonged to one of the most reputable food magazines in the world. Kit didn't and suddenly she was untethered, her mind searched for something to hold onto but it found nothing.

'Kit?' Piper said.

'I should leave,' Kit said. 'I shouldn't be here, *Hamper* never meant for me to–'

226

'Stop it,' Piper said instantly. 'Stop it. You're staying. Our room's paid for. No one will know. Stay, stay and take incredible photos that those closed-minded fools will never get to see.'

∾

The forest that surrounded The Priory felt damp and cool despite the mildness of the early afternoon.

'We always cut the mushroom stipe here, with a little knife.' Rosa knelt on the woodland floor, bare knees poking through the gap between dress and gumboots. 'And despite my proclivity for a plastic bucket, I always use a wicker basket for mushroom hunting. The spores need to fall through the gaps to propagate.'

The golden fungi came free in her hand. She took a small, soft-bristle brush from her basket and began to dust. 'Never scrub or peel a mushroom, you will only strip it of flavour. Any dirt can be dislodged with a brush, like this.'

When she'd finished, she started back the way they'd came, organic litter trailing behind her.

'Did you know that bordelaise is named after Bordeaux?' Rosa stood in the kitchen. 'Regional wines, mushrooms from our woods, deer slaughtered on Priory land …' She waved a glass of wine around. 'Can anyone think of anything as correct as a mushroom bordelaise with venison for lunch?'

Kit had already drunk a glass of the recipe wine, now she knocked back another.

'Are you alright, *ma chère*?' Rosa made a round of the table and stopped at Kit.

'Yes, delicious, wonderful,' Kit used the right words but spoke them too quickly. Instead of concealing her internal destabilisation like she'd meant to, she guessed she might have revealed it.

Rosa reached for the wine and poured Kit another.

'Bone marrow,' she announced and moved on. 'Nothing gives depth to a bordelaise like bone marrow. Never discard your bones – broths, demi-glace, sauces. If you don't have leftover bones, buy them from your local farmer, *non* waste.' She suddenly turned back to Kit. 'I forgot the garlic, *ma chère*. Could you collect it from the drystore, *s'il vous plaît?*'

Kit exited for the garden.

The wine had created a disjoint between her feet and mind. Her shoes felt like sponge cakes on the garden path, and when she reached the drystore she grabbed the doorhandle and pulled herself inside.

The shooter and groundskeeper was stringing up onions inside, and Kit announced herself by letting the door bang. He turned and gave her a once-over.

'Gabriel.' Her mind found his name and her mouth celebrated by saying it.

'*Oui?*'

'Garlic,' she said, then remembered he didn't speak English. She searched her mind for 'garlic' in French, but found nothing. They stood uneasily before Kit caught a glimpse of what she wanted.

She navigated bottles of preserves on the floor, then, by the window, stretched up.

Slowly, deliberately, Gabriel approached and when he reached the rows of high-hung bulbs, tugged a bunch loose into her hand. '*De l'ail,*' he said.

'*Ail*,' she remembered. '*Merci*.'

'*De rien*.'

Kit tried to manoeuvre around his too-close body. '*Scusi*.' Mistakenly she spoke Italian, blushed, and tripped on bottles of gherkins, then fumbled with them until they all stood upright again. She steadied herself on the corner of a table then found her way to the door without looking back.

'*De l'ail*.' She dropped the garlic onto the kitchen table.

'Ah, *merci*.' Rosa smiled. 'We need three times as much, *s'il vous plaît?*'

Kit's cheeks warmed as she cut across the grass. She opened the door to the drystore and to her relief, found that she was alone. She upturned a crate by the window, climbed to retrieve an armful of garlic – and narrowly missed straddling Gabriel on the way down. He was crawling from beneath the table, broom in hand.

He rose, eyes on her face, and his hand reached towards her to retrieve a garlic husk from her hair. He held her gaze as the fragment fell to the floor.

'*Merci, excusez-moi*.' She ducked by and out the door.

Wine, lunch, aperitifs, dinner, digestifs. An aged Cognac with cheese.

Kit's head swayed. Her silk skirt felt light. She peered down to check it was still there.

The evening class seemed to move in slow motion. When it was finally over, Piper hauled Kit to the pond and they walked to the end of the jetty.

'In you get,' Piper said.

'No, thanks,' Kit replied.

'You have to sober up before bed.'

'I've had too much, I'll drown,' Kit replied, and Piper chaperoned her back to the house.

'Stay out here for a while, then,' Piper said, and as she left for bed, Kit lay back on the steps, stared up at the swirling night sky, and listened to the breeze in the woodland.

When it got cold, she walked inside and found a reading lamp on in the sitting room.

'Fresh air?' Rosa gave Kit a once-over.

The French doors banged in the breeze.

'Fresh air, yes,' she said and watched Rosa reach for her glass of sherry.

'This is yours, *non?*' Rosa set the glass down again and held up Kit's camera.

'Oh … yes, it is,' Kit said.

Rosa patted the space beside her. 'I liked this one,' she said.

Kit moved closer, sat on the settee, and saw that Rosa had the camera set to playback.

'Was that intended or …?' Rosa gestured to the photo Kit had taken of the woodland.

Kit squinted at the screen before her breath caught. 'Oh I caught you, I didn't realise, I'm sorry.'

'Don't apologise. If I'm going to make love in the garden in broad daylight, I'm sure I deserve a little paparazzo.'

'I'll delete it.' Kit fumbled as she tried to take the camera.

'No, I want to have that photo,' Rosa said and continued to browse. 'Which publication do you work for?'

Kit felt woozy. The pattern on the worn African rug made her feel worse. 'I don't know,' she said.

230

Rosa studied her.

'I mean, I guess I don't work for anyone. The magazine who sent me "dissolved" our "bond".'

'Yes.' Rosa turned back to the camera, unperturbed. 'I thought these photos were too interesting to be commercial.'

Kit let her eyes linger on Rosa's face before she peered down, watched the photos tick by, and heard herself repeat Rosa's word. '"Interesting",' she said.

Rosa looked at her.

'What *does* "interesting" really mean, I often wonder …'

'I meant that they interest me,' Rosa said after some thought and Kit laughed despite not finding it funny.

Rosa must have sensed what was going to happen. She watched, waited, and it began.

'Fuck,' Kit half sighed, half groaned. 'Fuck,' she dropped her head back onto the hard upholstered lounge.

Rosa reached for her sherry and Kit plastered a hand over her eyes.

'Fuck, fuck,' she said.

Rosa put her feet up on a battered leather pouffe.

Kit curled into a ball. 'Fuck.'

'Are you finished?' Rosa sipped her drink.

'*Arggh*,' Kit groaned. She didn't feel finished, she felt overwhelmed and confused and saying 'fuck' felt inanely, fucking good.

'*Le problème*.' Rosa's voice was monotone. 'Tell it to me.'

Kit unfurled to stare up at the ceiling's crossbeams. 'I don't know where to start … I think I've lost myself …'

'*Non*.'

'Yes.'

'These photos are not the work of a lost person. These photos are *très bonnes*. I don't often see things that interest me but these photos: they interest me – a lot. They are *très sexy*, adventurous.'

Kit shook her head. 'They're lost … they made me lose my job.'

'Hurrah!' Rosa hooted. 'It is good to lose your job at a place that does not appreciate you or what you're good at.'

Kit stared at the blackness beyond the windows. 'I started to work in this way when I met a man. He–'

'*Non*,' Rosa said. 'This is your work, a man has naught to do with it.'

'He does,' Kit said. 'He made me feel–'

'*Non*,' Rosa shook her head, 'you're responsible for this work. You must own it.'

કૈ

Kit's neck hurt.

She blinked, saw daylight, shifted and almost rolled off the settee. A rug lay across her and a clock on the wall read midday. She swore and covered her eyes.

'Overdid it last night?' An elderly guest named Bonnie craned her neck as she trotted past.

Kit could hear others in the distance. She groaned.

'Tiger Balm for a headache,' Bonnie sang. 'And water!'

Kit saw Rosa later that afternoon. 'I'm so sorry,' she said. 'I drank way too much last night.'

Rosa gazed ahead, unperturbed. 'How did you sleep?'

'Like a drunk might.' Kit's smile was small.

'Come and see me before cooking class tonight, okay?'

જી

Half a dozen books were stacked on the kitchen table.

'*Bonjour*,' Kit said.

Rosa looked up, lips red, a fine rose-gold chain on her décolletage. 'I wanted to show you these,' she said. She handed Kit a book.

'Oh wow,' Kit examined it. 'Yours … one of yours.'

'*Oui*,' Rosa said. 'Unfortunately, *oui*.'

Kit began thumbing through the pages. 'It's wonderful.'

'*Non, pas super*,' Rosa said. 'I'm not proud.'

'The recipes are gorgeous.' Kit began to run a finger down a page but Rosa leaned over and took the book away.

'*Non*,' she said. 'You have made me feel *très* insecure.'

Kit smiled, uncertain.

'Did you know I am writing a new cookery book?'

Kit said she didn't know, offered her congratulations and asked what it was about.

'I thought I knew,' Rosa said, 'then I saw your photos last night and I changed my mind. Those photos … they made me feel differently. They reminded me of what I like. They reminded me of the way I like to see the world, what I like to think about, what inspires me.'

'You're kind,' Kit said after a pause.

'*Non*, just honest. The reason I wanted to see you was to ask you something. I wanted to ask if you would be the photographer for my new cookery book.'

Kit went to laugh, then stopped.

'Do you like this *photographie*?' Rosa fanned a cookbook in front her.

'It's–'

'*Merde*. Shitty. It was what I liked at the time but not now. Now I have seen what you do and it is *magique*. You're available, *non?*'

Kit shook her head. 'I'm sorry that you saw me unravel last night,' she said. 'It was pathetic, I don't need a job, or pity, I–'

'Pity?' Rosa frowned. 'If only I were that *compatissante*. *Non*. I ask you to do this *pour moi*. I'm not asking for your sake.'

Kit gazed down at the books then back up. 'If you're serious, then … I'm very flattered.'

'Good, I am flattering you. The world needs to see work like yours and I would be honoured to marry it with work like mine. Will you promise that you'll do it? I'll have my assistant call my publisher and they'll call you. Are we agreed?'

Kit wished she had a gracious, eloquent reply, but only managed, 'Yes, of course, yes, I'll do it.'

❧

'To learn how to craft a sausage is, itself, a worthy pursuit …'

The evening's lesson had begun.

Rosa set down an old tome, which opened to where she seemed to want it to, and her finger traced a coiled snake-like sausage in a photo.

'... but a sausage for our cassoulet is something we need. Duck confit we have and now a Toulouse sausage – made with the country's finest pork – will make a *merveilleux* cassoulet.'

Rosa was unapologetically strong and self-assured. She was everything Kit admired in a woman and now everything she admired in a woman seemed to admire her back. Rosa's belief in Kit burned at Kit's doubt, made her embarrassed that she had any.

A blast of cold air from the cool room preceded a pig's carcass.

'The key to a good Toulouse sausage is a heritage-breed pig, free-range, well maintained. We use a Basque pig, spotted black and pink, fatty and versatile.'

Someone retrieved a tray of cuts and soon pink, white-flecked threads of meat oozed from the nozzle of a mincer. Piper told Kit that she felt sick and left for bed. It felt like her friend had been long gone by the time Kit was wrist-deep in flesh that smelled of garlic and nutmeg.

'*Très bien*,' Rosa added wine to Kit's bowl. 'When you cook, imagine that you are taking a photo. Feel the food with mind, body, spirit. Enjoy it, *savoure-le*.'

She moved on and Kit stared after her. The world had felt like a dark tunnel, but Rosa was like a light at the end. She gave Kit permission to feel free again.

She stared down at the flesh between her fingers, felt it move and change. Nothing seemed to matter. It was only when someone turned off the radio that Kit glanced up.

Everyone had finished. Guests were audible in the scullery and hall but the kitchen was empty, and she looked down, saw that she was finished, too, and that a slick, shiny coil of meat lay on the table in front of her.

Kit reached for a tea towel and wiped her hands.

She plucked her shoes off her feet and flywire pressed her palm as she pushed the garden door wide.

The grass was damp between her toes. She stood still and sensed the vibration of the night.

She walked forward, reached the wide wooden sleepers that retained Rosa's herbs, then stepped up onto them. Her feet left dewy footprints on the sun-warmed timber. She walked along and heard soft cooing up ahead.

She stepped from one retainer to another, dropped to the ground when the last retainer ended, then padded across twigs to the chicken coop where she threaded her fingers into the wire and brought her face close.

Rosa's doves were easing themselves to sleep.

'*Bonsoir.*'

Kit was slow to turn and when she did, she didn't see him at first, crouched, checking the enclosure's wire door.

'*Bonsoir,*' she replied.

Gabriel straightened as he came towards her and she heard him speak his first English word. 'Fox,' he said, then, '*Un renard.*'

Kit slid her fingers from the wire, stepped back from the coop and felt her shoes slide from her hand.

The leopard slippers made no sound as they hit the ground. Kit watched them settle, and when she peered back up, Gabriel was close in front.

'Fox,' she said. Gabriel's hand slowly rose until Kit felt its warmth encircle her throat.

She stared into his eyes, sensed his latent brutality and felt herself grow wet. Then, because she was free to and because she wanted to, she answered a question he hadn't asked.

'*Oui*,' she said, and in reply he moved a hand to his fly, and another under her skirt. His mouth touched hers before he was inside her.

Kit climbed the stone steps of The Priory.

At the front door she glanced back, watched the bare back of Gabriel disappear into the night and knew that he'd sated her. Now she hoped she'd never see him again.

Her knickers felt small in her fist as she made her way up the stairs inside.

Piper was asleep, and as she closed the bedroom door Kit saw that the *Bove e Porcu* bag was out on the nightstand. Piper's arm hung limp beside it.

Kit went to pick it up and Piper mumbled. 'I already saw what was inside it,' she said, voice croaky. Kit stood, mind ticking over, then she climbed into bed and closed her eyes.

26

It was morning and the sun shone through the fine white drapes.

Piper was lying in bed, gazing at the bag on the nightstand.

'You've been hiding it,' she said.

'No, I haven't.'

'You have,' Piper said. 'I wouldn't have seen it if you hadn't left your suitcase open.'

'And you thought you'd take a closer look?'

'Why wouldn't I?'

Kit draped her arm over her eyes.

'It's your engagement ring, isn't it?' Piper's voice was flat as Kit rolled to face the wall. 'Why aren't you wearing it?'

Kit didn't reply.

'Would you like me to get it out of the bag so you can put it on?'

'No,' Kit said, and neither spoke.

Finally, Kit heard the springs of Piper's bed creak, followed by the sound of footsteps on the rug. Kit's mattress rippled as Piper climbed onto it and she felt her friend's skinny body slide in. They both lay without speaking until Kit finally rolled over to face her.

'I don't think I can do it …'

Piper frowned. 'Scott?'

Kit tugged at a thread on the pillowcase.

'If you're worried about him …' Piper began slowly, 'don't be. For someone else, he's the complete package. If you let him go, someone else will appear, instantly.'

Kit felt a pang but was surprised at how small it was. She put a hand to her forehead and thought of the night before, Rosa, the groundskeeper, the freedom that seemed so near to hand here.

She gazed at her friend and wondered which of her thoughts to say. She pushed up onto her elbow and studied the clock. 'Class is about to start …'

'No.' Piper rocked her head from side to side. 'No, I can't face that kitchen, I'll be sick again. You go, I'll try later.'

Kit slithered over her to get out, said she'd come back after lunch, then paused at the entry to the en-suite. 'Oh, and Rosa wants me to shoot her new cookbook.'

Piper opened her eyes. 'What?' she propped herself up.

'Rosa saw my photos and liked them … apparently. She asked me to shoot her new book.'

Piper flopped back. 'What the fuck?' she said then propped herself up again. 'What the fuck? She's the biggest-selling female food author in the world.'

'Is she?'

'Yes!'

'Oh. I–'

'Oh shush.' Piper waved Kit away. 'Stop showing off. It's too awesome, you're awesome, it's too much …' She put her hand over her eyes and rolled over.

Rosa smiled at Kit as she entered the morning lesson, late. Kit smiled back and felt the implicit respect ... the connection between them.

If nothing else was certain, at least Rosa was, in this kitchen, and Kit felt a strength knowing that beyond this moment, beyond this week, this place would be here for her.

Fresh peaches were strewn about the table. Kit set down her camera and sat on a stool.

Rosa lifted a peach, sank her teeth into it and wiped away the juice that ran down her chin. 'As ever, the garden tells us what we're cooking, and today we need to find a home for this late harvest of peaches.' She sucked the stone clean, wiped her hands on her apron and spread her fingers on a large marble tile. 'Pastry.'

Kit sensed an air of excitement about her.

'Pastry is my favourite lesson because if I'm lucky I have an assistant.' She reached for a large jar of flour marked *Farine*. 'We're going to make a peach galette with fresh frangipane, Priory peaches and my *préférée* sweet pastry.'

Kit put her fawn and white Mason Cash bowl on the scales. The flour was unbleached and fine and the butter a rich yellow. She chopped cold chunks into the bowl.

'You made it, *mon garcon chéri*!' Kit heard Rosa at the front of the room.

She looked up and watched as Rosa, with a flurry of French, greeted and embraced a man who'd come in through the scullery.

'My son,' she was flushed, 'my son has always been my best pastry chef and now peach season is my *favourite* as I know it's one of the rare times I can coax my *garçon* to get his hands dirty in my kitchen.'

Raph smiled from the front of the room. '*Bonjour*,' he said simply to the group.

Kit's legs seemed to disappear and she held onto the table to stop herself descending to the tiles.

Raph gazed about the room as if he hadn't seen it in some time and Kit's eyes slid over him, slow, lagging, disbelieving.

He took in the room: his mother, the stove, the radio, the windows, guests, and Kit counted down the seconds before he took her in, too. She glanced down but knew he'd seen her when she heard him cough and sensed his body shift, uneasily.

She glanced up and saw his hand fidget as his mother held his attention, her tone excited and warm.

Beads of sweat began to form on Kit's upper lip. She dug her hands into the pastry as profanities took shape in her mouth …

Fuck.

Rosa giggled affectionately and wiped flour off or onto Raph's nose, Kit couldn't see.

'I'm going to send my Raphaël around to check on you all,' Rosa's voice was steeped in pride. 'Please indulge me while I indulge my son, he's my one weakness.'

Kit's mind was in disarray, like a puzzle that had been ransacked by an ill-tempered child. She breathed … tried to cobble it together …

One of the women was laughing. Kit lifted her gaze to see Raph lean over the woman's dough. Unshaven, hair unkempt, wearing a now-floured hunting gilet, he seemed almost like the man she once thought she knew …

Fuck. Fuck. Fuck. Fuck. Fuck.

He was approaching. Kit wiped the sweat from her lip, leaving flour in its place.

He stepped from person to person and when she was the next, her body stiffened. Knowing he was in earshot she breathed, 'You do not know me, you do not speak to me and you do not come near me.'

His voice was disarmingly composed as he began, 'Kit, I had no idea –' but she stared him down. He moved obediently on, but the sense of him remained and she punched her hand into the heart of her dough to fend the feeling off.

'Has anyone made frangipane from scratch before?' Rosa returned from the pantry with a jar of almonds. 'These are from our most recent season, beautifully sweet. Raph, could you find the Disaronno, *s'il vous plaît*? We need amaretto for the frangipane … and our glasses,' she beamed.

The women in the group had grown animated on Raph's arrival. Now ripe peaches were being peeled and the energy amplified. 'Slippery little deviant!' a woman announced as a wet peach popped from her hand and she licked her fingers.

Kit felt nauseous.

Rosa circled the room, checked pastry, and paused by Kit, her hand smoothing along Kit's ragged-edged dough.

'*Exemplaire*. My son is a good teacher, *non*?' Her fingers sailed affectionately over Kit's shoulders as she moved on.

Rosa's attention was on her galette at the front of the room as she drew the lesson to a close.

'This is simple, *rustique*, French fare,' she said. 'No fuss. Tuck your peach slices in, turn up the edges.' Her well-used hands threw the pastry border over the rim of the fruit to frame the inner peach medley. '*Voilà!*'

Voilà!

The happy exclamation parroted itself in Kit's mind.

Kit walked into the scullery, attacked pastry remnants on her fingers. *Voilà!*

Rosa sailed by, swinging a bottle of crème de cassis by its neck.

'Quick *kir* in *le jardin*?' she asked Kit, bumping the garden door wide with her hip.

Kit stared after her, hands dripping on the floor as she listened to Rosa banter with the geese outside.

She followed mechanically, patting her apron, but froze when she saw Rosa seated at the garden table.

Raph was standing beside her. He held a cleanskin bottle of wine and two champagne flutes.

'Another glass, Raph?' Rosa said when she saw Kit.

Raph walked past Kit to the kitchen without meeting her gaze, and Rosa beckoned for Kit to join her.

Kit lingered by the edge of the table.

Raph returned with a third flute and Rosa gushed thanks and praise. She splashed crème de cassis and wine into the flutes then slumped into a chair.

'A rest, finally,' she held her cocktail aloft. 'Sit, *mes chers.*'

Kit stood motionless.

'*Relax ma chérie!*' Rosa insisted and Kit positioned herself uncomfortably on the arm of a wrought-iron chair.

'This is Katherine,' Rosa told Raph. 'You know how I love to pick a favourite? Kit is fast becoming it.'

Kit stared at the grass.

'She is also fast becoming a good cook. Did you see her pastry?'

'It was very good.' Raph's voice was low. Kit saw flour plume in the shearers' quarters, saw it fall to gather on the floor, on his stomach.

'And she takes *beautiful* photographs,' Rosa said. 'She captured Eduard and I making love in the woods. I think I'll frame it for our bedroom.'

Raph smiled and Kit ached at the sight.

'You've always had a proclivity for the wanton, *Mère*.' He took a sip of his *kir*.

'Speaking of wanton, last night I spied Kit making love to Gabriel by the chicken coop.' Rosa rested her feet on a neighbouring chair. 'The Priory is becoming quite licentious, *mon chéri*, you're missing out.' She poked her toe at her son and Kit's cheeks filled with blood as Raph's eyes met hers for the first time.

'And then of course we have Kit's pregnant *collègue*. How is she feeling today?'

Kit broke from Raph's gaze to meet Rosa's.

'Piper, *oui*?' Rosa said. 'I noticed she was not in class this morning.'

'Yes, she was feeling–'

'Unwell? She's pregnant, *non*?'

Kit stared.

'This could not be *news*,' Rosa tutted. 'Her breasts are forever bare under her blouse and all I can see are *petit*, very ripe *melons*, she is most definitely *enceinte*!'

27

Kit pushed open the door to their room. The beds were unmade but empty.

She checked the en-suite then sat on the bed, face damp from taking the stairs at speed.

She had waited … finished her *kir*, and pretended that 'Piper's pregnancy' was indeed not 'news'. She had sat and pretended that 'Raph being Rosa's son' was also 'no big news'.

Raph had cracked first.

He'd excused himself and Kit had felt triumphant like she'd won in a shitty, unwinnable game. Then she'd gone straight to her room.

Piper wasn't there. The room was empty and now Kit stalled, wondering whether to go back out into The Priory …

Instead she closed the door. She couldn't risk seeing Raph, risk again being reminded of all he'd once meant – and all he'd taken, and what more he was taking by being here.

She poured a glass of water from the jug on the nightstand, drank it, then another, and as a headache drummed, she covered her eyes and lay back on the bed.

Kit woke, disoriented.

It was dark and quiet.

She propped herself up, turned on the lamp and saw the bed opposite was still empty. A breeze billowed the bedroom drapes. She closed the window and checked her phone for missed calls. Reception was nil.

Kit went downstairs. A guest in the library raised his teacup, lowered it, kept reading.

The kitchen was dark. She'd missed dinner.

The long-awaited cassoulet had been made that afternoon and leftovers sat in a baking dish on the slow-combustion stove.

She picked at a bean, some sausage, and stepped out the side door into the garden. On her phone, reception bars climbed as she walked down the drive and neared the road.

'*This is Piper, thanks for calling, please leave a message.*'

Kit hung up, then waited, but the phone stayed silent. She stared through the dark gap the driveway made in the hedgerow … the world beyond veiled by the night.

She turned and walked back up the driveway.

Gabriel was coming around the side of the house.

'*Bonsoir,*' he said.

It occurred to Kit that he didn't know her name.

'Hello.' She made a beeline for the kitchen door but he fell in step beside her, let his hand brush hers. She stopped a metre from the door. 'Good night,' she said. '*Bonne nuit,*' she clarified, but he took her hand and spun her against the stone wall, hand tight on her arm.

There was a swishing in the grass and they glanced up. Raph.

Kit expected him to turn around, to walk the other way, but he kept coming, and halted only when he was a step away. Gabriel's expression changed as Raph spoke to him in rapid-fire French. Gabriel's face darkened, his shoulders tensed, and Kit thought he might assault Raph but instead he swore and walked away, knocking Raph as he passed.

Kit smoothed her clammy hands down the front of her skirt. 'What the fuck do you think you're doing?'

'I'm sorry, did I interrupt something?' Raph said.

Kit felt rage … wanted to slap, scrunch and kick him.

'You're a bastard,' she said. 'What you and AGVM did almost gave Dad a heart attack. I can't believe I ever trusted you. I can't believe we trusted you. Have you been laughing at us this whole time? Were you laughing at me?'

Raph's eyes flickered and he stammered, the sound uncertain and inadequate.

'I thought you were so much more than you are but you're *nothing*. You should know that it was never you that I wanted. I wanted something real, and strong, and I made myself believe that's what you were but there's nothing real or strong about you and you know Gabriel who was just here? Well when we fucked last night, all I could think was *thank God* I never shared this with you.'

'Thank you for making that so clear.' Raph's throat glistened with sweat but his expression had grown vacant and withdrawn.

'And don't worry, I have no plans to tell your mother what a coward you are. She presumably knows what a fuck your dad is, but you clearly still delude her. I wouldn't have come here if I'd known who she was and now I wish I'd never been here.' Kit walked away. She was almost at the door when she thought she heard Raph speak, but when she turned back, he'd already gone.

❧

Kit gazed at Piper's breasts.

She'd woken in the morning to Piper in the bed opposite – sleeping soundly, like she'd never been gone – and when Piper joined her in The Priory garden for breakfast, Kit wondered why she hadn't noticed her friend's two swollen orbs earlier.

Piper was jittery, fumbling with her spoon and coffee.

'Piper,' Kit said, mercifully. 'I know.'

Piper looked up from her breakfast. 'What?'

'I know,' Kit said. 'You're pregnant.'

Piper was expressionless until her face began to crumple, and Kit choked in surprise and stumbled around the table to hold her.

Piper couldn't speak through her tears. Kit held her until the weeping slowed. 'It's okay!'

'It isn't,' Piper spluttered. 'No, Kit, you don't know–'

'Calm down, it's fine–'

'It's Marc's.'

Kit wavered.

'It's Marc's,' Piper said. 'I've been sleeping with Marc.'

Kit's arms slackened and she slowly stood. 'What?'

Piper gazed up at her, eyes wide, skin pale.

Kit reached for the back of her chair and lowered herself onto the seat. 'What?' she said again.

'I'm pregnant!' Piper shouted. 'To Marc! We've been having sex.'

Kit covered her eyes with her hands so she could think. Finally she laughed. 'Holy shit.'

'Arrggh!' Piper shouted. 'Arrrggh!'

'Oh Piper …' Kit crawled back to her friend and flopped against her with a wasted sigh. 'You're the one. It was only a matter of time before this happened to Marc – and you're the one.'

Piper howled.

'Does he know?'

'No!'

'How long have you known?'

'Twenty-four hours!'

'That's it?'

'I'm totally fucking clueless!'

'Rosa knew!'

'*How?*'

'She's been clocking your mammaries. It's so the kind of thing she'd notice.'

Piper plastered her hands over her breasts. 'Fuuuck. It's just all of a sudden – they're these throbbing balloons.'

Kit tried to appear sympathetic.

'Are you angry?' Piper whispered.

Kit searched her friend's face. 'I'm not sure … I'm a little bit angry. I'm angry with Marc for being so cavalier and not doing what I asked, and–'

'I didn't do what you asked, either.' Piper's face seemed pained. 'I'm sorry. I was going to tell you, but I didn't know if it was going anywhere and–'

'Now it's gone somewhere?'

Piper's face contorted. 'Fuck.'

'A fuck'll do it,' Kit said.

'But I don't want a baby!'

'Don't you?' Kit said.

'Oooh I don't know.' Piper covered her face. 'I don't know.'

'Marc will do anything,' Kit said, knowing it was true only when she said it. 'He will. He'd do anything for you, I know he would.'

'I think I love him.' Piper peered up, expression complex.

Kit held her mouth closed, eyes wide. 'That's good,' she finally said.

'And he's your brother – I'm sorry, I'm sorry!'

Kit was quiet for a while. 'It's kind of lovely … at least it might be.'

Piper stared down at herself. 'Auntie Kit?' Her laugh wavered.

Kit took Piper's hand and closed her eyes as she squeezed.

'I just can't–I can't believe we're flying out tonight.' Piper flumped back. 'I feel so bewildered and disoriented. I want to stay and recover and I'm dreading morning sickness on the plane.'

'Our flight's tonight?' Kit blinked. 'I thought it was tomorrow.'

'It's Tuesday,' Piper said. 'Our flight's tonight. From Paris.'

It was raining when they left.

Rosa had been in the middle of a lesson so was unable to see them off. Kit smoothed her unhappy, frizzed hair as she climbed into the cab, the air warm and muggy.

Kit had lost all sense of time at The Priory. One day had bled into another, and now she felt unprepared to re-enter the real world so soon.

'It's a shame to leave …' Piper said, hours later when they were settling into their seats on the plane at Charles de Gaulle.

Kit stared down at her lap.

'Don't you think?' Piper said.

'Yes.'

Piper looked at her. 'You're not pining? I thought you and Rosa had become besties.'

Kit undid and redid her seatbelt.

'Kit?'

Kit fidgeted.

'Did something happen? Did you disagree?'

'No, she's amazing, but while you were off buying pregnancy tests yesterday, her son arrived.'

'She has one?'

'We were making pastry. Rosa became excited as this man, her son, joined–'

'That's a nice–'

'–and Raph walked in.'

'Raph?'

'He walked in. Walked straight into the class.'

'Go back …' Piper shook her head. 'So Rosa's son was going to come, but then Raph appeared? As in *Raph*?'

'Yes.'

'Wait … *what*? What the *fuck*? *Why*? From *where*?'

'He walked in from the garden.'

'But *why*? What was he doing there?'

'I don't know! He came to help his mum, I guess.'

'Who's his mum?'

'Rosa!'

Piper stared before she exhaled, 'Nooo …'

The air hostess walked past, checking their seatbelts.

'So Rosa goes to introduce her son and her son is …'

'Raph.'

'But he's an Arenberg!'

'He's both an Arenberg *and* Rosa's son.' Kit stared, mutually disbelieving.

Piper covered her mouth and swore through her fingers. 'Jimmy's article called him *French-American*. French-*fucking*-American. Oh Kit, *God* …'

Kit was silent.

'Oh, Kit … he's food fucking royalty.'

Kit turned to the window.

'I feel like I should have known this!' Piper said. 'I'm sorry, I mean Rosamonde Michel – his *mum*? *Shit*. Tell me *everything that happened*.'

Kit was quiet before finally she said, 'Nothing. Nothing happened. He strolled into Rosa's kitchen like the same Raph I've always known. I almost passed out then proceeded to sweat through a pastry lesson while half the women gagged for his attention. Rosa, in her naïvety, then had he and I sit through a "friendly" cocktail in the garden. I went searching for you later that night, saw him again, we exchanged unpleasantries, and that was that.'

'But was he surprised to see you?'

'I would say … yes.'

'So Rosa doesn't know about any of it?'

'No. She adores him.'

'That makes me like her a lot less.'

'I wish I felt the same.'

The plane began to judder as it powered down the runway and Piper reached for Kit's hand as the plane took off.

Twenty-four hours later, their cab from Melbourne airport neared Kit's Gertrude Street apartment.

Piper squeezed Kit's hand. 'I don't want to part with you.' Her smile was small.

'Why don't you come up?' Kit said. 'I'll make you a bed if you're not feeling well.'

Piper faltered. 'No, I need some time out. Oh God, I don't know what I need ...'

Kit climbed out and the cabbie unloaded her luggage. She leaned in through the window and kissed Piper's cheek. 'Bye, then.'

'Love you.' Piper had fear in her voice. 'Thank you for being so amazing about ... all this, with Marc, and—'

'The baby.'

Piper dry-retched and Kit tried not to smile. She put a cool hand on her friend's cheek.

'Thank you,' Piper finally whispered.

'Love you.' Kit squeezed her arm then watched the cab peel away. She watched the brake lights flash on and off, and when she could no longer see the car, she felt the truth settle.

On top of Kit's shaky foundations sat the weight of the truth. Piper and Marc, the only people Kit had ever let into her inner world, had begun their own inner world and Kit was going to be on the outside.

She was about to lose her best friend and brother – to each other.

28

Kit had promised that she wouldn't call Gossard Range until Piper had, because they both knew the pregnancy was not a secret Kit could keep from her family.

Five days following their return, five days into the lockdown and jetlag, Kit's phone remained silent.

Her life began to feel like a pirate map. The edges had begun to burn and she sat in the middle, watching flames approach. Her escape route via The Priory had burned. Raph's connection to it had lit the match and Kit had set it on fire.

She had begun with a phone call. Rosa had been busy, but she'd called Kit back, and when Kit heard her voice she'd almost changed her mind. Rosa had immediately asked when Kit would return to shoot the cookbook. Kit was silent before she'd told her story.

She said that an assignment had appeared, one that was important and pre-agreed, and that a schedule reshuffle had made the start date immediate and the end date uncertain. She sketched the story so convincingly that even she believed it and she concluded by telling Rosa that she'd recommend another photographer for her cookbook.

Rosa had been silent, then said, 'You mentioned a man when you were here last. Now I hear that exact same fragility and angst in you. Why are you letting a man stand in the way of something you want?'

Kit had been lost for words. Rosa added, '*Ma chère*, not one man on this earth is worth it,' and Kit had wanted to fall down with hysterical laughter and rage.

She wanted to tell Rosa exactly who this man was. She wanted to tell Rosa exactly why this man prevented her from coming to The Priory, why he prevented Kit from doing anything *ever* with Rosa. She wanted to tell Rosa that this was the one man on earth Rosa *would* do anything for.

'I appreciate your concern,' Kit said as she'd wiped a hot tear from her face, 'but this is about nothing more than a prior commitment. It's unfortunate that I have to decline your kind offer but I'm honoured that you thought of me and I'll happily recommend someone else.'

Rosa had been quiet. Kit had covered her face with a tissue, and finally Rosa had said, 'I'm in no great hurry. I'll call you in a month.' Then she'd hung up.

Kit googled how to block phone numbers, then followed the steps for Rosa's. She'd never speak to Raph again, nor his mother, and she sat for days in the middle of her burning-map-life and scanned for escape routes.

She opened *Hunger*, hopefully, but it only made her feel ill. She was glad when finally, on the morning of day six – her phone rang.

'Kitten!' Connor sounded brighter than she'd heard him in a while.

'Da-d …' She forgot not to answer.

'Where are you? I thought you were back a few days ago.'

'Yes …' She didn't have the energy to pretend. 'I'm just back.'

He told her to come up to Gossard Range because there was exciting news. She didn't ask if it was that he was going to be a grandfather.

'Dinner? Tonight?' he said. Kit hesitated before she agreed, then called Piper.

&

Ovate, white flowers bloomed on the magnolia that picketed the Gossard Range homestead. Kit pulled her Defender in and felt the cool valley air through the open window. She took her blazer from the back seat and someone stepped out from under the entry portico, coming towards her.

Piper's skin was bright, red hair full, and Kit said, plainly, 'You look beautiful.'

'I've done it.' Piper's expression was relieved.

'Marc?' Kit said. 'You told him?'

'Yes …' Piper exhaled. 'Finally. Today. After you called. I had a total fucking meltdown this week. I'm so sorry you had to keep the secret, but it's done now. It's happening. Marc and I are having a … baby.'

Kit pulled her friend close and they held each other.

'It's a miracle, really,' she said.

'If by that you mean it was instant and easy, then yes, it was,' Piper scoffed. 'Did you speak to Rosa this week? Are you going back?'

Kit hadn't expected the question. She faltered before she shook her head and turned towards the house. 'No,' she said. 'I won't be.'

'Really? Because of Raph?' Piper followed. 'Do you think it matters?'

'Does it *matter*?' Kit smiled ironically. 'I want nothing to do with him. And Rosa wouldn't want anything to do with anyone who feels how I do – about her son. I can't conceal that I fucking hate him.'

'It's such an incredible opportunity, though. Couldn't you just–'

Kit pushed open the front door and hurried ahead so she wouldn't have to hear Piper's useless words.

She threw her arms wide when she saw Marc. A part of her wanted to say, 'Woopsies! Aren't you a silly bee that visited one too many flowers! This is what happens when you don't cap your cock! Aren't you a dumb-dumb who couldn't keep it zipped! You just couldn't help your wittle self, woopsie doodle dandy!' But when their eyes locked and Kit saw his fear and hope, all she could do was hug him.

'Congratulations ...' she breathed into his collar.

'The junk works.' He laughed to conceal his anxiety, and Kit touched his face.

'Isn't this incredible news, Katherine?' Annalese stepped in from the garden with a handful of rosemary.

'Congratulations, Granny.' Kit smirked.

Annalese walked behind the kitchen island, and said, 'Don't ever call me that again.'

Piper power-walked away towards Marc at the drinks trolley.

'Well this was inevitable,' Annalese said when Kit joined her at the bench. 'Marc's humped everything in sight since he knew how. Thank God it's ended up being Piper who copped the mother lode. Imagine if it was one of those tarts at the winery? The word *termination* might have sprung to mind.'

Kit patted her mother on the arm. Her predictability gave Kit a strange comfort.

'Found it!' Connor strode in with a stray cobweb in his hair and set a dusty little bottle of 1913 Seppeltsfield port on the table. 'We'll break it open with dessert, to celebrate.'

'Hello,' Kit said.

'Darling, how's this news? These two almost gave me a *real* heart attack,' he chuckled.

'It was always my plan. An heir to secure the Gossard reign.' Marc grinned. 'You're welcome.'

Connor scoffed. 'I know my son, Piper, and this is not the kind of thing he plans.'

'Nor I.' Piper tried to smile, and it occurred to Kit that despite Piper and Marc being well and truly adult, unplanned pregnancy between two people who weren't in a relationship could deliver fear and disorientation at any age. Despite Marc's confident banter, there was an air of bewilderment about him and Piper. They resembled people who'd just endured a significant shock.

Connor was lively, his mood more *well isn't this jolly!* than *holy fuck!* Clearly, pregnancy held more gravity for women than it did for men. But her father's positivity permeated.

Marc became genuinely talkative, then Piper, and Kit watched her brother and friend begin to meld. Soon they'd be subject to the ultimate bonding and only in this moment were they realising it.

'I think it's my bedtime,' Kit said when her plate was empty.

'Now just wait, don't miss the toast,' Connor said, and Kit waited while her father divvied up the port. 'To babies.' He finally held his glass high. 'Mine and theirs.'

In the bed of her childhood room, Kit lay like a pencil in a box, staring at the ceiling.

A single glow-in-the-dark star was stuck in a far corner, having survived the teenage cull fifteen years earlier. Now it glinted from its dark nook whenever she came to stay.

She'd been reckless.

The feeling had been coming on and now it engulfed Kit with cavernous certainty.

Piper had goaded her. She'd always promoted a carelessness in Kit but now Piper herself was shutting down, settling, drawing in, gathering – preparing for the utmost responsibility of her life.

Piper was retreating. She was taking Marc with her and they were breeding, breeding both a human and a comfortableness, a cosiness of the kind Kit had spent much of the year casting off …

Now Kit lay alone like a solitary pencil, no other colours in the box.

There was a knock on the door. 'Knock, knock?' Her mother was already opening it. 'Are you awake?'

'Yes,' Kit said.

Annalese turned on the light. 'Have you lost weight? I noticed that your bottom looked toned tonight.'

Kit stifled a groan. She knew that the potential for a moment of intimacy tended to panic Annalese – her mother used nastiness to balance the state of play.

'I'm sorry.' She surprised Kit with an apology, closed the door and came to the bed. 'That was rude. I'm trying to be more considerate in what I say … and how I say it.' Annalese sat down. Why was she there?

'You know I've always been proud of you …' Annalese took Kit's hand.

Kit murmured, doubtfully.

'Well I'm telling you. I think you are beautiful, everyone does.'

There was silence as they both considered the unusualness of holding each other's hands.

'This must be hard,' Annalese said. 'For you.'

Kit waited for her to explain.

'Marc … and Piper,' Annalese said.

They heard Marc laughing loudly down in the kitchen. Annalese adjusted her hold on Kit's hand.

'I was wondering,' she said, 'how your wedding plans are going? You've been keeping the cogs turning while Scott's been gone, I assume? Let's remember that it's not all about your brother and Smarty-Pants-Up-The-Duff Red. *You've* got the wedding to look forward to, we all do.'

There was a wait. 'I'm not sure that's happening,' Kit said.

'Who? What? *Piper?*' Annalese's eyes were wide. 'Do you think she *might* have a termination?'

'No.' Kit frowned. 'The wedding.'

Now Annalese frowned.

'The wedding … Scott …' Kit said. 'I'm not sure.'

'Did he end it?' Annalese asked, voice high. 'Did *you*?'

'Not yet, but …' Kit hadn't gotten back to Scott during her stay at The Priory, nor since she'd been home.

'Don't be silly.' Annalese patted her hand. 'Don't be silly. Scott's good for you, you know that.'

Kit didn't know that. What she did know however was that suddenly the thought of him brought her a surprising comfort. Like her mother's bad behaviour, he was something Kit could rely on.

'I think you'd feel better if you settled,' Annalese said.

Kit wondered if she meant better if she settled *for* Scott or *down with* Scott and then the realisation dawned.

The fever was ending. Regardless of her mother, regardless of her wanting her mother to be wrong, Kit's rebellion had to end.

She never wanted to see *Hunger* again. It suddenly felt like a collage of everything she'd become – experimental, confused, something no one cared about – and it meant nothing.

She'd arrived home unemployed, unloved, without insight or direction, and her engagement ring was stuffed in a forgotten pocket of her suitcase.

'You're a good girl.' Annalese began to tuck the doona up around Kit's throat like she was a child. 'You know the right thing to do.'

The lights went out. Kit was alone.

29

Kit opened her eyes. She'd slept well, and breakfast was cooking in the homestead kitchen, she could smell it. She slid from the covers, and padded to the bedroom door.

A box sat on the threshold with a note on it, the handwriting her mother's.

I thought this was the perfect one for you, so I kept it.

Kit took the box back into her room and lifted the lid. She stared at the silken white fabric inside then exhaled, peered at the ceiling and saw the glow-in-the-dark star, still radiating in the dull morning light. She stayed gazing up until her neck hurt, then returned to the box.

A pale Delpozo dress.

She walked to the window, pulled the curtains wide and turned back.

Her pyjamas came off and the dress began to slide on. One foot, then the other, she carefully lifted the fabric over her body and smoothed the front with her hands as she studied herself in the mirror.

Her mother was right. It was perfect. Right then and there, Kit looked like the perfect person. She looked like the person other people wanted to be, a person who knew their path and had stuck to it.

Marriage meant that you'd made it. Like a baby, marriage was a life-long commitment and responsibility, and 'commitment and responsibility' commanded respect. In this dress, Kit commanded respect.

The year gone was behind her and this was the way forward. It was already happening.

She left the bedroom, walked towards the kitchen, and appeared from the mouth of the hall.

Connor said, 'Here she is!' then looked twice at what she was wearing.

Scott stared from the head of the table, face tanned and a flake of croissant on his lip. 'Kit …'

'Oh!' Annalese laughed in surprise. 'I didn't mean for you to put it on right now!'

'Scott–' Kit said. 'I …'

'I invited him,' Annalese said.

'When did you get in?'

'Last night.' Scott began to stand. 'Annalese called not long after I landed.'

Kit nodded, numb.

'Is that …?' Scott stared at the dress as he walked towards her. 'I didn't want to see you in it before the–but wow … it's stunning.' He folded his arms.

'I was right.' Annalese sounded smug. 'It looks perfect.'

Piper walked into the room and came to the table, staring at Kit … then Scott.

'No morning sickness today?' Annalese said.

'Not yet.' Piper sat down.

'Piper's pregnant.' Kit smiled at Scott. 'To Marc.'

Scott stuttered a laugh. 'Sorry?'

'Pregnant,' Piper said. 'To Marc.'

'How'd *that* happen?'

'One guess,' Piper said. She smiled drily as she gave Kit a What the Fuck is He Doing Here face.

Kit glanced away. 'What are we doing four weekends from now, honey?'

'Us?' Scott replied. 'I–'

'Let's get married,' Kit said.

Connor beamed and Annalese clapped her hands.

Scott went to her. He took the back of Kit's head with his hands and settled a kiss on her forehead. 'Let's,' he said. 'I love the idea.'

Connor had his arm over Kit's shoulder as, back in plain clothes, she walked with him to the Gossard Range cellar door. '*This* is the reason I asked you to come up yesterday, but we got sidetracked with baby news!' he said.

Along the cellar's central wall, an arrangement of wooden crates were stacked like shelves. Connor and Kit zigzagged through tourists and Kit read the blackboard sign:

Gossard Range Cidre Bouché.

'You started selling the cider?'

'Sold,' Connor said.

'What?'

'We launched it quietly on the weekend. Last bottle sold yesterday.'

'*Really?*'

'I'm surprised, too.'

'Did you sell it all here?'

'As well as the Barossa estate, and a few select purveyors in town.'

'Dad! Amazing!'

'I'm buoyed, I admit it,' he smiled. 'The publicity was great, it's boosted sales across the board, and the letterpress labels have been nominated in a packaging award.'

'Oh, *Dad.*' Kit hugged him.

'We got quite a bit of press which culminated in a lot of restaurant orders, half international. The reviews were fantastic, and that, coupled with the cachet of the recipe and limited run – for reasons best left unsaid – seemed to create a bit of a stir.' Kit must have appeared surprised because Connor added, 'It's not just any old cider, darling.'

'I know!' she laughed. 'And no sign of an Arenberg version?'

'Not as yet, but we await the cider deluge …'

They left the growing crowd for the courtyard, and started back up towards the homestead. The dogs joined them, Sergeant the deerhound falling in step beside Connor, who rested his hand on the animal's proud head.

'It was a blow to me too, you know, all that business involving … Raph,' he said.

Kit frowned. 'I know, Dad. You almost had a heart attack.'

'Yes, but I don't just mean Cannock Chase. I mean *Raph*. He made an impact on us all and I, well, I can only presume from what I've heard, but I know you two had a … "relationship" … of sorts. You haven't said, but I feel like what happened must have been hard on you, too.'

'There was never any *relationship*, Dad,' Kit choked, tucking hair behind her ear.

'I don't want to know anything. I just wanted to say that Raph's double-crossing … well it was big, on a lot of fronts. Here there'll only be this one batch of cider – we have no orchard, no farmgate – and for *you* …' he bobbed his head uneasily, then sighed and changed course. 'Anyway, I suppose all we can do is just keep on keeping on.'

Kit took his arm and they walked up the incline.

When they were almost back at the house, Connor turned to face her. 'No,' he said, resolute. 'I won't sweep this under the carpet. Tell me you're okay. Your announcement over breakfast was big. Tell me you're not just rebounding … from Raph to Scott, I mean.'

Kit managed to appear taken aback. 'Dad, what do you mean? I've only ever been with Scott this whole time.'

'I know, *I know*,' Connor fumbled. 'It's just … I don't know …' He gave up. 'Am I being silly?'

Kit gave his arm a firm squeeze. 'It's all fine, Dad. It's the right decision for me and for Scott. You don't need to worry.'

Connor looked hard at her and she smiled to prove she meant what she said.

'Well … good,' he stammered. 'If that's so, I'm delighted.'

At the front door, Kit paused. Her feelings – usually akin to multi-coloured ribbons that danced around a maypole – had suddenly stilled. In place of the maypole a cavern had appeared. Doubt, uncertainty, fear and hesitation … those feelings had disappeared, the cavern had swallowed them. In their place was a lightness. An emptiness.

Scott gazed warmly at her as she walked into the lounge room and Kit smiled, wondering what else this strange cavern could make disappear.

'What are you doing?' Piper said.

Kit had answered Piper's call during the drive home from the winery.

'Still driving,' she spoke loudly to be heard over the engine. 'Have you left yet?'

'No, I meant: what are you doing with *Scott*?'

It had started to drizzle. Kit flicked on the windscreen wipers.

'What?' she said.

'I said: what are you doing with Scott? I thought you were ending it!'

'No,' Kit said, 'I'm not ending it.'

There was silence on the other end of the phone before Piper finally spoke again. 'Kit …' she sounded worried. 'Kit, did you see what he did in there? He kissed you on the forehead.'

'Piper.' Kit exhaled.

'Kit.'

'What?'

'What's going on?'

'What do you mean?' The cavern perpetuated a detachment. It created a magically vast distance between Kit and the chaos of others, Kit and the chaos of … herself.

'I'm worried,' Piper said. 'I feel like you must be breaking down … or something.'

'Piper. You're projecting your insecurities on to me.'

'No–'

'You're worried about yourself and now you're projecting it all on to me.'

'Fucking hell. Are you–'

'Last night went well,' Kit diverged.

'Sorry?' Piper said.

'Marc,' Kit said. 'He took it all very well. You must feel happy about that part being over, and Mum and Dad, they seemed very happy. Did you talk to Marc? Do you think you'll move in together?'

'We're not talking about this, Kit, we're talking about–'

'Marc will do whatever you want,' Kit said. 'He fell for you the moment he saw you.'

Piper was quiet before she said, 'Why four weeks?'

'What do you mean?'

'Why four weeks until you get married?' Piper said.

'Oh, because four weeks is the minimum time for our Notice of Intention,' Kit said. 'But we've changed it to November. Eight weeks. Annalese and I discussed it before I left and she'd prefer more time to get the garden ready. Scott saw the garden and decided it should be there, at home. It's as beautiful really, as the Barossa, just more of a private, domestic beauty which I think Scott felt added an exclusivity.'

'It's going to be *eight* weeks?' Piper said. 'Thank God. That's enough time to get out of it.'

'Pardon?'

'Thank God. That's enough time to get out of it.'

'I don't want to get out of it, Piper, I want to get on with it.'

'Kit!' Piper sounded as if she was hyperventilating. 'Does your family have any idea how much you and Scott don't work? If they did they would not be encouraging you.'

'Piper. I know you have doubts about people's capacities to take care of one another, doubts about people's ability to have simple, uncomplicated relationships, but what you need to do … is grow up.'

Piper was speechless.

'You've taken your new path and now I'm taking mine,' Kit said. 'They may not be what we expected but it's the way it is. I can't know what's right for you, nor you for me. Why don't we just try to be happy for one another?' Kit's sentiments felt like those of a wise person. For the first time in a long time she felt peace and clarity and she exhaled as she tapped the indicator and turned a corner.

'Are you having a breakdown?' Piper said. 'I don't understand anything you're saying.'

'I don't expect you to understand,' Kit said. 'We're both moving in new directions. I hope I haven't surprised you, I know you're probably already feeling uncertain and unstable, and–'

'I'm not feeling unstable, Kit. I actually feel extremely grounded. I feel more grounded than I ever have and …'

Piper rambled on and Kit let her. There was no need to listen. She didn't need Piper to litter her way with crumbs of doubt and distraction.

'Kit?' Piper said. 'Are you listening?'

'I was just wondering if you'd checked in at work this week,' Kit said. 'How is *Hamper*?'

'Who gives a fuck! I just said–'

'Piper, please, stop.'

'Kit … Kit … look, just listen. You know how much I care about you–'

'*You* know how much I care about you.'

'Yes, so please hear me. I'm only saying what I'm saying because I want the best for you.'

'I want the best for you.'

'Well marrying Scott is not what's best for you, Kit. It is NOT.'

'Perhaps you don't know what's best for me, Piper. I don't say that to be rude but I don't think you do know what's best.'

'I'm being honest in a way no one else can be. No one knows you like I do …'

The rhythm of Piper's words mingled with the rhythm of the windscreen wipers.

Kit watched, mesmerised as the wipers swept the water off the glass and into the wind.

All the uncertain times were over.

All the craziness had ended and here Kit was at the end … calm and contained.

'Be happy, all will be well,' she said when she noticed that Piper had finally quieted.

'*What?*' Piper spat.

'All will be well,' Kit said again. 'You and I are both going to be fine and neither of us needs to worry. Everything's fine.'

The phone went dead, reception was full. Piper had hung up and now she would be wallowing in self-perpetuated angst.

It didn't matter. Kit drove on, contained and assured. She no longer needed to rely on them: Piper or Marc. They had their own journey ahead and they were already self-absorbed and bewildered by the monumental consequences of their actions. Kit was the only one in possession of clarity.

This felt good, a relief.

The freeway opened up, Kit coasted onto the six-lane motorway and turned on a TED Talk.

Her fingers curled gently around the steering wheel, the composed orator heightened her sense of equanimity, and she knew that the crazy times were definitely over. All would be well.

30

All this time, Kit had made life difficult for herself.

She had made it difficult by limiting her photography and styling to food. Food was unpredictable, difficult to prepare and disorderly, with varying colours that made it hard to set the light.

If she were to sufficiently commit herself to Scott, burying *Hunger* was the place to start. She didn't know what it was ever meant to achieve anyway and whatever it was ... it had failed.

Scott was delighted when she told him her plan to shift her focus to furniture and design photography, and Kit realised the power of two becoming one. When she ceased bucking away from him they made a potent pair, just as Scott had predicted and wanted all along.

The new dynamic also meant she could worry less. He led and – with her camera – she followed. She liked to slump into the comfort of his art direction, the correctness of his mind and his ability to encourage a well-crafted shot from her. Capturing the lines of man-made shapes was controllable, all Kit had to do was align angles with angles.

More than she had before, Kit stepped into Scott's community of friends. Most were other designers who also continually needed their work photographed, and this saw Kit segue from *Hunger* to a different online magazine – a digital publication she built to showcase industrial design. The space featured new designers and eventually, Kit imagined, would begin to earn through advertising.

Scott's collaboration with Fermi had made his profile soar, negating his initial wish to make the wedding a vehicle for promotion. His increased workload also meant that the wedding had become something that they both just wanted 'done' and they agreed to reduce the guest list to family and close friends only.

They shopped together for Scott's tux, ordered wedding bands from *Bove e Porcu*, and Kit felt safe. She'd returned to what mattered and from this secure centre point she set the co-ordinates for her future. There would be no wilderness or unknown where she was going.

Not only did the impending wedding make her glad, Marc's impending baby did, too. She felt glad not just for herself, but for Connor, who needed the diversion.

Following the discontinuation of the *cidre bouché*, negative rumblings began. Gossard sales slowed and Jimmy Hillinger, who had initially lauded the cider on *thegastronome.com*, wrote a speculative piece detailing the instability of Gossard since the 'infamous tussle' with giants AGVM.

Sweet Cider Sours
O, Gossard, wilt thou leave us so unsatisfied? Today we examine the fallout from Gossard Range's infamous tussle with giants AGVM as we assess how something so promising simply failed to fly.

Soon after my first <u>key report</u> that revealed Gossard's plans for a new product, <u>this marvel</u> appeared – a traditional cidre bouché made using long-secreted Gossard ancestral techniques. The hype proved not to be misplaced, the product lived up to its presumed distinction, so why we ask, has it gone?

Somehow, as I report <u>here</u>, heads at Gossard Range allowed historical rivals AGVM to claim Cannock Chase – Gossard's one and only source of heirloom cider apples as well as their truffle farmgate. Gossard have long been known for their quality and nous, so does this gaffe mean they're losing their edge?

<u>*This*</u> *previously published photo of Kit Gossard and Raph Arenberg captured at Gossard Range earlier this year makes one wonder if more is afoot. With invitations to a wedding between Kit and prominent designer Scott Baldwin circulating as we speak, we can't help wondering if a lover's quarrel between Kit and Raph was at the heart of the Gossard–AGVM conflict.*

Whatever the reason, this setback will prove uncomfortable for Gossard. Though a short run can imply a product's exclusivity, a product cut short implies scandal. For a brand whose credibility relies on confidence and consistency, this kind of fluctuation and instability will no doubt come at a cost.

That said, we look forward to those Gossard/Baldwin wedding pics …

Kit felt impervious to the inanity, although she was glad the wedding would distract Connor from the gloom. The cavernous space she had continued to cultivate within gave her shelter. She imagined it like a black hole where feelings could be discarded and never seen again. Scott's complete ignorance of the food industry helped, and Kit encouraged it, felt closer to him when they embraced and ignored the same things. Jimmy's musing was just one of the many goings-on which Kit now paid no attention.

Piper persevered with her anxious, hormonal behaviour, but this didn't perturb Kit either. If Piper and Kit's bond weakened it would allow Piper and Marc's to strengthen. In between Piper and her brother was not where Kit wanted to be.

Marc was predictably distracted by his upcoming responsibility. Kit avoided asking him what plans he was making. She didn't want him to feel judged or suffocated, and she couldn't see how her opinions on matters she had not herself experienced would be helpful, anyway. When Marc called and put anything to her, she told him to put it to Piper and when he pressed Kit about her life, she told him the truth: that it was easy, without complaint.

Annalese sent Kit daily updates of tasks she or her contractors were performing around the homestead: hedge shaping, flower planting, branch removal, border trimming, gravel raking, window cleaning and roof spraying, all in preparation for the big day. Kit enjoyed this connection with her mother: a goal shared.

If the busyness ever felt like it was getting too much, Kit wandered to the Japanese bath house down the road from the apartment, where the soft clop of wooden implements and the sound of trickling water was a failsafe way to replenish her sense of equanimity.

She and Scott were enjoying themselves so much that time flew.

Six weeks passed. Two weeks before the wedding, their 'pre-moon' – their honeymoon in advance of their nuptials – was upon them.

Scott's agenda was full following the wedding, so he'd suggested that pampering, tanning and relaxation *before* rather than *after* the big day made sense, and the idea for a pre-moon had emerged. His thinking was practical, Kit appreciated this, and eleven days before the wedding, they boarded a flight to Thailand.

ॐ

'Perfect.' Kit smiled as they disembarked their twelve-hour flight to Phuket and were greeted by their waiting chauffeur.

The room at their resort was decorated traditionally with lotus flowers, water features, coloured silks and meditating deities. Kit was delighted that their outer environment reflected the harmony of their internal one.

Scott initially fussed about the humidity, Kit reminded him to swap jeans for shorts, and subsequent complaints were nil. Her patience and insights were abundant, solutions to Scott's concerns neverending, and where his fussiness might at one time have irked her, it now gave her purpose.

She'd purged her internal world and had begun to fill it with her love for him. All the neuroses in the world wouldn't have been enough to overwhelm her, and Scott's were only trifling. She couldn't wait for their mutual devotion to be made official by law.

A tropical fruit platter was delivered to their suite.

Kit considered reclining on the bed to eat it, but instead took the tray to their patio where sticky furnishings wouldn't disrupt Scott's enjoyment of the day. He came to stand beside her and she sensed that his energy was coiled, his mind not yet in the place his body was.

'This is nice,' he said.

'Yes,' Kit smiled. 'How about you take a swim … relax.'

Scott didn't reply. Kit ate a slice of mango, and offered him some pineapple. Scott sniffed it and said, 'I think I need a coffee.'

Nothing in the resort matched the coffee Scott was used to so they bought an icy sugared beverage on the street. Sugar in lieu of caffeine wasn't wise but it was an easy way to see them both through this initial phase while Scott slowly unwound.

'How are you?' Scott asked as they strolled along the beachfront boulevard, and despite his arm over her shoulder, Kit was surprised that he was thinking of her.

'What do you mean?' she said. He shrugged and sucked on his straw. Kit added, 'I've never been better,' and they leaned in to kiss each other.

'This is heaven,' Scott said a few mornings in. He'd begun to unwind, and the emptying of his mind was making space for new ideas.

Each morning was spent on the balcony with breakfast. Scott used the time to draw in his notebook, and by mid-morning he'd sketched enough ideas for he and Kit to critique until lunch time.

Scott was happy, therefore so was Kit, and when they ventured out beyond their resort, she gladly volunteered to photograph him for his popular social media feed. In the photos,

Scott pensively examined ad hoc local furniture – '*No such thing as downtime*' – and lounged beneath thatched sunshades in swim trunks – '*Researching umbrella design*'.

He asked for a photo with Kit so he could caption it 'Inspiration', but Kit declined. She'd readily taken a back seat, and that was where she wanted to stay. For this reason she didn't mind Scott's agent or others calling through their dinner and dates – after all, Scott's growing success would soon be her own.

'Where shall we buy a place together?' Scott said one night as they walked home from dinner along the beach.

'Huh … I haven't even thought.'

'Do you *want* to buy a place?' Scott looked at her, and when she saw that he seemed uncertain, she laughed.

'Of course!' She stood on tiptoes to kiss him.

'Well,' he said, 'do we buy near where we are now or maybe look at something abroad? I think we're going to need a Euro bolt hole but with the trains and flights, pretty much anywhere on the continent would do. I suppose it's more about where we want to settle …'

Settle. The word sank into Kit's psyche, emotion stirred, and she blanked her mind until the feeling faded.

Her phone rang. She lifted it from her pocket, saw Marc's name, put the device away, and said to Scott, 'Yes, let's talk more about where we should settle …'

The following day, Marc called again. Again Kit ignored it, and this time he left a voicemail message.

'Kit, it's me, Marc … I was calling about your–your wet weather plan for the wedding. I'm getting some things sorted, like you asked, but I need to talk some things over … logistical things. Call me back when you can, as soon as you can.'

Kit had left clear wet weather guidelines, along with anything else anyone might need to know, in her wedding folder at Gossard Range. She had spent twenty minutes telling *and* showing Marc and Annalese and Connor this, and for this reason, Marc's call went unreturned.

The voicemail messages clocked up and five voicemails in, Marc finally dropped the wet weather guise. 'Kit, Kit, could you just call, please? I just … just call me. Call the fuck back.'

Marc's tone matched exactly the unsettled tone he'd adopted since her wedding announcement, was a tone Kit didn't care for, and like the others, this call too went unanswered.

Piper called too and her messages at least didn't waste time with pretext. Her dubiousness about Kit's 'pre-moon' and what awaited her at the end of it was plain.

'It's Piper … again. My last message got cut off so I'm going to say this *fast*. Kit, this shouldn't be happening. None of this should be happening. I know that I must seem like some dark fly swimming in your sunny cocktail but I'm not trying to be. I'm trying to tell you what's right – for you. I know you, and–'

The message cut out, subsequent calls from her brother and friend went ignored, and Kit felt untouchable.

But the calls didn't cease.

Piper's and Marc's names appeared again and again on her phone, slowly wearing something away, and Kit felt like she was contracting a virus. Psychological bugs of disquiet took hold, they quickly bred, and Kit's well-cultivated cavern was suddenly neither dark nor deep enough to swallow them.

She woke in the night, covered in sweat.

She tore off her bedclothes and stood in the shower, the water washing away the heat and anxiety, but back in bed, nausea ticked on into the night until she was sick before sunrise.

Scott diagnosed food poisoning. He was usually right, so Kit agreed.

Then the following night she woke again, body blanketed in perspiration and she lay curled in the dark, night air chilling her flesh as the nausea rose and once again she was curled over the toilet bowl.

'It's a strange parasite,' Scott insisted, and despite now knowing he was wrong, Kit agreed.

There was a parasite but it wasn't strange – Kit knew it well.

Gossard Range and the wild man in the hazelnut thicket.

In her fever, the sense of him had been formidable, his wildness palpable, hallucinations of him coloured by food – pagan, abundant and brimming like the still-life images of Bluebeard's Picnic and Rosa's kitchen.

The vision appeared the next night and respite only came at daybreak when Kit's apprehension and feverishness faded and she sat pale and depleted, up-taking juice by the pool as the bright of the day burned off the darkness of the night.

The last night passed and it was time to go home.

The honeymoon was over and it was time to get married.

31

Not quite a season had passed since Kit had tried on the wedding dress in the homestead bedroom at Gossard Range, and now the stage for a Yarra Valley wedding was being set.

Not far by road for the select family and friends invited, the estate had become the perfect venue, and when the day arrived, the atmosphere was perfect late spring in the valley. Sun shone on the trees in the homestead garden and the air was fresh with the scent of warming citrus.

Annalese had demarcated a pretty space for the ceremony, and for the reception, a table sat between two beds of the vegetable garden, the produce from which had been selected for Annalese's menu plan.

Mid-morning, Kit was at the reception table, adjusting the décor, when she heard Piper's voice and saw that her friend had arrived early.

Piper didn't have much to show by way of a belly yet and she wore a pair of soft, cropped lambskin shorts with a sumptuous white angora knit. Kit thought she looked beautiful, but didn't say so.

'Hello,' Piper said, face pinched as she navigated the garden until she reached Kit, motionless by the table. 'I came a little early to see if you needed help with … anything.'

Kit gazed at Piper before she replied, 'No, thank you.'

Piper didn't leave like Kit had hoped, so she strolled to the head of the table and began rearranging the place setting there.

'I'd very much like to be of assistance, if I can,' Piper said.

'Thank you,' Kit said again, 'I can't think of anything at the moment.'

Piper fidgeted, then walked away, and Kit resolved that Piper's arriving ahead of time would be the first and last thing that would put her out that day.

Annalese appeared and as Kit went on arranging the table, her mother tailed her – correcting anything she thought was incorrect. Because of the resolution Kit had just made, she said, simply, 'You're always such a help,' and exited the garden to get ready.

Inside, the main room was full of flowers and food, and assistants bumped into each other with plates and vessels.

Kit had been without an appetite since her return from Thailand the previous day, but now, confronted with this sheer volume of edibles … she wavered.

Careful hands wrapped, basted and layered …

Lobster, crab cakes, scallops wrapped in prosciutto, stuffed piquillo peppers …

Soft green and white blooms rested with willow branches and piles of fruit, and Kit's eyes roamed the unwieldy landscape before she stepped forward and raised her hand. Her finger made its way down the soft, mossy stem of a branch until it reached a forgotten raspberry on the tablecloth and–

A shout rang out from the garden.

Kit stopped.

She glanced towards the window and saw Annalese berating a man who was erecting a canopy. She watched her mother's arms wave about like a malfunctioning robot, then turned slowly back to the spread in front of her.

This feast was an homage to colour and chaos. These were both things Kit no longer cared for, and she let her hands fall limp by her sides before she left the table behind and walked towards the bedroom.

The Delpozo dress had hung on the back of the robe for three days, and the storage creases had fallen from the full skirt. Kit looked the dress over, the bodice slim with sheer organza that covered the chest and capped the shoulders with tiny sleeves.

She slid the dress on, raised the zipper, slid her hands into natty pockets at the hips then stood to attention in front of the mirror.

There was a knock on the door, before Piper let herself in uninvited. Kit didn't take her gaze from the mirror but she heard Piper help herself to a seat on the bed.

'I don't need any help,' Kit said, still not turning. 'Thank you.'

Marc appeared in the door. He too strode in without invitation and positioned himself in front of Kit, arms folded.

'You look hostile.' Kit smiled, making light of her brother's stance.

'No,' Marc said. 'I'm not hostile. You, however, have been very much so, for the last two months. You've been avoiding me, us, both of us.'

Kit tried to see past him to the mirror, but he blocked her. She raised a hand to rub a knot that had formed in her neck.

'I haven't been avoiding you, Marc. Could you please move?'

'You have been hostile *and* avoiding Piper and me.' He stood motionless. 'And now you're not leaving this room until I hear a sane explanation for what the fuck is going on.'

Kit sighed and pinched her neck. 'Marc, can we just let each other be?' she said. 'Can we let each other be for five minutes? Adults mind their own business, adults have private lives and personal space. We're adults. How about we stop getting in each other's way and start getting on with things, yes?'

Marc stared at her before he just said, 'Jesus. Fucking. Christ.'

Kit squeezed at her neck to dissuade the knot but it didn't seem to be working. She stretched her shoulder and turned to the window.

'Don't look away, Kit.'

Kit stretched again.

'Kit.'

Kit ran her hand up the nape of her neck and slowly turned back.

'What the *fuck* has happened to you?' Marc's face contorted.

'This is just the kind of sensationalism I've been avoiding.' Kit gazed at him then swivelled again towards the window. 'You and Piper are so anxious about your own situation, that all you can do is project your anxiety onto me and *my* situation. I've got it together, Marc. You should get it together, too.'

Marc started to laugh. 'You've *got it together*? Only a deranged person says they've *got it together*.'

He was no longer blocking the mirror. Kit took the opportunity to take her hair down. She combed it with her fingers.

'As we all know,' Piper said from the bed, 'I'm pregnant. I'm pregnant and none of us planned it. It's unsettling. We're all nervous.' She paused. 'But we're all going to be fine.'

'I know.' Kit's expression neared serene. 'I'm neither unsettled nor nervous, it's all wonderful.' She went on combing her hair.

Marc stepped towards her. 'Kit, you've had a big year,' he said. 'We know that.'

Kit extended her neck as the knot laced itself up towards her skull.

'This year,' Marc said, 'you woke up.'

A braid … or a bun?

'Not only did you wake up, you *got* up. You explored. You looked around, sought more, then shit went down. Dad got sick, certain things didn't work out, you realised that nothing out there is predictable, and you got scared.'

Kit leaned forward to check her teeth in the mirror.

Marc yanked her back by the arm. 'Wake the fuck up,' he said. 'If you don't get your head back out of this hole you're going to suffocate, and no one in this room wants to watch you wither and die.'

Kit pulled away but Marc grabbed her, hugged her tightly and squeezed. 'Kit, admit it, *you do not love Scott.*'

Kit stared angrily up at him, struggling, and shouted, 'What the fuck would you know about love? You fuck anything that moves!'

She expected Marc to flinch and release her but he didn't. His hold was like quicksand and the more she struggled the tighter it got.

'Even on my wedding day I *will* punch you,' she spat.

Marc released her, arms wide. 'Yes! Yes! Punch me! Hit me hard so that I know there's an ounce of my sister still alive in there.'

Kit ran out into the hall and didn't look back.

Carpet, floorboards, decking, gravel, her bare feet carried her to her car and she leapt inside.

The gate into the old sheep's paddocks was closed but unfastened. Kit bashed the Defender through and at the shearers' quarters, left the car running and got out.

Grapevines fell down hills in the distance, wind swept up them, and Kit's dress rustled as she walked towards the shearers' quarters, found cobwebs spanning the partially open doorway and saw that leaf litter had gathered beyond the threshold.

A marble pastry tile, mismatched kitchen implements, radio atop books ... all Raph had left behind shared a dust blanket.

Half-full bottles stood like sentinels on top of the fridge, and Kit took one, felt the residue of the decaying room cover her palm and wiped her hand on her dress. She put the bottle to her lips, alcohol burned her throat and she winced, wiped her mouth, and tugged open the fridge door.

Old butter sat forlorn on a shelf inside and she retrieved it.

She went to the small pantry, heard something scuttle, tugged the cupboard wide, and found flour. White trailed from mouse holes as she dragged the bag of finely ground wheat onto the bench. A flour cloud billowed as she upturned the bag.

Air sputtered in the pipe as she turned on the tap, filled a jar, and upturned the water onto the flour. She tore silver skin off the butter and engulfed the yellow flesh with her fist, scrunched until the canary-yellow fat slid through her fingers and her fingernails cut into her palm.

She smashed it onto the bench, reached for a rolling pin, and the tired shaft dented the timber bench as she beat the butter to nothing, then mashed the flour with her hands.

Finally she screamed and cracked the marble tile against the sink.

She spun around and saw *Walden*, forlorn atop Raph's pile of forgotten books.

She fell to her knees.

She crawled forward and appraised the book like a dog might a bone, then rested her head upon it.

She lifted the book from the stack and the grease on her fingers collected the grit from the cover.

Pages fanned. Dust drifted.

Kit rose and her legs carried her to the bedroom and up onto the bed.

Raph Arenberg.

Pencil named the owner.

Notes and underlines … grey pencil filled the pages:

'Every morning was a cheerful invitation to make my life of equal simplicity, and I may say innocence, with Nature herself.'

'We need the tonic of wildness – to wade sometimes in marshes where the bittern and the meadow-hen lurk … we require that all things be mysterious and unexplorable, that land and sea be infinitely wild …'

Every word he'd valued by way of a pencil line, she read.

'If a man does not keep pace with his companions, perhaps it is because he hears a different drummer.'

There was a shadow at the bedroom door. Kit's stomach turned over. She glanced down and up again but he was still there.

She pressed her finger to the page she wished to read and stared down at it. The shadow stayed. Her eyes rose once more, saw that he remained, and the book slid from her hand.

Raph walked forward and picked it up. He dusted his hand across the cover and sat it on the nightstand. Kit wanted to speak but had no words.

He turned back, gave her a once-over, glanced around the room, then began to move things about.

'*What* are you doing?' Kit finally managed.

He lifted the edge of the mattress then yanked at the nightstand's unwilling drawer. 'Getting things.'

Kit didn't know what was happening so repeated his last word in a hollow whisper. '*Things* …?'

'Yes, that I left. Don't worry, I'm not staying. I'm on my way to the airport.'

'You've come … to get … *things*?'

'My dog, my–'

'*Dog?*' Kit felt like she was coming to. She slowly pulled herself upright on the bed. 'Your dog?' she said again. 'It's … it's too late for that. That dog's Dad's now.'

Raph stared at her longer than she expected then pulled something from his pocket. 'Give that to Connor.' He put an envelope on the nightstand, then shunted about the room, searching for something.

'Here it is, now you can leave.' Kit waved *Walden* at him.

Raph ignored her. 'Stand up, please,' he said.

Kit didn't move.

'Move, please,' he said. Kit slid reluctantly sidewards, but the mattress beneath her was bare. Raph crouched, peered under the bed, swore, then glanced about. His gaze finally fell on Kit.

He began to speak, then cleared his throat. 'You're wearing it,' he said.

Kit looked down at herself, at the cascades of wedding white. She didn't know what he meant.

She watched as Raph slowly came forward and suddenly she knew.

Her hand snapped to her wrist, covered the watch that had been there almost every day since she'd found it. Her cheeks warmed, fingers fumbling as she tried to free herself from the part of him she'd shamefully held onto. She wanted to throw it across the room and watch it shatter, see his face when it did. Her nails pried at the steel, the clasp was rigid, unmoving.

Raph reached out. His fingers took the catch on the back of his watch. He almost undid it, then paused, and the timepiece settled back against her skin.

She stared at his hand as it went to her wrist.

His finger touched the soft skin that covered her veins, began to move, his single finger became fingers, his fingers became his hands, and both hands gripped Kit's arms as his gaze met hers.

'I hate you,' Kit said.

Raph tried to pull away but she grabbed his neck, wanting to cry, to scream, to have and hurt him. He took her wrists and pinned her back against the bed, eyes searching her face and Kit saw the wild man she'd wanted so long, so much.

She struggled.

He loosened his grip but that wasn't what she wanted.

She arched her body towards his and he released her wrists, seized her, pulled her against him, and as he kissed her, she wrapped her legs around him.

Raph lifted and swung her against the wall. The sound of chiffon shredding on splinters brought her near to climax.

He lifted her hem, pushed inside her and she screamed and grabbed at him as she came.

He held her there, breath raging, skin damp, and she felt a separation between body and mind as she began to fall, caught by the softness of the bed, and there she sank, drifted, and knew only one thing: that until that day, that moment, she had never known herself.

32

Kit woke to the sound of bird's claws on the old tin roof.
She was alone, her body splayed out. She shifted, then slowly rolled over and came to sit. The fabric that clothed her looked like snow that had been visited by animals, children, a cook, a chimney sweep …

Everything was still and Kit knew he'd gone. She glanced about the room.

On the nightstand was the envelope he'd left, and she crawled across the bed to retrieve it. The packet was fat in her hand as she read the name that addressed the front. *Connor.*

She turned the envelope over, broke the seal, and removed the wad of paper inside.

A letter with the day's date preceded the rest.

Connor,
I came by to pick up my remaining belongings, as well as to leave this note and package.
Please accept my apology for the overdue nature of this and for my sudden departure. It was necessary to achieve the

delivery of the enclosed: an ownership contract for the lands and orchards of Cannock Chase.

Let me firstly say that in regards to AGVM's assailing of Gossard Range, I am in part responsible and for that I apologise. A year ago my father announced two wishes: one, to retire; two, for me to lead AGVM. Things have since been difficult.

To explain, despite its privileges, my life has long existed within the walls of my father's. It wasn't until I took stock a year ago that I realised how little of my life was mine and how little of it I enjoyed.

My mother, whom you do not know, is an enigmatic, pagan character, the kind of woman my father will never understand, and one whom he has never paid adequate respect. Until recently, when he offered me the leadership baton, I hadn't realised how much of my mother's way of being I had been denied. When I did realise, it came with the understanding that her *values were the ones that inspired, she was my most valuable influence, and it was a life like the one she has led, not my father's, that held any meaning to me.*

Dialogue between my father and I eventually failed and I took leave from the company.

'You want room for your thoughts to get into sailing trim and run a course or two before they make their port,' a wise man once said, and this was what I needed, room.

I sought solitude but power is my father's most valued asset. He could not understand my so easily giving it up and he used, and still uses, his power to remind me of the power I have lost in the hope that this will see me rejoin him.

I sought Gossard Range because I knew that within your borders was the last place in which my father would seek me. I also knew that, ironically or not, it would be a place where I'd find a kind of comfortable familiarity.

I hoped only to stay long enough to gather my thoughts but instead, found myself belonging, and your shearers' quarters became a haven in which I felt I may, one day, have found myself.

Unfortunately, my father became aware not only of my whereabouts, but of your intentions for Cannock Chase. I presume he delighted in acquiring land and ventures intended for you, whilst also parading his power in front of me, showing me what he wields that I cannot, unless I'm by his side.

It was for this reason that I left Gossard Range at speed and without explanation. I apologise for the lack of warning in this regard, but I did not want to entangle you more than was necessary, nor offer you potentially empty hope regarding Cannock Chase. I admit that a part of me also hoped I could return, still anonymous, and carry on the life I'd come to enjoy.

I'm glad however that I am not offering you false hope today. The enclosed deeds to Cannock Chase are irrevocably yours. News of the demand for Gossard cider has reached me, so I can only assume that the world-class orchards offered by Cannock Chase are not something you will pass up. Much fulfilment of my father's wishes was required for me to procure these deeds, so do please accept them.

I was distressed to hear of your ill health and I'm pained to think that I may have been the cause of it. I apologise again for my long period of camouflage, but I hope you now understand

my need for it. During my time at Gossard, you facilitated my
better coming to know myself as a son and man and for that, I
thank you.

The above said and done, I can leave you and your family in
peace.

Yours,

Raph

Kit stared at the sign-off.

She folded the letter, put it in the envelope, saw *Walden* where
Raph had left it on the nightstand, and when she picked it up she
noticed he had left his watch, too.

She slid it off her wrist and turned it over.

For Raphaël, from your dad, Elliott.

She glanced at the time. She'd been asleep for two hours and
it was twenty minutes until the ceremony. She gazed at the letter,
her hands … the dress.

The claws on the roof had stopped and in their place: rain.
Pellets of water were thunking slowly and steadily on tin, and Kit
turned to the small square window to see flecks of water become
sheets, and then there was no distinction between the sound of
one drop and the next.

She put her hand to the back of the Delpozo dress, felt the
fabric hanging in shreds, and found skin where there shouldn't
have been any. On the wall, white threads danced on nail and
splinter, snagged where Raph had held her.

The dress came off, an oilskin coat slid on, and, a handful of
white silk in one hand, *Walden* and the watch in the other, she
left the hut and reversed the Defender down the drive.

She parked a distance from the homestead and slid on foot around the side of the house until she reached the citrus grove.

Everyone was huddled by the tables, sheltered beneath the canvas canopy. Kit saw Piper on the outskirts checking her phone, and willed her to look her way. She stared from behind the lemon tree but when Piper refused to look, Kit plucked a piece of fruit, pitched it, then ducked to hide … and waited.

A hand landed on Kit's arm. Piper was there, ushering Kit further behind the bush.

'Christ! I've been trying to call you – where the hell did you go?'

Kit watched the rain build in Piper's hair then stream down her face. She started to smile and Piper, after at first seeming uncertain, smiled too.

'Tell me honestly …' she began, slow and serious. 'Have you just taken drugs?'

Kit smiled, slowly.

'Have you?' Piper frowned as she looked Kit over. 'What's with that coat? Where's your dress?'

'I think it's broken.'

'Broken …?'

'A little broken, yes.'

There was a beat before Piper's hand rose high over her head and she said, 'High. Fucking. Five.' Kit's hand rose to meet Piper's and their palms slapped wetly together, clasp soggy and tight. 'So what's the plan?'

'I don't have one.' Kit glanced to the gathering and saw Scott, patient in his tux.

'They think you're getting ready,' Piper said. 'Except Marc, he's out searching for you.'

Kit wiped the water off her face. 'Could …' she began, 'could you get Scott to meet me in the car?'

'In your car?'

'Out the front,' Kit said, and Piper began jogging back to the gathering.

Water streamed from Kit as she returned to the Defender, squelched into the driver's side, and watched little puddles form at her feet.

There she waited … time slow … car silent. Water blanketed the vehicle like a cocoon. Through it she saw the front door of the homestead open, and Scott appear.

He popped an umbrella, strode towards the car, pulled the passenger door open, caught a hit of rain, and swiped water from his face as he clambered in.

'Kit.' He stared at her, eyes wild.

She gazed at him.

'Kit?'

She leaned over and gently kissed his mouth. 'You look nice.'

He gave her a once-over. 'You look like shit.'

Kit laughed.

'Where's your dress?'

'Your feet are on it.'

'What the fuck!'

Kit leaned forward, tugged then brushed ineffectually at the thing with her hand before she met his gaze.

'Scott …' she began. 'You're such an amazing person.'

'Oh Jesus Christ,' he said.

'What?'

'I *knew* you would do this.'

'What?'

'Fuck it up and throw it all away.'

'Scott–'

'I knew it. You've been feigning love for me for months – months and *months*. I've been wondering what the fuck you've been doing. I thought I was going insane.'

Scott had noticed. He never noticed anything.

'You knew?'

'I'm not a fucking idiot!' he said.

'But … do you really care about me, Scott?'

'*Jesus*, Kit!'

'I mean do you *really* care about *me*?'

He stared at her.

'*Me.*' She thumped her chest with her fist.

'*Me!* Me! Me!' Scott shouted. 'What the fuck are you talking about?'

'No, not "me, me, me"!' Kit shouted. '*Me!* You only care about me in relation to you. You only care about me in relation to *your* life, in relation to *your* work. I don't think you do actually care about *me.*'

'Are you out of your fucking mind?'

Kit stared at him.

'I give you everything you need …' Scott was almost panting, bewildered.

'And what is that?' Kit said.

'I don't know? Everything? A home. Friendship. Guidance. Inspiration. Support. I–'

'Yes.' Kit took his hand. 'Yes, you give me those things. I'm so thankful for your friendship, guidance and support. I love those things–'

'So what the fuck are you talking about?'

Kit turned to the window, before she glanced back. 'Freedom and inspiration,' she said. 'I don't get that from you.'

'Here we fucking go–'

'How can you inspire me, Scott? How can you let me be who I need to be when you don't understand me?'

'Fucking hell.'

'You don't really love *me*, you never touch *me*, you don't want to get to know *me*. You like the *idea* of me, you like me when I like you, you like me when I fit in with you. I'm not blaming you. It's my fault. I thought I wanted these things. I thought I'd be happy if I fitted in. I thought how we were was how I wanted it. I thought if I compromised, let myself be led, I'd find my way.'

'Of course you have to *compromise*,' Scott spat. 'It's called being in a fucking *relationship*.'

'Do you compromise? Have you ever compromised?'

'I've never had to! We've always been going the same way.'

'I don't want to go that way anymore!'

'And what fucking way do you want to go?'

'My way.'

'Jesus, you're so selfish.'

'No, Scott, you're selfish. You've only ever wanted to be in a relationship that's about you.'

There was silence.

'I think we should go the ways we want to go,' Kit finally said.

'And what's that supposed to mean?'

'It means that we might have to go different ways … separately.'

Scott shook his head. 'I have no idea what the fuck you want.'

'This.' Kit lifted her shredded wedding dress and knew that if she smelled it, it would smell like rain … and sex. 'This is what I want.'

'And what's that?' Scott spat, exasperated. 'Something that was perfect that now you've trashed! That's exactly what you've got, Kit, that's what we've got, that's what we are.'

'No, Scott. What I want is passion, I want filth, I want the unexpected, I want the vandalism of all things right and correct, I want–'

'Then you're absolutely right,' Scott said. 'You want exactly what I cannot give you. You want everything I'm not, and I think you've known that for a long time.'

'This goes two ways! It's not me you want or love.' Kit started to cry. She watched Scott cover his trembling mouth with his hand. 'I'm sorry,' she whimpered and reached for him.

He couldn't reply but he nodded, squeezed her hand and finally said, 'I'm sorry too.'

Their families appeared under the portico of the Gossard homestead. They stood shoulder to shoulder, necks craned, each trying to not be pushed into the rain. Kit was glad the windscreen had fogged.

Scott suddenly gave a short laugh. 'Jesus,' he said, 'I knew you'd fuck with me.'

'Scott …'

'I'm sorry,' he shook his head, and there was silence before he spoke again. 'I guess I just mean that I've never quite understood you. Just the other day I was asking my agent, saying that you'd done, or said … something … and I didn't get it, and thought a woman might, but even she–'

Kit surprised herself with a laugh. 'Your agent Alexi? Oh my God. You two understand each other better than anyone could understand either of you. You're the same. Of course neither of you would understand me.'

Scott frowned like he didn't like what she was implying.

'I'm sorry. It just seems so obvious now. Alexi.'

'There's nothing going on if that's what you're insinuating.'

'No, no,' Kit said. 'It's just that you and she … I hadn't realised before how perfect you are for each other.'

Scott scowled and looked away but his face twitched and Kit guessed that maybe this wasn't the first time he'd thought it. They were silent before Scott leaned forward, then, with his finger he scrawled slowly backward in the fog on the windscreen:

Not Just Married & Never Will Be

He looked at Kit, they smiled at each other through tears, and even from within the car and at a distance, they heard the murmur rise up.

They sat around the table, drips rolling off the canopy despite the rain having ceased.

Kit's respect for Scott remained. The respect was mutual and their conversation stayed between only them.

That a wedding had been skipped and that their close friends and families now ate food intended for a reception may not have gone unnoticed, but the group's silence was an improbably congenial one.

Kit sank into the peculiar comfort that her mother's food bestowed. Piper sat in the groom's chair beside her, Scott between the two mothers who both doted on him.

Kit cocked her head to see the pale curve of Piper's cheek. She knew that there were no words worthy, but said anyway, 'You stuck by me.'

Piper's cheek rippled into a grin. 'Well, I really couldn't have conceived of you losing your shit like you did,' she said. 'But, I think once a person finally loses enough shit, then they find something.'

'I love you, P,' she said.

Marc's head peered through from behind. 'What am I missing?'

'Just the wise musings of your baby boat.' Kit patted Piper's stomach. 'And I would thank you, too, but the only reason you were ever born was to keep me on the straight and narrow–'

'Or *off* the straight and narrow.' Marc sniffed. Kit reached out and took his hand and he added, 'So where were you for two and a half hours while I crawled the valley-side looking for you?'

Kit took a mouthful of food so that she wouldn't have to answer. She still wore the oilskin – Raph's envelope padding the inner breast pocket. 'I'll tell you later,' she said to Marc, then got up and walked towards their father.

'Hello darling.' Connor patted the arm of his chair as she neared. 'I must say that's an unusual choice of wedding dress.' He eyed the damp, brown wax of the coat as Kit sat down.

'I thought you'd like it,' Kit said.

'Yes, just my thing.'

'I have a surprise for you,' she said and Connor looked nervous.

'No offence,' he said, 'but I'm not sure I can take many more surprises from you today, darling.'

'This won't distress you, I promise.' Kit reached into the jacket, withdrew the dry envelope and handed it to him.

He read out loud: 'Connor ...'

33

The wind moved gently through the branches of the apple trees.

Kit watched her father in the distance – bend and reach, bend and reach – as he inspected leaves, bark, fruit and soil. It was the day after the wedding and the air was still damp, the new foliage was washed clean.

'It's a shame,' Connor strode back towards her. 'No one's been here since Earl sold it. It all needs a bit of TLC.'

'But it's yours,' Kit said.

'Yes,' Connor sounded uncertain. 'Though I'm not sure how I feel about that. Poor Raph, what he must have gone through … he didn't do this out of love for *me*, that I know.'

'I think that's exactly why he did it.' Kit's eyes roamed the orchard before they settled back on Connor. 'He obviously has a lot of respect for you.'

Connor rolled up his sleeves. 'There's more to it than that, Kit, we both know that.'

Kit didn't know that. She didn't know anything. Raph was gone. He'd left her in the shearers' quarters. He'd left her, his dog, his watch, his book and the deeds to Cannock Chase, and gone.

Kit had tried to make him feel hated and it had worked – she'd pushed him away.

'I wonder what he'll do now.' Connor's arm folded as he scanned the trees. 'I wish he'd given me the envelope in person, we could have spoken.'

Kit stared at the ground.

'Well.' Connor put his arm around her. 'Big year, eh?'

'Big year.'

'And what's next, hm? Where are you headed?'

'Somewhere fun?' Kit kept her voice light, her arbitrary words for Connor's sake only.

'For me, perhaps a new batch of cider? More truffles? Nuts? I'll have to head up and see how the rail tunnel's looking.'

Annalese wasn't in the house when Kit and Connor returned. Kit found her outside, packing down the wedding tables.

'I'll do that,' she said. 'I'll do it before I go.'

'No,' Annalese replied. 'I know where everything goes.'

They hadn't really spoken yet and Kit wondered if they'd ever speak again. Her mother had wanted so many things that Kit had failed to deliver.

She took a few steps then stopped. 'Mum–'

'You don't need to say anything, darling.'

Kit hesitated.

'I understand.' Annalese kept working and Kit wondered if this was a test, wondered if she should stay or go.

Annalese looked Kit in the eye then walked towards her, hands up. Kit flinched but the hands gently settled on her arms.

'You and I …' Annalese began. 'We're different.'

Kit wanted to laugh at how true the statement was.

'That man,' Annalese said, 'Raph – the winery hand – he was a calibre I didn't understand ...'

Kit tried to grasp what was happening.

'I'm one for becoming fixated on trivialities,' Annalese said. 'I really just saw all the social and material provisions that Scott offered. I couldn't have imagined anybody better suited to you than Scott.'

Kit was failing to work it out. She'd have to wait.

'But when I saw you yesterday,' Annalese said. 'When you emerged on your wedding day – no dress, sodden, dirty, hair like a nest and eyes brighter than I'd ever seen – I understood. I understood that I didn't understand. I understood that I don't know you, Kit.'

Kit stared.

'I've always wanted you to be someone you weren't. Do you know why?'

Kit knew this wasn't a question.

'I can't be sure ... but sometimes I think it's for lack of imagination. Any time in your life that I saw you straying off what I saw as the right course, I thought you were making a mistake. But the reality, I see now, is that you were off on your way to something much bigger. Somewhere different to anything I could ever imagine or understand.' She paused to search Kit's face and Kit blinked at the unfamiliar woman in front of her. 'I'm sorry I've held you back.'

'Mum ...' It took Kit a moment to find words. 'You haven't held me back.'

Annalese tittered. 'No, I suppose I haven't. Look at you! Look at the man you fell for. An *Arenberg*? I thought *I* was a gold-digger! I don't know how you saw the glint through the filth.' Kit's gaze fell. 'I'm joking,' her mother added, quickly. 'You're not as silly and acquisitive as me ... You're a good girl, Kit, and I don't mean well-behaved. I wish you were well-behaved but I think maybe you're good in other ways. That might have to be enough.'

Kit allowed her mother to walk her out.

The ruins of the Delpozo dress were still on the floor of her car and Kit's hand tangled in the still-moist fabric as she tried to tuck it out of sight.

Annalese told her not to bother. 'I've already seen it.' Her voice was familiarly strained. 'I came out last night to see where you'd put it and see whether – despite whatever you'd done – it could be saved, with drycleaning.'

'The dress or the wedding?'

'Well, I do know a bloody good drycleaner ...' Annalese smiled and Kit laughed.

'I'm sorry about ... that,' Kit said. 'I did love that dress, it was beautiful.'

The ragged white shreds lolled from their grave under the seat.

'It was.' Annalese sighed. 'You looked lovely in it.'

'Another day, perhaps.'

'I'm not having *anything* to do with your next wedding, darling.'

'Thank God,' Kit teased and Annalese rolled her eyes.

Finally, Kit climbed into the Defender. Annalese closed the door, Kit fanned a wave and her mother blew her a kiss.

Kit braked. She wound down the window.

'Please don't be so nice,' she said. 'It makes me nervous.'

'Oh shut up,' Annalese said.

2

Kit lay in bed, blinking at the clock. Gertrude Street was noisy.

Scott's home had recently become her own, so the Gossards' Gertrude Street apartment had gone unused, and now it felt like it.

The unfamiliar smell of her own duvet was disorienting. Kit wondered if she should have stayed at Marc's cottage back on the estate. He'd offered, but despite the comfort he and Piper would provide, she needed to be by herself, to think and find her bearings.

The world she found herself in felt old, whereas she herself felt new. She was raw and unbranded, her reality unfamiliar – she had to be alone to come to terms with it.

She stared at the clock until, with the faint scent of sourdough, her stomach compelled her to rise.

'Newlywed!' Beth, the owner of the downstairs bakery reminded Kit that other people knew something of her life. The woman threw her arms wide, then clapped, repeating, 'Newlywed, newlywed, newlywed!'

Kit shook her head.

The woman's expression began to fall. Kit nodded, encouraging it to fall completely, and the woman's face was blank by the time Kit met her at the counter.

'You and … Scott?' the woman stammered.

'No …' Kit said.

'No?'

'I'm not married. I'm sorry.'

The woman's hand went to her mouth, a gaggle of staff came to flank her. The well-meaning faces that Kit saw almost daily, stared, eyes wide.

'It's fine.' Kit almost laughed. 'It wasn't meant to be, it's all fine.'

'What happ–' the owner began, then, 'are you alright?' She reached for Kit's shoulder.

'Yes, yes.' Kit realised her smile might seem callous and said simply, 'I'm fine … we're fine. Our parting was a long time coming … obviously bad timing, but …' She laughed, but the marionettes in sweet little hemp aprons covered their mouths.

'I'm fine, really.' Kit didn't laugh again. 'Don't feel bad, Scott and I are in a good place.'

'Where is he?' one said, and Kit realised how alone she must seem. She went there most mornings with Scott, for bread and coffee, and that she was now alone must make her seem vulnerable … and exposed.

'He's–' Kit hesitated. 'I'd guess he's on his way to Italy,' she said, and there was a sad, group exhalation as though they'd hoped for redemption and Italy had thwarted it.

'He'll be back,' Kit said. Their eyes brightened and *she* felt sad. 'I'm sure he'll be back. His place is just up the road, and you've got the best bread in the neighbourhood.'

The owner suddenly scattered the flock, bustled through

to the baskets that lined the back wall, and stuffed loaves into paper bags.

'Seeded sourdough and a spiced fruit.' She squeezed Kit's hand as she gave the bags to her. 'Gratis. And come down for a chat any time. We're always here.'

Kit walked out onto the pavement. She'd wanted a macchiato but had wanted to escape more.

'I didn't expect to see you up and about this morning, *Mrs* Scott!' Robert, a camp neighbour, tripped over his dogs' leads in front of her as he tottered forward for a kiss. 'I suppose an appetite does rouse one from even the *sexiest* of times.' He patted her loaves. 'How was the big day? Photos?'

Kit stared down at his dogs. 'Big,' she smiled. 'A big day.'

'Did you look *amazing*?'

'At … times.'

'Oooo. *Wardrobe* troubles?'

'A few …'

He tittered as though this thrilled him. 'Well, I expect photos ASAP. But I'll let you get back to your beautiful *husband* for now, and tell him yes, I'm still keen on those Louis Ghost chairs he's getting rid of.'

Kit watched the dogs shepherd the man up the street then she walked upstairs to the apartment, sat on the couch and ate bread from the bag while staring at the wall.

There was a knock on the door. Felicity from over the road appeared surprised when Kit answered.

'I didn't expect to see you!' She beamed. 'I was just going to push this through your mail chute.' She handed Kit a small gift with a wedding card attached. 'Congratulations to you!'

'No ...' Kit said, as she'd said to the bakery owner and should have said to the doggy neighbour. 'I'm so sorry but Scott and I called off the wedding.'

Felicity didn't seem to know what to say. Kit pressed the gift back into her hands. 'Thank you, that was such a kind gesture but I can't take it.'

Felicity began to speak then instead took Kit's hands and magnanimously laid the gift back in them. 'No, you take it, it's yours,' she said. She closed her eyes, her hands encircling Kit's, and Kit waited as they shared what she assumed was meant to be a moment of grief.

Eventually, Felicity let go of her, beamed again, and turned to go down the stairs.

જી

The person's flesh reminded Kit of cottage cheese. She watched the white, soft dimples and, as a mist hovered around them, wondered what this stranger might have looked like young.

She'd walked a short way from the apartment to her long-standing place of respite. Now, as the naked woman opposite wiped sweat off her own face, Kit wondered if she was seeing her own future: an aged woman alone in a Japanese bath house.

There would be worse things than being alone now. She'd now known unimpeded passion and honoured her deepest desire. She'd taken what she wanted from Raph and left Scott behind. If she had to be alone forever now at least she'd been true to herself.

She closed her eyes, heard her wedding dress shredding on nails, and opened them again.

The unknown woman lifted herself from the water. Kit watched the body ripple hypnotically as it lumbered onto the tiles, then shut her eyes again.

34

Life began to return to normal.

Connor and Marc were occupied at the winery, Piper with *Hamper*, Annalese with very little.

Kit wondered what her normal was now, wondered how she was going to return to it. She felt like a child on holidays with the adults still at work.

She wondered if Rosa had tried to call again and considered removing the block on her number, but didn't. Rosa was forever bound to Raph and that was not a problem Kit knew how to solve.

She didn't tell Piper what happened in the shearers' quarters on her wedding day. Piper would encourage her to go after Raph, to repair, redeem and reconcile after all his letter had revealed, but Kit couldn't. Her feelings for Raph had always been deep and powerful. But now knowing exactly who he was, she realised how many women in the world must feel the exact same way about him. Everything about Raph might now be known to her but did she really know him?

Kit wouldn't chase Raph Arenberg.

She would find the strength to explore a life of her own making, not one made by others.

'A job? At the bath house?' Piper said.

'Yes,' Kit replied.

'Why? What's there? What will you be doing?'

'I don't know,' Kit said. 'Whatever they want me to.'

'I thought only Japanese people worked there.'

'I had the requisite aura … They like me.'

'Why?'

'Why do they like me?'

'No, why are you working there? Why don't you call Rosa? Have you heard from her? You could do anything you want to …'

❧

Kit didn't need to do what she wanted to, she needed to do what she needed.

The solitude of the bath house made her feel uncomfortable and that made it the exact place she needed to be. For hours she went without talking. The simplicity and discipline of the place made her feel lonely, and for that reason she stayed.

Self-containment: she would perfect it.

A life unaffected by others: she would achieve it.

A call came through some weeks into her employment.

'Kit!' the caller said when Kit answered. 'It's Sarah, from Henry Publishing. I was calling because Rosamonde Mich–'

Kit feigned reception loss by muffling the phone's mouthpiece as she cut the call short, then she blocked Rosa's publisher's number, too.

Kimono robes, shiatsu and tea rituals.

Rice paper, tatami, calligraphy, timber, lacquered black.

Starched towels folded in half, into quarters, into eighths.

Slippers were tucked into pigeonholes, legs were crossed on the floor and the days at the bath house ticked by.

☙

A familiar woman entered a bathing suite not long before closing. The cottage-cheese body seemed to bob before it settled into the bath.

Kit said, 'How are you?' because the woman seemed alone, like she felt.

The woman sighed, then her face changed as she smiled. 'I'm so happy to have a moment to myself!' she announced.

Suddenly Kit recognised her. 'Oh, Dova,' she said. The woman laughed, embarrassed to be recognised in the nude.

'Sorry,' Kit put up a hand, 'we've met – we actually met some time ago – at those magazine awards, I was your biggest fan …'

'Oh – yes,' Dova's face brightened. 'Yes, you work for *Hamper*. I remember your lovely face. You were married to that designer – I have his candelabra.' She seemed pleased to have recalled so much.

'Scott–'

'Baldwin, yes.' Dova clapped, puzzle complete, and Kit wondered whether to tell her that she didn't work for *Hamper* nor had ever married Scott.

'So, you're in town again?' She chose to postpone the telling. 'For work?'

'Yes,' Dova sighed. 'I'm contracted for a shoot nearby. I had no idea this bath house was here but thank goodness! What a discovery! I wish I knew of something similar in Cape Town.'

'Cape Town? Is that where you're based?' Kit perched on the edge of the bath.

'Yes, with my husband and our triplets. We had IVF five years back and our family of two became five overnight!' She hooted and Kit smiled. 'And would you believe that they're all out here with me, at our short-stay? I come here every day after work just for one single hour alone. I mean I know most people wouldn't drag their family halfway around the world, but work now means nothing to me without my family and my family seems a chore without my work. Life's too short to deny myself, I figure, so I indulge in everything!' She sank low in the water, monologue complete. 'Are you getting in?'

'Oh –' Kit faltered '– no I'm working – I work here.'

Dova looked confused. 'I thought you were a photographer? Don't you work at *Hamper* magazine?'

'No …' Kit said. 'Not anymore.'

'What's the story?' Dova frowned. 'Are you out of work?'

Kit shook her head and said, 'Not exactly, I guess I'm taking a … hiatus, of sorts.'

Dova huffed and nodded like she understood, then quieted as her gaze settled on Kit's face. 'But *is* it a hiatus?' she said, suddenly.

'Or are you opting out? Because if it's the latter, give that up right now. I'm not big on advice but I do rate joy and there's not a lot of that on your face. You look … lonely, to be plain.'

Kit quickly stood and tidied Dova's towel to distract herself from a need to cry.

'Sweetheart.' Dova tried to catch Kit's eye. 'Life's a mess. Once you embrace that, you'll be able to get on with it.'

Kit couldn't speak but nodded to show she'd heard. 'Well … I'll let you get back to your hour of alone time,' she finally said.

'Yes … and I would say that I'll see you same time tomorrow but I kind of hope I won't, if you get my meaning.'

Kit managed a laugh as she pressed the neat towel down onto the tiles and walked away.

The next morning, Kit arrived at work, walked to where Dova had been, and stared at the empty bath.

By removing herself from life, Kit had thought that she'd grow independent and thrive, but Dova was proof that the reverse could be true. Despite the apparent tunnel-vision dedication and independence that Dova's work implied, her life was chaotic and filled with others.

Kit turned, walked away, signed out at reception, and never returned.

❧

The number sat in the list of answered calls on Kit's phone. She gazed at it, then dialled.

'Henry Publishing, Sarah speaking.'

'Sarah, it's Kit Gossard.'

There was a pause. 'Oh, Kit! You exist!' Sarah sounded surprised. 'How are you?'

'I'm well,' Kit said. 'And you?'

'Great, great. I've been trying to reach you all week.'

'Sorry. Problems with my phone …'

'I hate that!' Sarah laughed and Kit mimicked it. 'So … a week or so ago our Paris arm called. They were chasing a Kit Gossard, they linked you to Gossard Range, and they thought we might be able to hunt you down. I drink a lot of Gossard wine but had no idea you yourself were a photographer! I love your online magazine.'

Kit wavered.

'*Hunger*?' Sarah prompted.

'Oh, yes–'

'It's incredible.'

'I–'

'Why have you stopped doing it? I see you've been curating a furniture design site with someone called Scott–'

'Both projects are actually dormant now.'

'Why? Why didn't you publish more issues of *Hunger*? Excuse the candour, but your furniture photography pales in comparison …'

Kit hesitated long enough that Sarah spoke again.

'Have you heard of us before? Henry Publishing?'

'Um … non-fiction?'

'Yes, high-end coffee table books mainly, food, art, design. Rosamonde Michel is our bestseller and I hear she's a friend of yours.'

Kit smiled. She was ready to accept the offer. She inhaled …

'It was Rosa who put you on our radar,' Sarah spoke first. 'Paris are in the midst of producing her new book and she's stalling until she has the photographer she's after … you, I'm told. Now I'm looking at your photos and I see why she's waiting. Your work's sexy stuff.'

'Thank you … Rosa actually asked me some months ago to shoot for her and I was incredibly flattered, but things got in the way and–but now …'

To know Rosa was one thing. To be asked to work with her was another, and to turn down an opportunity many would kill for was nothing more than self-sabotage.

Dova had been right. Life was too short to deny oneself. Life was too short to be lived unaffected by others, particularly when others were Rosamonde Michel. Kit was going to say 'yes' to Rosa and she couldn't wait.

'… but now I'd be thrilled to take up the offer,' Kit finished.

Sarah seemed to falter and Kit wondered if she'd spoken too soon. She suddenly realised she had no idea why Sarah had actually called.

'You mean you'd *like* to shoot Rosa's book?' Sarah cut in.

'Well … of course, I would love to, but I understand if that's no longer–'

'No, that's *definitely* something that's still on the cards for Paris. To be honest I think it's only ever going to happen if you do it. They'd fall over themselves if you agreed.'

'I mean–well yes–I'd love to … obviously,' Kit faltered.

'But sorry,' Sarah said, 'that's not the reason I've been hounding you, funnily enough.'

There was silence.

'Sarah?' Kit said.

'Sorry!' Sarah returned. 'Sorry, I got lost in your photos. Anyway, yes. The main reason I called was because Henry Publishing has a proposal. After seeing your work, we want to produce a book based on *Hunger* by Kit Gossard. Your own book, Kit.'

35

The thick sheepskin lining of his coat curled above his collar, fringed his jaw, and his khaki Musto shooting boots left footprints in the shallow snow.

Fingertips numb, Kit fumbled with her lens focus and brought her target into range. His mouth and nose were pink from cold …

He adjusted the weight of the animal across his shoulders then walked towards the bench, swung the boar down, brushed his shoulders, checked his rifle and walked towards the building.

Kit stood still, waiting as he disappeared into the house.

She slid from her hiding place and walked to what he'd left behind. Blood dripped from the boar's head, crimson freckling the white snow.

She positioned herself on her back beneath the bench. The animal became nothing more than pinstripes of coarse, brown hair, lines divided by slats of timber, trotters hung off one end of the bench. Kit gathered the hairy rows and hooves into a shot.

The house door opened. Kit lay still, listening as cold radiated from the snow at her back.

The door closed again and she cocked her head, saw boots. The boots sunk one after the other into the thin carpet of white and Kit watched, heart drumming. The footsteps arced away from her but Kit stayed motionless until she heard a vehicle start then drive away. She rested back, pulse slowing.

It was always going to be a risk, coming back to The Priory. But for now the risk had passed.

He'd come and gone, the danger momentary, and now she was alone again, with Rosa.

Almost two months had gone by since Kit had agreed to shoot Rosa's book, as well as signed on with Henry Publishing to produce her very own.

Henry Publishing had loved what they'd seen. They'd said they'd not seen a collection like it – photography that concerned food but not remotely cooking. Now *Hunger* – the book – would soon be realised.

Kit crawled from under the garden bench and walked towards the kitchen door.

Rosa turned from the sink. 'My son came by, you only just missed him,' she said.

'Oh?' Kit peeled off her fingerless mittens.

'He said he killed a wild boar, did you see it?'

'Yes.'

'They're such interesting, antiquated animals … Did you get a photo?'

'Yes, I did.'

'I'll have Gabriel butcher it. Perhaps a ragu? A boar ragu with the truffle papardelle I dried in autumn … I wish I'd told Raph to wait and meet you but I was so surprised to see him I forgot.'

Kit was silent. 'We've met,' she finally said.

Rosa paused. 'Oh yes, yes of course, summer. *Kirs.* That was a lovely day.'

'How–' Kit's lips were frozen. 'How is he?'

'Raph?'

'Raph, yes.' Kit said the name as though it wasn't altogether familiar to her. 'He lives near?'

'*Dieu seul le sait!*' Rosa replied, which Kit was sure meant 'only God knows!' 'He roams. I didn't even know he was coming today until he appeared in the kitchen with a rifle in his hand.'

Kit hadn't expected to see him either.

It was early February and she'd been at The Priory for some weeks, taking the photos for Rosa's book. Rosa had once said that peach season was the only time she got to see her 'boy'. There were no peaches mid-winter but inexplicably, there'd been Raph.

'I think he's pining,' Rosa said. 'For what I don't know but he's not been himself for some time.'

Kit walked to the sink so Rosa couldn't see her face. She turned on the taps and fiddled with the temperature.

'He disappeared a year or so ago now,' Rosa said. 'At first I thought something might be wrong but then I was surprised to get a letter from him, then another, then more, and with each letter, he sounded more and more … I suppose … content.'

Kit stared at the water blanketing her hands.

'I was surprised because *contentment* and *my son* are two ideas I'd never put together. His father has seen to it that Raph carries the weight of the world on his shoulders.'

Kit stepped back from the sink and pressed her hands against a grey towel.

'But in these letters … well, he's always written eloquently but he sounded … *je ne suis pas sûr* … he sounded … different.'

Kit's eyes stayed on the weave of the smoke-grey linen. She couldn't meet Rosa's gaze because if she did, Rosa might see what Kit hid: Raph's story, the one that Rosa had just sketched but that Kit had the means to colour in.

'Then I suppose I was disappointed when he eventually appeared in early autumn and he didn't seem at all content. He was distracted and uneasy, and now – now he's distant, at best.'

Rosa sighed.

Kit dared to look at her but Rosa was gazing out the window. 'Anyway,' she said. 'Enough about that. I'm glad you got the extra photos you needed for your book. It's quite something that we got snow at all.'

Though she'd come to The Priory to take photos for Rosa, Kit had been keen to take some for herself, too. Henry Publishing had structured her *Hunger* book seasonally and the Winter quarter was lacking. Kit had hoped that visiting The Priory in the heart of winter would remedy this, and in the past two days of snow, it had.

Rosa stood up. 'A slice of *tarte aux pommes*? I used Ceylon cinnamon quills, they'll warm us.'

Kit made a coffee while Rosa cut the apple pie. They sat opposite one another at the kitchen farm table, and as though two and not twenty minutes had passed, Rosa said, 'My guess is that he's skulking at Château Rivière.'

Kit's eyes rose. 'Château Rivière?'

'I think he likes to lie low there at times. It's the old family house where Raph was raised for a time. He bought it from his father, years ago. He thought I might like it kept in the family but I don't. I haven't been back in twenty years. I can't imagine why he'd keep the place.'

'Is he–' Kit hesitated '–is he coming to the party ... tonight?'

'I *asked* him to,' Rosa sighed, 'but he won't show. He's too much like me, ventures out only under duress.'

That afternoon, Kit sat stiffly on a banquette in the main room of The Priory.

Raph wouldn't leave her mind: the wild, bloody animal ... the majestic, quiet snow.

Two staff carried an old chaise to the outskirts of the room and another appeared with an armful of magnolia branches that he began arranging in an old brass canister: all preparation for the wrap party for Rosa's book that night.

Rosa had just described Raph as distant. She'd outlined a side of him that Kit had not seen, and she thought of the joy he'd found at Gossard Range, then how it had been taken away.

She saw his boots press into the thin veil of snow, remembered the depth of his frown, sensed the pain that Rosa had described, then her insides began to cave. She'd held strong for so long but now she'd seen him, she didn't know why she'd been resisting.

She was in love with him. She was powerfully and inescapably in love and had been since he'd first said her name. She'd been resisting for reasons of prudence and pride but *life was too short to deny oneself.*

Rosa had said that Raph was pining. Kit was too, when neither needed to be.

She walked to the kitchen and told Rosa she was taking the car into the village.

Rosa could have afforded any car she wished, but she still drove the first car she'd ever owned, a 1960s Citroën Bijou that Kit thought looked like a small cream bunny with no ears.

The mottled grey sky hung low as The Priory land fell away. Kit typed the location that Rosa had unwittingly given away into her phone, and the drop-pin landed.

Château Rivière, Limeuil.

She drove onto the main road and activated her phone's navigation. The roadside was patchy white, green and brown.

The car sputtered along, low to the ground, and Kit overshot turns, turned back, turned too early, and after a good while she was on the last road – an unsealed lane that drew parallel to a small *riviere*, an offshoot of the Dordogne, where the château stood.

Château Rivière. The entry was overgrown, the way closed, and the car idled by the gates. Finally Kit shut off the engine, sat watching her breath mist in the cold air, then got out and approached the entry. The pedestrian gate was unlocked, and she started up the drive.

She could see why Rosa no longer wished to visit.

The elms that lined the drive remained impressive but the cream-yellow stone of the once-grand château was now stained sooty, and timber frames were all that remained of tall, ground-floor windows. The weeds of the former lawn had given up – flattened beneath snow – and the faint sound of the stream was the only sign of life.

Kit made her way up the drive until she reached the house. She peered in each window, but inside was as desolate as out.

Rosa had been wrong. No one had lived at Château Rivière for a long, long, time.

Kit surveyed the comatose estate. He wasn't there. Rosa hadn't promised he would be but Kit had felt he must be. Something about the way Rosa had spoken of Raph and the place felt like they would be here, together.

She took the gridded pathway towards stone outbuildings and stables by the front fence.

The atmosphere of the day was changing, the air felt no longer dry but damp, and Kit sensed it might soon rain.

She was nearly at the stables when she heard a sound.

The sound came again – a voice – and her gloves felt suddenly hot and tight as she stumbled forward, anxious, hopeful, as she realised that *of course* this forgotten corner was where he belonged.

There was movement in a low, stone window. The soft glow of a lamp lit the face of the man she'd come to find and she stepped forward …

Pale, barely clad curves filled the window as someone passed by inside.

The woman reached out, caressed Raph's hair. He reached for her, and Kit tried to look away but his head began to turn and as Kit ran, she knew he'd seen her.

The Citroën was slow to turn over. She pumped the accelerator, the engine roared, and the car shot away, down the lane from Château Rivière.

ॐ

'You were in the village a while.' Rosa had gotten ready for the party by wearing the same dress she'd been wearing for two days, adding red lipstick and brushing her hair.

Kit slid her umbrella into the stand by The Priory's front door and put the Citroën keys on the hall table. 'I'm going to have a shower before everyone arrives,' she said.

She climbed the stairs to her room, turned on the copper taps in the en-suite, then waited for the water to steam. It had been a fantasy. Elaborate, but nothing more.

Women's minds. They made men into things they were not. Kit thought she was smarter than that, but she wasn't.

Raph wasn't a wild man seeking to be tamed. He was a *wild* man, that was the end.

Why she'd thought he felt more for her than physical attraction she didn't know. He loved Gossard Range, the land, the freedom he found there. That, not Kit, was what he cared for.

Women presented themselves, men took them. Raph was no different. Kit had presented herself and he had taken her. There was nothing more to it and she'd never been given reason to think there was.

Despite the generosity and nobility he'd shown towards Connor, this was a man – an animal – who took what he wanted when he wanted it, Kit, that woman, another …

She'd given in, run to him, but he wasn't waiting, pining, wondering.

They'd fucked, she'd slept, he'd left. Lust was acceptable, love wasn't.

The story had ended.

36

Rosa's guests were being outdone by her food. No one looked or smelled as good as, or attracted more attention than, what was on the plates.

Kit stood by the back windows, watching sleet hit the woodland and picking at her four-cheese gougère as guests tumbled through the front door, laughing as they shook off the weather. Listening to everyone's French was like listening to an instrument, sound without explanation. Kit was surprised when she heard a word she recognised.

'Kit!' Edwina, Rosa's editor at Henry Publishing, touched her elbow. 'Congratulations.'

'Oh, I'm so glad you were happy with the photos,' Kit smiled.

'We were so excited! And our designers were thrilled. Your style is going to have a huge influence on the final design of the book. The photos are an inspiration.'

'I admit it is hard to take a bad photo of Rosa's food ...' Kit took a bite of her gougère.

'I doubt that, though Rosa is of course brilliant. I foresee you shooting many more books for Rosa in future.' Edwina smiled and sank toasted bread into baked brie stuffed with garlic.

Kit couldn't wait to leave the next day.

Before seeing Raph that morning she'd actually considered putting off her flight. Then she'd seen him, him with the other person, and the only place she'd wanted to go was the airport and home … home … home.

'And you're also working on your own book,' Edwina said. 'What a year it will be for you.'

Kit smiled, nodding.

'It's very exciting,' Edwina prompted. Somewhere behind them, the front door opened and closed again, and though Kit heard the sound, she didn't register it until the tone of the conversations around them began to change.

She turned her head and Edwina did the same, but they were ill-placed to see. Then Rosa laughed in surprised delight and Edwina stood on tiptoes to see what was happening by the door. 'Oh! Raph is here.'

Kit stared at her.

'Rosa's son,' Edwina explained.

Kit glanced around for an escape then hid behind a woman nearby.

The woman moved, Kit moved with her, but their movement made an opening in the throng and suddenly Kit had a clear line of sight towards him …

Beads of water glistened on the oiled shell of his shearling jacket. His boots were thick with mud. He hadn't closed his jacket and Kit could see the flesh beneath his drenched white T-shirt.

He glanced around the room. Rosa bustled forward to wrap him into a hug and he allowed it without ceasing to scan the crowd. His eyes swept over Kit … tracked back … settled upon her. He gently slid from Rosa's embrace.

Hands of greeting extended towards him as he walked through the room but he didn't see them, his eyes only on Kit.

Edwina was beside her again and she felt the woman's hand on her arm as she said, tone high, 'Kit, is he coming over?'

Just then the front door swung open. A sodden man appeared and Kit's eyes broke from Raph's to look at him. The man announced something in breathless French, so fast Kit didn't understand, and the crowd gasped, bumping into one another as they readied for some kind of action.

'*Merde.*' Edwina shoved her plate onto the sideboard. '*Merde,*' she said again. 'Albert, the head of Henry Publishing. His car's gone into a ditch.'

The assembly jostled out the front door and a dozen men jogged down the driveway, Raph at the fore.

Edwina popped an umbrella, hooked Kit's arm, and they shuffled with a second wave towards the darkness at the end of the drive. An Audi was cast sideways in the deep ditch that ran between the road and the firs that hedged the property.

The spotlights that illuminated The Priory's entry sign were enough to see by, and more men than seemed necessary climbed into the sludgy trench to wrestle the car.

Raph took hold of the driver's door, wrenching it wide. Someone reached out. Raph gripped the arms and extracted a man, who whimpered as rain caught a cut on his forehead and washed red down his face.

'Oh thank God,' Edwina said. 'He's okay.'

The men climbed from the trench, and one helped Raph support Albert up the drive. The car stayed behind in the ditch.

The party slowed when they reached The Priory steps. Kit waited as everyone squeezed through the door, and when the last person was inside, she followed and shut the door behind her.

Rosa appeared with first aid. Albert was seated by the fire looking sheepish, and someone medically minded began asking him questions as the music began, signalling to the guests that all was well.

'I can't believe that!' Edwina tittered as she offered Kit a glass of champagne.

'Thank God he's okay,' a woman said.

'It's *so* dangerous this time of year.' Another woman ate two canapés one after the other, adrenaline high.

'We should all have come in a van together from the airport!'

'I think Albert has a holiday house here and he was coming–'

The speaker stopped short. Someone had pushed in from the crowd and stood before Kit.

'Are you married?' Raph was covered in mud, water dripping from his jacket to the floorboards.

The women stared at him, then Kit.

'W-what?'

'Are you married?'

'Am I–'

'It's a simple question, the answer should be too. Are you married?'

'No,' Kit said.

Raph's eyes narrowed, jaw tight. 'Why were you in a wedding dress?' he said.

Kit blinked, overwhelmed, lagging, dizzy.

Raph repeated the query. 'Why,' he said, 'when I saw you in the shearers' quarters, were you wearing a wedding dress?'

The throng began to murmur and Kit gave an exasperated laugh. '*Why?* Because it was supposed to be my fucking wedding day!'

Raph stared before he grabbed her hand. He parted the crowd as he led her at speed from the room, through the kitchen, into the garden, and onto the stone path. When they pushed into the quiet shelter of the drystore, the springs on the door slammed it shut behind them.

He let her hand fall. 'Why did you come to my house?' he said, breathlessly.

Kit felt weak and shaken.

'Why did you come to Château Rivière?' he asked.

Kit's head shook. 'Why do you think?'

'Tell me!'

'Because I wanted to see you!'

'Why?'

Kit swore and grabbed the doorhandle but Raph held it closed. 'Why?'

'Do I *really* need to tell you?'

'Do I really need to ask again?'

'I wanted to see you because despite being rejected, later screwed and finally cast off by you, I can't seem to rid myself of you. I want you, I've always wanted you–'

Raph kissed her.

His hands held her head and fingers combed through her thick, wet hair. He tasted like something she'd forgotten and wanted to remember … forest … woodsmoke … childhood …

She pulled away. 'What are you doing?'

He frowned.

'You were just with someone else, some woman, at your house.'

'So?'

'You were just at your house fucking some other woman.'

'No, I wasn't.'

Kit's laugh was incredulous.

'I intended to, but I didn't. I saw you.'

Kit remembered his hands reaching for the flesh of the person she didn't know. 'I don't believe you,' she said.

'It's the truth.'

Kit held his eyes, waited for them to flicker away. They didn't.

'Why?' she said. 'Why have you come here?'

'Because,' Raph's gaze remained steady, 'because when I left you that day in the shearers' quarters, I thought I'd never see you again … *you* who's consumed my every thought this past year, *you* the kind of woman one never finds twice.'

The sleet beat down outside.

'When I first went to Gossard Range all I wanted was to ignore and be ignored. Then you appeared. You were categorically unignorable, and in spite of it all I had to know more. I found a woman I'd never come across before, one who was complex, enquiring, and free from pretensions, one who wanted me not because I was an Arenberg but because I was nothing like one. I'd come seeking nothing and I found everything. You interrupted my solitude and upended my resolve. You were this magnetic, earthy woman looking at me like I had something that you wanted and it was all I could do not to give it to you–'

Now Kit kissed him. She couldn't help it. His brow had been furrowed, he'd leaned in close to make sure she could hear every word he was saying, and as his mouth spoke all the words she wanted to hear she couldn't help but want to taste it.

She kissed him and after a moment, he kissed back. Their mouths slid over one another and Raph's hands seized her wrists, crushed them until it almost hurt.

His hand rose to her neck.

His fingers peeled back the damp hair that clung there and his mouth took Kit's throat. Goosebumps feathered across her skin.

He pushed at the shoulders of his coat, let it fall off his arms, then laid it out on the workbench behind them.

Kit stood still as his hands unhooked the fastening of her silk palazzo pants. Neither of them heard the rustle as they fell to the floor. Raph lifted Kit up, set her down on his jacket, and soft sheep's shearling pressed against her bare flesh.

A boning knife lay nearby. Kit watched as Raph picked it up and slid it between the skin at her hip and the lace that covered it. He tugged the blade, and the threads split apart, hung loose; he cut the other side, took the severed piece of lace between his fingers and pulled it away. He stood back to look at what he'd revealed.

Kit gazed at him, edging her legs open. He made a strange, hungry sound like she'd never heard before and came at her, cupped her vagina with his hand, her mouth with his, and she felt herself filled up with his fingers.

She moaned, he hesitated ... pushed deeper ... and Kit sunk her teeth into his lip before they both stilled, sensing their proximity to one another.

Kit's hand slowly rose, took the hem of his T-shirt, found his flesh damp and patchy red from the cold, and pressed her head against his chest. It rose and fell, her mouth opened, tasted the savoury, unfiltered rain that softened his skin, and her hand went to the muscles that led beneath his waistband – to the cock she hoped would be fucking her soon.

Raph took her chin, tilted her head up to look at him, and when her eyes met his, Kit felt his fingers began to move back … forth … back … forth inside her until her breath caught.

He freed his hand and took the edges of his jacket.

He drew it towards him, Kit slid slowly with it, and when her wet cunt was perched on the edge of the workbench, Raph let go, unfastened his pants, held her head with one hand, her thigh with the other, and filled her.

Raph sat on the floor, watching her. He was shirtless, back against the stone wall, boots still on his feet.

Kit's bare knees were pulled up to her chest. Raph's jacket big enough to both sit on and hug around her, and she tugged it against her body before she dug her spoon back into the jar.

'Good?' he said.

'I know you know it is.' Kit carved a scoop of velvety chocolate and hazelnut paste from the jar he'd selected from a shelf.

'Homemade Nutella. I ate bottles of it growing up.'

'I bet you did.' Kit licked her finger and Raph watched her for a while.

'I had that Jimmy Hillinger fired,' he said suddenly, listlessly. 'He was the one who leaked Connor's Cannock Chase plans to AGVM. He also told them where I was. I got him fired for unethical journalism.'

Kit nodded slowly without words. The sleet had begun to ease and the faint sound of music was just audible, away in The Priory.

'I want to come back to Gossard Range with you …' Raph said.

Kit smiled at him with the spoon in her mouth. He didn't smile back.

His expression was drawn and uneasy and Kit slowly set the spoon down.

'I want more than anything to come back with you,' he said, 'but I can't. We have to end this.'

Kit lowered the jar.

'I was trying to tell you …' Raph's voice rasped. 'I was about to but …'

Kit shuffled forward to touch him but he pulled away a little.

'I'm sorry,' he said, 'I shouldn't … we shouldn't …'

Kit's heart began to race. 'What are you doing?'

There was a wait before Raph said, 'Kit. My father and I made an agreement. When I returned all those months ago – to see what I could do to get the Cannock Chase deeds back for Connor – I had to … I gave up some things.'

'You what?'

'I promised my father I'd resume my position at AGVM–' Raph's eyes rose to meet hers '–and that I would succeed him.'

'No.' Kit stared. 'Raph, you don't even want this.'

'Of course I don't. I couldn't see another way.'

'But–'

'Kit, when you found out who I was, you didn't like it. You didn't want me near you, you were engaged to be married, and …

in light of that, this decision seemed like the right one, the only one. If I'd known then how you felt–'

'No.' Kit's head shook.

'It's already in motion. I start next week.'

'No!' Kit choked and Raph swore and looked at the ceiling.

'Please … please don't.'

'We can move around, together,' Kit stumbled over her words, 'we can work around it. What will you have to do? Where will you be based?'

'Far away from you,' he said.

'No, I–'

'I want to be far away, Kit. I know the person I'm going to become and it won't be someone you'll like.'

Kit half laughed, half choked.

'I'm not joking. You'll hate me like Rosa hates my father. I've been that man before and I didn't like him. It'll be worse now. I can't be the person I am now and do the job I have to. I don't want it to happen to us. You deserve better.'

'Don't fucking tell me what I deserve–'

'I'm telling you what I want and it's over. You have to leave. It's finished.'

'You can't control this, you're not in charge of this!' Kit spat. Angry tears scorched her cheeks.

'I'm in charge of myself, and I'm telling you I can't see you again. Please don't make this harder for me. I shouldn't have come to find you tonight.'

Kit cried and Raph reached out to crush her head into his chest. 'Don't,' his voice shook and she knew this was the last time he'd hold her.

37

Four months later, Kit stared at Raph's hand as it held a sandwich.

The meat lolled out of the bread, the food almost in his mouth, and his free hand gripped the steering wheel of Connor's E-Type.

'I'm pleased they chose that for the cover photo.' Piper smoothed her hand across the image. She held the last remaining copy of *Hunger* by Kit Gossard, all other copies sold. Kit's book launch was drawing to a close and she and Piper were the last left in the literary café near the library in town.

'And *wow* that Rosa wrote the foreword.' Piper skimmed the opening pages. 'You'll sell half a million from that alone.'

'I'd laugh if I didn't know you might be right.' Kit smiled.

'She didn't want to come?' Piper said.

'It's spring at The Priory ... too busy.'

'Do you ever ask her about Raph?'

Kit stood up.

'S-sorry,' Piper stammered, 'I shouldn't have–'

'It's fine.' Kit pulled her hair into a ponytail. 'I'm fine. Look at all this. It's amazing, aren't I lucky?'

'You *are* lucky,' Piper patted Kit's book then held it proudly aloft. 'It's good that they called it *Hunger*. Did Marc tell you some of his other suggestions?'

'He said the book was porn charading as art and that I should have called it *Have Hole, Need Fill* or *Cooking with Beaver*. My editor appreciated the suggestions.'

'That's m' baby-daddy.' Piper patted her swollen stomach, then squatted awkwardly to rummage in her bag as Kit began packing up her things.

'I might see if I can catch Rosa when I'm in Paris next month.' She put her pens and business cards into a box. 'I'm not sure if she actually ever leaves her little corner of the world, but if she did come to my Paris book launch, perhaps we could–'

Piper squeaked.

Kit's head turned. Piper was squatting over a small puddle on the floor.

'Holy … fuck.' She blinked up at Kit.

'Did–'

'My water just broke.'

Kit held Piper's hand in the back of the cab.

'Why didn't you answer before? I called twice,' she said.

'I was in the orchard with Dad, had to check something in the last of the light. The launch was great, wish we could have stayed longer.'

'Feel like coming back into town?'

'I can't–'

'Well you have to.'

'Why?'

'You're going to have a baby.'

There was silence.

'You're about to have a baby,' Kit said.

'I'm–'

'You're having a baby!' Kit laughed. 'Run! Drive! We're almost at the hospital.'

Marc swore. 'Jesus, fuck, is Piper okay?'

'A-OK.' Kit was smiling. 'She's waving at you. No sweating or swearing – yet.'

'Give me sixty minutes,' Marc panted.

When Kit hung up, Piper winced and covered her face.

'Arrgggh …' she groaned. 'It's started.'

Three days later, Kit sat on the couch in Marc's cottage, gazing at the tiny white cocoon with the face in it.

'I want to eat her,' she said.

Marc had been inspecting Kit's new camera lens. He put it down, picked up the wool-wrapped nugget and Kit wanted to cry at how good it felt to see him with his baby in his arms.

'I want to hoe down on her arm like it's a drumstick,' he said.

Kit cupped baby Violet's head with her hand. 'I have to go. I'll come back later when Piper's woken up. I'll bring her a treat of some kind.'

'I doubt she's even sleeping. She's probably on her phone googling "ways to show your child you're cool".'

Kit kissed Marc and Violet then walked towards the door.

'I liked your new camera gear by the way,' Marc called after her. 'I think it bodes well for your next project, whatever that may be.'

Kit smiled. 'I'm going to walk across to the orchard, see how the cider harvest is going.'

'Violet Gossard says bye-bye.'

'Bye-bye, baby Gossard.'

Kit walked through the orchard, a book and a rug under her arm.

The pickers stood on ladders, baskets of apples at their feet. Kit picked one out, smoothed her finger across the faintly powdered skin then sunk her teeth into sweet, crisp flesh.

Connor waved and she raised her hand with a smile.

She'd left her sunglasses back at the homestead. The day was warmer and brighter than she'd anticipated, and she kept on, heading for the shadowy respite in the distance. The grass thinned as she strolled into the hazelnut grove, an alley of trees made cool by foliage.

The earth had begun to colour with fallen leaves and she thought how their decay would soon fertilise the heady black fungi the Gossards would harvest and consume in winter.

She let her rug fall then lazily tugged it square.

The occasional shout was audible in the distance. Pickers laughed and called out, making Kit feel at ease. She lowered herself onto her stomach and sat the book in front of her. It had been in her old room at the homestead. The fabric hardcover had a dustiness to it that no amount of wiping could remedy and she read the name written inside as she had once before. *Raph Arenberg*. The pages were patterned like a doily, holes made by silverfish.

Raph's old watch hung on her wrist and she gazed at it, too. The watch and the book – remnants of a lost thing, a thing she hoped to forget, hoped never to.

She skimmed through the pages then parted the book in the middle and slid her nose in. It smelled like sawdust but she wanted it to smell like him, and she inhaled, wanting one, last … something.

Her phone beeped with the arrival of an email.

Kit's nose remained in the book. She held her face there until she grew bored … then lowered the book to the rug.

She reached for her phone and opened her mail app.

Subject: *This Week On thegastronome.com*

Kit had failed to unsubscribe from Jimmy Hillinger's blog. His posts had become more frequent since his sacking from *Hamper* and each time *thegastronome* email appeared in her inbox, she deleted it. This time, she opened the email and scrolled down to the 'unsubscribe' link.

The newsletter promoted the blog, featuring a preview of each post, and Kit hesitated then scrolled back up to a heading she knew she must have misread the first time.

Gossard vs. Arenberg 4.0

She hadn't misread. Jimmy had titled one of the posts thus. Kit frowned and prodded the heading until the link opened in her browser and the article loaded fully down the page.

Gossard vs. Arenberg 4.0
Perusing one of my favourite Parisian foodie sites this
afternoon, my interest was piqued by this <u>article</u> and I realised
I was overdue for an update on our favourite heartbreak kids.
Though recently thought to be lying low, a little digging reveals
that much, in fact, has developed of late between should-be-foes
Kit Gossard and Raphaël Arenberg.

Kit and Rosamonde Michel – renowned cook, recluse,
director of French Art of Food at The Priory and most
notably Raphaël's mother – *have purportedly become close,*
collaborating on significant publishing projects including Kit's
new photography venture Hunger *and Rosamonde's upcoming*
A Woman's Place.

Next, despite earlier accounts of hostility, the titles of <u>orchard</u>
<u>lands</u> surrounding Gossard's Yarra Valley estate have now been
reported to be under Gossard ownership, not Arenberg, as was
<u>reported</u> last year. Not only does this mean that we're in for a
relaunch of Gossard Range's previously ceased cidre bouché,
but I find myself enquiring: why the sudden accord between
houses Gossard and Arenberg?

The aforementioned Paris article may reveal …

The article broadcasts this scoop from <u>Heavy Weights</u>
who reports that Raphaël Arenberg has stepped down from
AGVM. Yes … you heard right. The report cites an insider's
disclosure that AGVM heir and French-American playboy
Raph Arenberg may no longer be the successor to his family's
mammoth corporation. The burning question? Why oh why oh
why!?

Gossard Range Cidre Bouché, re-release date & details <u>here</u>.
Hunger, *by Kit Gossard now available <u>here</u>.*

A Woman's Place, *by Rosamonde Michel pre-order <u>here</u>.*

Kit sat up, agitated. She re-read the post then stared at her phone, wanting it to elaborate.

'I thought you'd already read that.'

Kit startled and dropped her phone.

'Haven't you?' Raph leaned down and took *Walden* off the rug. His deerhound licked Kit's face. She spluttered and Raph commanded Sergeant to stop. When he did, Kit gazed up at the man standing over her. Raph stared down.

'Raph?'

'Kit.'

Kit tried to find words.

'I left AGVM,' Raph said simply and Kit climbed shakily to her feet to stare at him.

'What?'

'I've left AGVM.'

'What?' Kit repeated. 'How? Your father, your agreement–'

'He doesn't compromise. It went the whole way, one way. I'm no longer his successor, nor do I hold a stake, share, title or position at AGVM. My father's pride won, our relationship lost.'

Kat stared, mind racing.

She reached out and pressed her hand against his chest, testing the reality of his form.

His hand took hers. He held it still, took her arm, drew her in and when she was near, face almost touching his, he said, 'I have come with nothing, hoping to regain everything. You are everything. You are everything and more and I want you.'

Kit was silent before she whispered, 'I want you, too.'

'I want to marry you,' Raph said.

The words rang out into the silence and Kit drew back.

Raph gazed at her. 'I first came to Gossard Range seeking to be free and unbound, and now I return seeking the opposite. I want to be yours.'

There was a pause before Kit leapt on him. She blanketed his torso with body and limb, burrowed her face into his neck, and inhaled the smell she'd long craved.

He took her head, held her face where he could see it. He kissed her hard on the mouth, fell with her onto the rug, and Kit laughed as he pinned her there, savaged her face, neck, chest, and Sergeant barked, uncertain if danger or play was afoot.

Raph stilled and stared down at her. 'Well?'

'Well?'

'Do you have an answer?'

'To what?'

'My question.'

'What was your question?'

Amusement flickered across Raph's face.

'I asked you to marry me,' he said.

'You did?'

'Yes. Will you?'

Kit gazed at him then suddenly rolled away, and on her feet began to run, bounding across the floor of the hazelnut grove. 'As if a Gossard would ever let an Arenberg have them that easily!' she called back and began to sprint, knowing she was being chased. Sergeant overtook her moments before she felt herself taken to the ground.

Raph crushed her into leaves the colours of sundown.

'I'm sorry,' he said, 'but an Arenberg always gets what he wants. Unfortunately for you this Arenberg wants only one thing, and you can be sure he'll get it, however long it takes.'

Kit laughed, breathless. 'Fine,' she said. 'Have me.'

Acknowledgments

Very few can live an artistic life without one thing: belief from others. Sorry to give you all away, but everyone here has shown indispensable belief in my work so it's all your fault, you guys.

Thank you to my literary agent Jacinta di Mase whose energy and insight made this manuscript just what it needed to be right when it needed to be it. Thank you to my team at HarperCollins who made this long-journeying writer feel like she'd arrived. The perception and sensitivity of Mary Rennie, the patience and precision of Nicola Robinson, and Anna Valdinger who got excited first. Thank you to the design team and everyone behind the scenes, it's your belief that will get this book where it needs to go.

Thank you to the incredible women in my life who provide me extraordinary support and friendship – your strength and complexity inspires me. I am grateful for the research advice from Ryan Hodges, Troy Jones and Pierre de Masse.

To my competitive, high-achieving family – siblings Tess, Bryn and Bede – thank you for driving me mad, it's been essential. To my wise and creative parents Jenni and Chris Overend – you have been the bedrock which made me feel like nothing was ever out of reach.

Lastly and most importantly I want to thank James Reid. You're the first to read, the last to read, the one who reads me inside out, upside down, by day and by night. Your brain is made of squares, mine from circles, I love the knots we tie ourselves in, may we never be untangled.

Sunni Overend is a graphic design graduate, and the daughter of the late, award-winning children's author Jenni Overend. Sunni worked briefly in creative advertising before building an online fashion store and concurrently wrote several contemporary fiction manuscripts. In 2015 she signed a two-book deal with HarperCollins Publishers and now lives with her architect husband in Melbourne where she writes full time.

FEBRUARY 2017

The Golden Child
Wendy James

With the move back to Australia and all that entailed, did Beth miss something with her daughter?

MARCH 2017

The Fifth Letter
Nicola Moriarty

Joni wants her friends to go back to how they were before. But are things already too toxic?

APRIL 2017

The Scent of You
Maggie Alderson

Perfume blogger Polly is in crisis. Will her husband's absence break or make her?

DECEMBER 2016

The Pretty Delicious Café
Danielle Hawkins

Lia may have found a match. But her café, family and life keep getting in the way.

DECEMBER 2016

Lyrebird
Cecelia Ahern

How will talented but reclusive Laura cope in the glare of reality television?

JANUARY 2017

The Dangers of Truffle Hunting
Sunni Overend

Kit has it all — talent, partner, career. So why does she hunger for something … more?

Spend

Summer

with MORE people you **actually** *want to be with.*

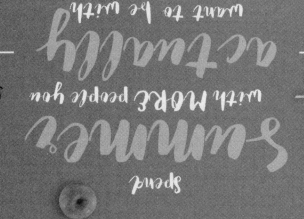